BITTER PILL

A J LINNEY

Copyright © 2024 A J Linney

The moral right of the author has been asserted.

Apart from any fair dealing for the purposes of research or private study, or criticism or review, as permitted under the Copyright, Designs and Patents Act 1988, this publication may only be reproduced, stored or transmitted, in any form or by any means, with the prior permission in writing of the publishers, or in the case of reprographic reproduction in accordance with the terms of licences issued by the Copyright Licensing Agency. Enquiries concerning reproduction outside those terms should be sent to the publishers.

This is a work of fiction. Names, characters, businesses, places, events and incidents are either the products of the author's imagination or used in a fictitious manner. Any resemblance to actual persons, living or dead, or actual events is purely coincidental.

Troubador Publishing Ltd
Unit E2 Airfield Business Park,
Harrison Road, Market Harborough,
Leicestershire LE16 7UL
Tel: 0116 279 2299
Email: books@troubador.co.uk
Web: www.troubador.co.uk

ISBN 978 1 80514 471 7

British Library Cataloguing in Publication Data.
A catalogue record for this book is available from the British Library.

Printed and bound in Great Britain by 4edge Limited
Typeset in 11pt Minion Pro by Troubador Publishing Ltd, Leicester, UK

For Kevan.

The love of my life, my best friend
You believed in me when I didn't
Your love completes my soul.

Remembering

My Sister, Pamela
My Brother, Stephen
My Niece, Alison

You were all too young to leave us.

PART ONE

PART ONE

ONE

Lexie

14 March 2013

Lexie's iPhone chimed a text message as she manoeuvred her Audi through traffic on the M40. *No time for distraction*, she thought, pushing her foot down to navigate through the volume of vehicles, while at the same time trying to avoid speed traps.

'Oh, come on. Come *on!*' she shouted at the drivers cruising in the middle lane. Accelerating into the outer lane, she gained enough momentum to pass them. Her team meeting was scheduled for three o'clock and her last appointment had overrun, thanks to Dr Chan, who'd kept her waiting until morning surgery finished. Some GPs irritated her with their sense of self-importance. Did they never consider her deadlines?

Their receptionists were worse, asserting their authority and making her wait. Normally she would meet with the whole practice and provide a deli lunch – bribe food, some would call it – but to Lexie, it meant sales. A personal touch was rare in today's climate, but for Lexie it was essential to get the doctors on side, to push up her sales and meet her targets. The thought of lunch, or the lack of it, made her stomach growl. She'd eaten an orange and a yogurt for breakfast. There had not been time for lunch. The lack of food, combined with tension, had brought on a headache. Lexie reduced the volume on the radio.

Bruno Mars' 'Locked out of Heaven' faded into the two o'clock news. The newsreader did little to improve her mood, droning on. She sighed, tapped a button on the steering wheel to power off the radio and located the message icon on her mobile, her attention wavering between the road and the screen, her curiosity conquering thoughts that she might be breaking the law by doing so.

Where are you? Three little words on the screen, seeming so innocuous.

She had not seen him since the row. She frowned, not wanting to think about that now. Reaching the A40, she headed towards Middlesex, massaging her brow as she went. A strong coffee might top up her caffeine level, but time was ticking, plus it wouldn't help her pounding headache. She steered with one hand, while she reached across to the passenger seat and rummaged in the front pocket of her briefcase for a packet of ibuprofen. Her manicured, white-tipped fingernails skilfully popped out two tablets from the blister pack, one-handed, and popped them into her mouth. She lifted a bottle of Evian from the water holder and swallowed them with a shudder. Her nose wrinkled at the bitterness of the cheaper variety of drug she marketed to keep costs down. She wanted medical practices to use their budgets on innovative, more expensive drugs.

Ting! Ting!

Lexie glanced again at the screen, where a question mark had appeared. Oliver would have to wait. Her schedule was too tight for interruptions.

When Lexie pulled into the car park at the headquarters of RestrilPharma, she breathed a sigh of relief and turned off the engine. She slipped on her suit jacket, grabbed her Tuscan saffiano leather laptop bag and locked the car.

She sprinted across the car park, despite her high heels, dodging the puddles from the earlier rainfall. Rounding the corner towards the tinted glass façade of the pharmaceutical offices, she climbed the steps and hurried through the main doors.

At reception, Lexie flashed her identity badge to a portly man leaning over the desk, conversing with a woman, whose long acrylic fingernails were pointing to a clipboard. He glanced up, nodded and resumed his business. Lexie passed them and boarded the lift, staring at the highlighted buttons, willing it to climb faster. As she approached the top floor, she wondered if Julian would be attending. She glanced at her watch: 2.50. Time for a quick refresh in the restrooms before meeting the delegates.

*

Two hours later, and much less stressed, Lexie was happy to be finished. It had been a successful meeting, albeit brain draining, and she couldn't wait to get home. She was glad to learn she'd remained top distributor in her area, and her performance – and her bonuses – were well above the averages of other reps. The company continued to shine in the marketplace, and it felt good to be a significant part of its success. Her expression softened as she made her way out through the double doors of the meeting room and headed across the plush-carpeted landing to the lifts. Her sales figures had exceeded even her own expectations. Lexie always pushed herself to improve her personal targets in the rapidly advancing industry, even if it meant sacrificing her social life.

'Congratulations, Lex.' Her rival, Sebastian, joined her at the lifts. 'On track for the promotion, eh?' He said it through gritted teeth, reminding her of Basil Fawlty. It pleased her immensely.

'You know I deserve it.' The corners of her mouth lifted. She stepped into the empty lift, and he followed. 'I must say, you didn't contribute much to the meeting today.'

'My area won't always be behind yours, don't you worry.'

'Believe me, I won't.'

'I see Julian's in China with Amelia? You know, the redhead with the big…?' He held cupped hands in front of his chest. 'She's really flying high, don't you think?'

Lexie smiled to herself. 'Clearly not high enough.'

'Difficult for him to concentrate on work when she's around.'

'And that's precisely why I'm still top in sales. Boys will be boys, eh?' Lexie raised a mocking brow and left Sebastian open-mouthed as she got out. Despite her confident retort, he had hit a nerve, though it wasn't enough to put a dampener on her mood.

Back in her car, Lexie put her bags on the passenger seat, relaxed and puffed out her cheeks. She'd planned a quick visit to the gym, but today she needed extra motivation. Exercise was a long way from her mind.

Her thoughts drifted to Oliver. Tucking her hair behind her ear, she reached for her phone, took a deep breath and tapped his contact details.

'You're through to Oliver,' his smooth voice announced on the answering service. Lexie ended the call, tossed the phone into her handbag and pushed the car key in the ignition. As she reversed, the phone rang.

'Shit!' she said aloud, braking and fumbling in her bag to grab it.

'Lexie?' said Oliver. 'Sorry I missed you. I was on voicemail.'

'No, *I'm* sorry for not leaving a message. I couldn't speak earlier because I was running late for a meeting.' The excuse sounded feeble, even to her own ears. She could have sent a text.

'No apology required. I figured you were with a client or something. You OK?'

Lexie wished he'd come to the point. 'Fine, and you?'

'Good, thanks. But you sound tense, Lex. Are you sure you're OK?'

'Yeah. Long day, Oli, that's all.' There was a pause and Lexie resisted the urge to fill the silence.

'I was wondering if you'd eaten?'

Lexie squeezed her eyelids shut. She was not ready for this.

'I'm just leaving Brentford and—'

'Look, Lex, have you got plans or not? It's a simple question, let's not waste time on trivialities.'

'As I said, I've had a long day and—'

'You've no plans then? Right, I can meet you en route, in Woodstock maybe, and we can have dinner?' He said this with the same air of authority he used in his military job. 'You still need food however busy you are. Woodstock then?'

'Where and what time?'

'The Ivy Bridge? I'll be waiting.'

Lexie was too tired to protest, and it was too late now, she'd agreed. The whole situation was just so awkward…

TWO

Pippa

Pippa's fingers flicked through her medical repertory as she researched remedies for an elderly man who was presenting with long-term chest problems. She noted down some of the recommended ones in the margin of his notes but remained unconvinced they'd hit the mark.

This client's symptoms troubled her, and gut instinct told her she needed a different prescription. Unsatisfied, she tucked the folder into her briefcase so she could continue later at home.

She checked her Moleskine diary for the next appointment before glancing at the clock: five minutes to go. Enough time for a drink, she thought, standing and stretching out her tense muscles.

Pulling a cup from the dispenser, she filled it with water and drank. The chill hit her stomach and instantly refreshed her. Pippa disposed of the cup and crossed to the filing cabinet.

The morning clinic was busy; time was flying by. So far, in addition to the previous patient, she'd seen two follow-ups: a middle-aged woman experiencing frequent migraines and a teenage boy suffering extreme anxiety. Both had improved. A young lady expecting twins, wanting to go over her birthing plan, had been next. Then a new case, a man who'd been referred with drug and alcohol problems.

The diversity in clients' conditions certainly meant Pippa's professional routine was never boring or predictable.

She selected the final set of notes from the drawer, scanned the paperwork and opened the door to the waiting room.

'Mrs Jenkins?'

A tired-looking woman nodded and stood, pulling a young boy to his feet. Pippa showed them through to her office.

'Take a seat.' She motioned to a chair beside a small table, on which stood a vase of mixed daffodils, a square box of tissues and a plastic stand of leaflets.

'Hello, Charles.' Pippa smiled reassuringly.

The boy remained silent and trailed behind his mother, clinging to her coat. Pippa waited for her to be seated and sat opposite them. The room was decorated in pastel shades, easy on the eye, creating a welcoming ambience.

'I'm sorry. He's so shy,' blurted the woman. He buried his face deeper into the folds of cloth while she stroked his hair. 'It doesn't help that he's tired. He's not sleeping because of this cough.' A red flush crept up her neck. 'He's got two inhalers now, but they're not doing anything,' she said, hoisting Charles onto her lap. 'I'm worried about his poor chest, but the doctor said it's an asthmatic cough and steroids are the way forward.' She sighed, lifting her palms in defeat. 'So, when I was telling one of the mothers at the nursery how dissatisfied I was, she recommended I come to you.' The mother spoke so fast, she barely paused for breath. Her hand rubbed the boy's leg erratically. Pippa wondered if she needed a prescription too.

'Do you know much about homeopathy?' Pippa asked in a soft voice.

'Not really, but I've seen her girl's eczema improve since she's been coming here. So I thought I'd give it a try for Charles. I'm getting desperate.' She blinked rapidly and her cheeks flushed. 'I mean... Oh, that didn't sound right at all.'

'It's when most people do come, either out of desperation or with long-term disease. Hopefully, we'll soon have Charles feeling better, won't we?' said Pippa, tapping the back of Charles's hand and smiling warmly.

He jerked his arm away, towards his mother.

'I'm sorry.' More blotches appeared on her neck as she soothed him.

'Don't be.' Pippa sat back to create a comfortable distance. 'Now, I received your form, so we'll go over this together first if that's OK?' Mrs Jenkins nodded.

'You may wonder why I ask certain unrelated questions, such as Charles's favourite foods for instance. This is to build what we homeopaths call a "constitutional picture". And that's because everyone is unique, which affects what we prescribe.' Pippa saw her brow wrinkle. 'It means I can home in on what the best treatment for your son may be. Feel free to ask any questions. Would you like a glass of water before we start?'

'No thanks, we're fine.'

'First I'll go over what to expect.' Pippa reached forward to select a pamphlet. 'And you might like to take this to give you some background, if you fancy a read later,' she said, handing it over.

'Thank you, I will.'

'Right, let's work through these questions, and then I'll go through a treatment plan with you.'

*

By late afternoon, as Pippa was writing up her final notes for the day, Sandy, the practice's osteopath, knocked on the door and she peered into the room.

'Sorry to disturb you, Pippa. Gillian's daughter, Debbie, phoned and asked – well more like demanded – to speak to you.' Sandy leaned against the doorframe and folded her arms. 'She wasn't happy and started questioning me. I told her I'm not her mother's therapist and Gillian's not my patient and even if she was, I wouldn't be able to talk because of patient confidentiality.' Sandy shook her head, causing her curly auburn ponytail to swish from side to side. 'She wasn't having any of it. She sounded irate and wanted me to fetch you. I apologised and told her you were with a client. I said I'd pass on the message.'

'Did she say why she was so upset?'

'Something about her mother refusing chemotherapy. Gillian's been admitted again.'

'I'll call her before I leave. Are you off now?'

'Yeah, my turn to do the school run today. His Lordship is working late. Do you want me to grab Alexander when I pick up the twins in case you have to call in on Gillian?'

'It should be fine, thanks. I'll call you, though, if I'm going to be late. Will that be all right?' Pippa knew Gillian wouldn't want her to drop everything to go to the hospital, but she wanted to see her. 'If you don't mind, I could leave him with you later for an hour?'

'Whatever suits. Better get going. Catch you later.'

Pippa sat back and twisted a copper ringlet around her finger, wondering about Gillian. She sighed as she stood up to clear her desk, mentally preparing herself for another altercation with Debbie.

THREE

Lexie

Lexie approached Oliver, who was perched on a bar stool, sipping a pint of Guinness. He put her in mind of the man in the Diet Coke advert: lean, toned and handsome. He rose to greet her, giving her a peck on the cheek.

'I see you already ordered,' said Lexie, accepting the gin and tonic he handed to her. He raised an eyebrow and grinned. 'I saw you arrive, so I was ready.'

'Mm, just what I needed.' She took a long sip, enjoying the light, refreshing tang on her taste buds.

'Shall we move over there?' Oliver pointed to the lounge area, defined by heavy damask curtains on thick wooden poles and soft lighting from bold-coloured lamps. 'The suite beneath the window looks comfy.'

Lexie turned to look and nodded. She took the lead to the oxblood chesterfield, positioned by a low mahogany table. Choosing the single armchair by it, she set her drink down and slipped off her Jimmy Choos.

'What a relief to kick those off,' she said, massaging her toes, relaxing back into the seat. The ambience soothed her mind.

Oliver folded his tall frame onto the firm leather of the two-seater.

'Not surprising given the height of those heels.' He nodded at the shoes. 'Hardly made for comfort.'

'Perhaps a pair of brogues would complement my outfit?'

'Erm… maybe not.'

Lexie retrieved her drink, chinking the ice around in the glass. She squeezed the lime with the cocktail stirrer, smiling as she did so.

'What are you thinking?'

'Your insight into my preference: lime, not lemon.'

'I aim to please.' He matched her smile. 'Besides, our absence doesn't mean I've forgotten, though I almost ordered Bombay Sapphire instead of Hendrick's.' He sat back and crossed his right ankle over his left knee. 'You know, Lex, your face completely changes when you smile like that. You appeared so tense when you arrived. The effect of a G&T is amazing… plus there's the charming company, of course.'

Lexie shook her head. 'You're full of yourself, aren't you? Now, do you want to tell me the real reason we're here? And don't bother giving me bullshit.'

'Tut tut. And I thought we were meeting for a pleasant dinner. Talking of which…' He motioned for a waitress to approach.

Lexie suppressed a sigh.

The waitress handed them bound copies of the hotel's menu.

'The table's ready when you are. Take as long as you need to browse, then go through to the restaurant. Table 7, to the left of the alcove.' She smiled briefly at Lexie before fixing a longer gaze on Oliver, who seemed to be oblivious. 'Is there anything else I can do for you, sir?'

Lexie was surprised to feel a jolt of irritation.

'No thanks, we're fine at the moment... Claire,' he said, reading her name badge. 'Unless you would like another, Lex?' He turned to face Lexie.

'Not for me, thank you. I'm driving.'

'I could always pick you up from yours in the morning and drop you back here to fetch your car?' Oliver leaned forward, took a sip from his pint and ran his tongue across his top lip to lick the froth.

The waitress's eyes followed his every move. Lexie couldn't blame her; she was only young and unaware of her immature flirtatious actions. Oliver turned heads wherever he went, and it was not difficult to see why. His smile was dazzling, and whenever he wore uniform, his effect on women was even stronger.

'I'm fine for now, thanks.' Lexie reached down to put on her shoes. The waitress took it as her cue to leave and Lexie perused the menu.

'Mm, the duck with juniper berries sounds good,' she said, peering at Oliver over the top of the menu. 'I suppose you'll be predictable and have the rib-eye steak?'

'Too right,' he answered, scanning the menu. Satisfied, he closed it and put it down. Moments passed and the awkward silence of unspoken recriminations stretched between them.

'Shall we go through?' Oliver asked, rising. The niceties were finished, and the atmosphere had changed. Both understood the need to talk. Lexie retrieved her handbag and Oliver offered her his hand.

Lexie was pleased the restaurant was more private. The subdued lighting matched her mood. Table 7 sat in an alcove in the corner, away from other diners, yet allowing an open view of the area. Oliver pulled out a chair for her and sat down opposite.

'Wine?' he asked, picking up the black leather-bound folder.

'I told you I'm driving.'

'Loosen up, Lex. I'm not your enemy.'

'Why are you here?'

'Because… there's unfinished business since you two—'

'And your role is?'

Oliver's mouth tightened into a thin line.

'Come on, Lex. You're not making this easy. It's ridiculous, you two drifting like this. Let's face it, we all have disagreements from time to time. But to let opinions come between you… I thought you were above all that.' He turned and beckoned the waitress.

'I don't need mediation. Does she know you're here?'

'No, I'm off the Brize Norton base.' He turned his head as the waitress approached, pen poised.

'What can I get you, sir?'

As he gave the order, Lexie noticed shadows beneath his cobalt eyes. She'd seen him looking drawn like this before, following his last trip to Afghanistan, but now he looked different somehow.

She listened as Oliver ordered Rioja to accompany the meal, hoping it was for him alone, but as the tension built between them, she realised she needed a drink too.

There was no early client appointment the next day. If she indulged, she could accept Oliver's offer to collect the car the following morning or order a black cab. Once they were alone again, he turned to face her and rested his chin on his hand.

'How did it come to this?' he said.

'Pippa's changed—'

'We all change. People don't go through life without change, Lex. Life is hard enough.'

'I'm tired of her slating my career!' Heat burned her cheeks. 'She spends her time pandering to new-age hippies and alternative health freaks. Not to mention self-indulgent, middle-class housewives. Well, I live in the real world. Suffering the daily commute, bargaining with pompous GPs who can't wait to throw in the "budget" word at every opportunity.'

'Come on, that's not fair, Lex, Pippa's a respected homeopath.'

'My job is science-based, Oli. Pharmacology, real medicine that saves lives.'

'And busting sales targets… and making shit-loads of money.'

'Now who's not being fair?'

'Is it not the truth?'

'I make money, so what? I earn it. I work hard. All this bullshit about vaccinated children becoming autistic and drug companies out to get us. She's gone too far with this conspiracy nonsense.'

Tension knotted her insides. Her breathing was short and shallow. She bit so hard on her lower lip she tasted the metallic hint of blood.

The waitress returned and Lexie focused on her as she removed the cork and poured a small amount of Rioja for Oliver. He picked up the glass, swirled the wine and sipped, nodding his head in approval. She promptly filled both glasses in silence, then secured the napkin around the neck of the bottle and placed it on the table. Lexie took an immediate sip following her retreat.

'Changed your mind on the wine then?'

'Cheers.' Her tone was laced with sarcasm. She twisted the stem and stared at the contents of the crystal glass. She was tired and irritable. It wasn't Oliver's fault, she thought. Sighing deeply, she tasted some more; smooth on the palate, she decided. She swallowed slowly, savouring it. 'Nice wine choice.'

'Good. You look like you're enjoying it, considering you said you didn't want any.' His grin emphasised the dimple in his chin. 'Be careful not to snap the delicate stem.'

Lexie smiled, despite herself. 'Do be quiet. Sarcasm doesn't become you.'

'Who, me?' Oliver pointed to his chest, adopting his expression of innocence. 'Sarcastic?'

Lexie raised her brows.

'How long are you home this time?'

'Only a couple of weeks' down time, then Josh and I will be training some new recruits in night flying at RAF Odiham.'

'How is Josh?'

'You know Josh. He'll stay at Odiham. He's married to the job.'

'Doesn't he ever visit his brother?'

'No, not since their parents' funeral. I guess he still

blames Jordan for their deaths. He was driving over the limit and Josh can't let it go.'

'That was three years ago.'

'Four actually.' Oliver sighed deeply. 'He never talks about it now. Anyway, talking of family, are your parents still enjoying France, Lex?'

'They're loving it. It's not quite a year yet, and they seem so settled.'

'And Hugo?'

'Mother said he's settled well. They were worried at first, especially with his condition, but he seems to be doing fine.'

'Miriam always did cope well with him.'

Lexie's mind drifted to thoughts of her brother, and how his autism had dominated their lives.

'It certainly is quiet without him.'

'Do you miss them?'

'Of course.'

'Still no intention of moving over there yourself?'

'You know me, my work is here.'

'There is more to life than work, Lex.'

'Says he, whose life is dominated by the RAF. You're almost as bad as Josh.'

'Not for much long—' Oliver coughed, reaching into his pocket for a handkerchief. Lexie poured mineral water into a glass and handed it to him.

'Here, take a drink.'

'Thanks.' He gulped back the water. 'Though it does dilute the alcohol somewhat.' He put the empty tumbler down, then shared out the remainder of the Rioja.

Lexie was aware of the wine going to her head, so

she poured water for herself. At last, the meal arrived. It wouldn't do to continue drinking on an empty stomach.

During the meal she focused on safer topics of conversation, enjoying the food and an easier atmosphere. It felt natural between them.

Once the meal was over, Oliver put down his napkin.

'Excuse me, I'll be back in a minute.' Rising, he left the restaurant.

Lexie took the opportunity to check her phone: no messages, for a change. She slipped it back into her handbag. Her head was woozy but more relaxed. She was enjoying Oliver's company. He had lightened her mood and made her laugh with his great sense of humour.

Oliver was known to fictionalise his many experiences, making light of serious situations. Lexie loved that about him. She loved to hear his stories, even if she had heard them before. Oliver was a great social entertainer – his release mechanism from the horrific atrocities he had witnessed in his career.

Where had he got to? He'd been gone a while now. She glanced around at the other diners, daydreaming scenarios about them, wondering what their lives were like.

She signalled to the waitress and ordered two large cognacs. The warmth of the first sip had just hit the back of her throat, when Oliver returned.

He sat down and eyed the brandy.

'I guess neither of us will be driving now,' he said, raising his glass. 'I've asked if there are rooms available. Perhaps that's the most sensible option. You're looking more relaxed now and I'm enjoying our evening.'

He leaned back and clasped his hands behind his head.

Lexie's eyes fixed on the firm muscles of his chest stretching the fabric of his shirt. Oliver had an amazing body, she found herself thinking.

'Besides, I can't be arsed to drive either,' he added, meeting her eyes.

Lexie turned away quickly.

'And... have they?' she said, picking up the starched linen napkin and folding it with precision, waiter-style.

'Yes. Are you happy to stay then?'

'Fine by me. I haven't charged any accommodation to my expense account yet this month. I've covered lots of miles instead. What about you though? Haven't you got to go back? Don't you have to check in or something?'

'No,' Oliver laughed. 'I'll go and book the rooms. Shall we go through to the bar?' She nodded.

Back in the bar, Lexie chose the sofa, feeling mellow. Oliver returned carrying two more cognacs and two room keys.

'You're in room 15 and I'm 17.' He handed her a key and a brandy and seated himself beside her, brushing her thigh with his.

'Thanks,' she said, slipping the key into her bag.

He leaned forward to place his glass on the table and she noticed how his skinny jeans clung to his taut thighs. Lexie took a sip of the brandy, rested her head back and closed her eyes. For the first time in a long time, she started to unwind, happy Oliver had booked rooms. She supposed they could have ordered taxis, but the mood spurred her on. Besides, she was fed up with driving and it would be good to have a decent drink for a change, even though she was already tipsy. She opened her eyes to see Oliver looking at her. He had his arm tucked behind his head, looking comfortable.

'You're beat,' he said, leaning closer, stroking her hair. 'Want me to escort you to your room?'

He wore Paco Rabanne's *Invictus*, one of her favourites. The masculine scent teased her senses. Her gaze fixed upon his firm bicep, moving as he stroked her hair. She didn't want to look into those deep questioning eyes, but she was drawn to them, not wanting to move either. God, he was sexy.

'I... erm... I'm relaxed sitting here.' Lexie's breath quickened. Somewhere in her brain, alarm bells rang. Her eyelids were heavy; her body relaxed, like an addict reaching a high.

'I think the cognac is going to your head, Lex. You can't get your words out. Come on, let's call it a night.'

'It's not going to my head at all,' she said, sitting up straight. Though the alcohol made her dizzy, it was his nearness that was unsettling her. She almost wished they were back in conflict mode. But she didn't want the night to end, not yet. 'I'm going to the restroom,' she announced.

Once there, she leant against the wall and took a deep breath, before bending over the sink to turn on the tap and pat cold water on her face. What was wrong with her? Oliver was her friend. Just a friend. She reapplied lipstick and combed her hair. More alert now, Lexie made her way back to the lounge and sat down. She crossed her legs and tapped her foot as tension hung in the air.

'Agitated?' Oliver glanced at Lexie's foot, breaking the silence.

'Why would I be?'

'Unless you've started smoking bud, I'm guessing that's not a cannabis tic? And you know as well as I do, there's something going on. Something neither one of us can understand. But it is happening, isn't it?'

'I don't know what you mean,' Lexie said, tapping faster.

Oliver reached across and placed his warm hand on her thigh to still her.

'You always do this when you're out of control.' He moved closer. 'So?' he asked softly, his mouth close to her ear, his breath on her cheek.

Her breathing quickened in response. As she turned, her face was only inches away from his and his gaze was intense.

'Well?' His voice was softer now. 'Why so restless?'

Their eyes locked.

'I… I'm not.' Oliver's eyes roamed down to her mouth and Lexie moistened her lips with her tongue.

'Do you have any idea what you're doing to me, Lex?' His eyes smouldered, his breathing deepening as the seconds ticked past. 'This can't happen.' He moved back. Lexie's senses shifted to high alert. Blood pumped through her body as her heart stepped up its beat. She wanted this. Oliver's thumb tentatively stroked her thigh. She swallowed again. She could find no voice. Everything around them held no significance. She didn't think about anyone else. There was only this moment, and her body's reaction dulled her mind to all sense of reason. She couldn't deny this electricity charging them, this new current of desire.

His hand reached up and gently caressed her cheek. She watched his pupils dilate, shrinking the cobalt irises of his eyes, eyes that were now darting between her eyes and mouth. Lexie bit her bottom lip as anticipatory desire heightened. She knew she was taunting him and could see his resolve slipping.

'Fuck it,' he said, bending to find her mouth.

He kissed her, slowly at first. When she didn't resist, his tongue found hers, probing inside her mouth. He tasted of cognac and his kiss was as fiery. She clenched her legs together as she became aware of a tightening sensation at the apex of her thighs. She couldn't control what was happening, and she had no desire to do so. His kiss deepened, penetrating every part of her mouth, sliding over her tongue. His hand clasped the back of her head, pulling her closer, kissing her feverishly.

He pulled away suddenly.

'I'm sorry, Lex... I—'

'Don't be.'

This time she pulled him, kissing him back. Reason had vanished. She didn't want to think. There were no consequences in the here and now, only this sensation dominating her body and allowing caution to evaporate. Hot desire burned her as he responded, and she heard a low groan escaping from his throat. His hand slid up to her breast and her nipple hardened in response. His finger teased it through the fine silk of her blouse, and she pressed into him, allowing the sweet torture of his delicate touch. The simple sensation had her longing for more. The strong thud of his heart vibrated through her as his arms tightened.

He lifted his head. 'I'd better take you to your room. I can't trust myself.' He pulled away and stood.

Lexie looked down, trying to conceal a smile as she observed the strain on his jeans. Oliver followed her gaze before quickly resuming his seat and laying an arm across his lap.

Lexie grinned, glad to be the cause of his arousal. It made her feel sexy. It had been too long since she'd had such feelings aroused in her. She wanted him, and her disappointment hung heavy when he'd pulled back.

'Ready when you are.' She finished her drink and stood.

'Good to go? I'll escort you.' He cleared his throat.

'I meant… I'm ready.'

Their eyes met.

'Are you saying what I think you are?'

'Yes.'

'Are you sure?'

'I'm sure.'

*

As Lexie opened bleary eyes, she turned her head to confirm she was next to Oliver; it wasn't a dream. She'd known it in her gut though, even before she was fully awake. She inwardly groaned as the events registered in her foggy brain now the drink had worn off.

Lexie studied him for a moment as he lay sleeping beside her. The light of dawn revealed a pallor to his skin the alcohol had disguised the night before.

Oliver always looked vibrantly healthy – strong, toned and tanned from the outdoor climate of Afghanistan. Today, dark shadows beneath his eyes showed in stark contrast to his pale cheeks.

Lexie massaged her temples. Her thoughts were all over the place, and her mouth felt like sandpaper as she swallowed. She needed water, and she needed to move. She craved space too. What she didn't need, was to be lying in bed with Oliver.

When she rose tentatively, Oliver remained deeply asleep. A fleeting thought came to her: Oliver usually slept light. His natural body clock awakened him at sunrise, having nothing to do with the regime of the forces.

He still didn't stir as Lexie dressed quickly and furtively. She had just pushed a hand beneath the quilt, trying to find her panties, when Oliver coughed and turned onto his side, facing her. His eyes remained closed. She eased her arm silently from beneath the cover, in fear of him waking. She tiptoed across the room, keeping her eyes fixed upon Oliver all the while, and released the door handle to make her way out.

Lexie let herself into the pristine room where she should have slept last night and headed straight to the bathroom to slip off her clothes.

Relieved by her solitude, she stood in the shower, enjoying the full force of the water cleansing away their mingled scent of sex. She soaped her body, the lather washing away her sin. Her eyes closed, reliving the moments Oliver's hands roamed over her, where suds now descended. She sighed, leaning her back against the cool tiled surface, trying to block out the memory.

Passionate sex should never have happened, and to be friends with benefits was certainly not their style. So why did it happen? She'd enjoyed his attention and flattery, basking in the glory of his need for her. Was it because the sex was stolen? Or because Oliver was out of bounds? It was definitely nothing more than lust, of that, she was certain.

Heat scorched her face as she relived her wantonness, standing up against the wall, begging Oliver to take her. He had been so hot, and her own need so strong.

Why Oliver? Had Sebastian's comment about Julian and Amelia provoked instinctive retaliation?

Not wanting to explore the psychology of it all, Lexie stepped out and wrapped herself in a towel. The mirror had steamed up, but Lexie didn't mind being unable to see her reflection.

She cleaned her teeth – grateful for the complimentary toothbrush and paste – towelled herself dry and dressed, except for her missing panties. She'd been so desperate to leave Oliver's room quickly and silently a search would have been impossible. She grimaced at the thought of Oliver finding them.

Feeling more presentable, after a quick titivation of her hair, she left the room and checked out. She would not face Oliver yet; she had to put distance between them. Driving home, Lexie took the scenic route to Chipping Norton. Mortification consumed her as events replayed in her mind. Yet, she had no regrets about the time spent alone with Oliver. It was a basic instinct both had given in to, for reasons she couldn't fathom.

It would be easy to blame Oliver for taking advantage of her inebriated state, but in truth, the blame lay with them both. She had enjoyed every second of their time together, relishing the feelings he awakened in her, under the influence or not, and she hadn't denied her pleasure.

She drove through lanes and cut through small villages, characterised by homes built in the classic Cotswold stone of quintessential England. Lexie never tired of the stunning beauty of the Cotswolds, and as she drove past fields where lambs were suckling and trees were budding into new life, she thought how Oliver had made her come alive again.

Throughout the journey to Charlbury, her mind darted from negative to positive and back again, trying to find clues as to what kind of person she really was. Struggling to concentrate, she drove slowly over a small bridge, beneath which a small stream trickled, before picking up a more reasonable speed past the park where the sun cast its morning glow on the Japanese flowering cherry trees.

She turned into Acacia Road, where pink and white blossom brought spectacular colour to the tree-lined pavements. She parked, gathered her bags and sprinted up the steps to her apartment.

Once inside, she leaned against the door for a moment and expelled a deep breath, so glad to be in her own safe haven.

Her internal dialogue still warred within her, but for now she allowed gratification to have the upper hand. To ease her guilt, she decided to view the experience as just sex. Not wise, logical or emotional, but simply sex.

She reached into her bag for her phone and sent Oliver a text.

FOUR

Oliver

Oliver was getting used to being woken by his cough. Still half asleep, his hand automatically went to his mouth as an odour of stale sex wafted up his nose from beneath the sheets. In the depths of his semi-conscious brain, a memory surfaced. Lexie!

His eyes shot open as realisation dawned on him. She'd left.

He pushed himself up and turned to see the clock displaying 6.45. He leaned against the headboard and blew out his cheeks.

Thrusting back the sheet, he sat on the side of the bed, elbows balanced upon his knees, head in his hands. Minutes later, he headed for the bathroom, showered and dressed.

Pulling back the curtains, he opened the window to let fresh air in, then called her mobile. No answer. He picked up the phone, dialled reception and asked to be put through to room 15. Still no answer. Oliver replaced the receiver, wondering if Lexie was showering. Or maybe she had gone down for breakfast? Perhaps she couldn't face him and had left the hotel.

He slumped on the edge of the mattress and rubbed his chin with his thumb and forefinger. As he looked up, he saw a black lacy thong near the door, and he groaned aloud. They hadn't even reached the bed. The evidence of their frantic need brought on an enormous wave of guilt. He couldn't allow the maids to find it and he certainly couldn't take Lexie's underwear with him! In haste, he picked it up and binned it.

Frustration built as he tried to rationalise the situation, calming the feelings of shame bubbling inside. In his mind's eye he pictured Lexie's vulnerability, something she disguised from the outside world, but he knew her better than most.

'Julian is history,' Lexie had told him at dinner, reverting to her default mode of independence.

'And why's that? It wouldn't be because his divorce is final and he wants commitment from you, would it, Lex?'

'I'm not the settling-down type.'

'So, you've thrown yourself back into work, obsessed with targets, I suppose?' Oliver had stated rather than asked. 'You have nothing to prove. You never socialise or go anywhere since Julian.'

'Drop the subject!' Lexie had demanded, so he did, and Julian hadn't entered his mind after that. Nor had Pippa…

What a fuck-up! In the fresh light of a new day, regret filled him. What the hell was wrong with him? Lexie was as much to blame. She didn't stop him, did she, almost begging him the way she did? But it didn't make it right. What a disaster! Mortification emanated from his every pore.

He left the room, descended the stairs, and peered into the restaurant – only businessmen and one couple present. He strode across to the receptionist.

'Would it be possible to tell me if Miss Philips has checked out, please?'

'Certainly, sir. Do you happen to know her room number?'

'Fifteen,' Oliver answered, drumming his fingers on the desk, waiting.

She tapped a few keys on the computer and raised her glasses-framed eyes to him. 'Miss Philips has checked out, sir.'

Oliver sighed. 'I'll settle my bill then, please. Room 17.'

'Seventeen?' she confirmed, reading the screen. 'The bill's been paid, Mr Sanders.'

'Are you sure?'

'Yes, sir, there's nothing to pay.'

Sitting behind the wheel of the Discovery, Oliver pulled out of the car park and joined the traffic, with no clear destination in mind. He needed to drive somewhere, anywhere, quiet, to get his head together. His brain seemed detached from reality.

En route through the Chilterns, he branched off and drove away from the main road, towards an area of woodland he knew. He stopped at a peaceful spot near a babbling brook, parked beneath a huge willow tree and sat for a while. Oliver came here whenever he needed head-space – often after returning from a conflict zone. He thought of it as his private sanctuary when he needed solitude.

When he opened the window, the sound of stillness

relaxed him. There was the odd swish of tyres passing, but no heavy, deafening traffic. Sighing, he pressed the button and sealed the window, then left the car.

Oliver pushed his hands into his pockets and started walking. He coughed as the cool air reached his throat. His chest ached again. The cough had lasted weeks and grated on his nerves.

After walking a short distance to the water's edge, he became breathless and a tightness in his chest prompted him to rest. He halted at a rickety wooden bench and sat, crossing his ankles. The wood seeped the dampness of the morning dew into his clothes, but that was the least of his worries. He should go home but wasn't officially due to get back for another day.

Oliver couldn't face Pippa, yet.

He stared ahead at the water meandering over uneven rocks, falling into a miniature waterfall. Its sound brought therapy to his unsettled mind. He was mesmerised by its magical continuity as it glided around old, stunted trees growing on the bank. The tranquillity calmed him, and his lungs relaxed into a gentle rhythm, taking in the petrichor scent of the damp woods.

His thoughts drifted to Pippa and a sudden wave of irrational anger accelerated his pulse. Pippa: quietly composed and suffused with serenity. Always finding the answers, never allowing stress into her life.

Perhaps that's why he fucked Lexie? They were both hungry for the passion, both desperate to feel alive. Words had not been necessary; they'd both wanted some kind of release. The uncertainty of the future weighed him down, and last night, he hadn't wanted to think; he'd wanted to feel.

Oliver shivered. He rubbed his arms vigorously. His body temperature kept fluctuating too. Night sweats and chills. He'd wanted to ask Lexie what she thought about it but lost the chance to confide once their tense conversation took over.

The alcohol had served to lighten the tension, but in retrospect, had only fuelled the fire. He checked his watch. It was still early, and he needed coffee. Standing, he brushed down his jeans and took a slow walk back.

As he walked, the soft sound of the trickling stream offered peace, unlike the war zone of destruction and death he was familiar with, though even that seemed preferable to his dilemma now. It was good to be back on home soil. There was nowhere like England for its beauty, in his opinion. He spotted a blackbird rummaging beneath the leaves for food. Oliver inhaled deeply, filling his lungs with air devoid of city fumes. The action induced another coughing spasm, startling the bird, which hopped into a hawthorn bush. He should have shown the same caution last night.

The kiss had been a huge mistake, but something inside of him had needed a release. An unidentified emotion… Fear perhaps, or loss of control? A whole myriad of emotions filled him, and he was not dealing with any of it well.

By the time Oliver reached the car, his legs felt heavy, his body drained. He wondered where his energy surge had come from last night.

He got into the car and glanced at his Galaxy. A message highlighted his inbox. He paused, rubbing his chin before opening it. He would have to look at some point, he supposed.

Thanks for last night. No regrets…

No regrets? What the fuck did that mean?

He pressed the delete button and leaned his head back. He hoped it meant last night had been a one-off.

Lexie was not the one who was married.

FIVE

Lexie

'So, who's your friend?'

'Which one?'

'Come on, Lex. You know who I'm talking about. The curvy, copper-headed gorgeous babe over there.'

'Oh, you mean Pippa.'

'She's so tiny... and cute,' Oliver said, raising his eyebrow in appreciation. 'Is she attached?'

'No.'

'Hmm.'

'Oh no you don't, Oli, she's a good friend and you know I don't make friends easily. I'm not having you mess that up,' Lexie admonished, wagging her finger at him sternly.

'Who, me?' He adopted a look of innocence.

'Yes, you. Besides, you're going away again soon, there's no point in getting cosy. Save that for your other conquests.'

'How come I haven't seen her before?'

'I met her on campus. She's different, interesting actually, unlike most people here.'

'Look… she's coming over.'

'Hi, I'm Pippa.' She extended her hand confidently towards him and smiled.

'Oliver.' His hand reached out to meet hers, drawing it to his lips, holding it a moment longer than normally acceptable. 'Where's Lexie been hiding you?'

'Sorry?'

'I thought I was acquainted with all of Lexie's friends. I'd definitely remember meeting you.'

Lexie watched Oliver give Pippa one of his most dazzling smiles.

'And who's this charmer, Lexie?' Pippa's expression was coy.

'Oliver and I go way back.'

'We certainly do… through our parents mainly, and college.'

'So, this is your friend from the RAF?' Pippa finally broke eye contact with Oliver to look at Lexie.

'You know of me then?' Oliver diverted Pippa's attention back to him before Lexie had time to respond.

'Lexie told me all about you.'

'Well, we must chat over refreshments, for I must learn about you too. Obviously, it's unfair to have imbalance, surely?'

Lexie watched their exchange in fascination, feeling like an intruder, so strong was the chemistry between them. They stood transfixed, as though they were the only two people in the room.

*

Lexie stared hard at the photograph in her hand, replaying the scene in her mind when Oliver and Pippa first met.

Oliver had fallen for Pippa so fast. As for Pippa, she had spoken of nothing else.

Lexie had never been made to feel like the outsider though, and as they all matured, it was never a case of three being a crowd. They were equal in their mutual bond of friendship, and their chosen career paths enabled a quality of balance between them.

The photograph of their graduation ceremony took pride of place on the shelf, and as she studied it in her hand now, she reminisced. They looked so young back then. Pippa was stunning. The snapshot had captured her beaming smile as she stood proudly in the centre, looking tiny compared to Lexie and Oliver.

The picture reminded her of happier times when she had played Cupid, arranging dates for them and places to meet.

How could she face Pippa now? Even the thought made her queasy. It was just as well they'd become estranged, but she still missed her. Now, Lexie had betrayed her in the worst way possible. She sighed and moved the photograph into the drawer of her bureau.

Lexie needed a real drink. At the drinks cabinet, she poured a generous Remy Martin, inwardly berating herself for her agitated state, thinking about the row that had tainted their mutual affection. She knocked back a gulp of brandy, casting her mind back to their last evening together at the wine bar…

'You're a money-motivated career junkie, who forgets how to live, shutting out anyone who gets close to you. You're emotionally dysfunctional.'

Pippa's words still stung. Was she emotionally dysfunctional? Oliver always said she had no heart. They knew her too well; Lexie didn't expose her inner self freely.

Nothing fazed Pippa though, her emotions well balanced and controlled, instinctively knowing what others needed.

Lexie tried to block out her thoughts. She crossed the room to the kitchen and checked the cupboards, then the fridge. It held a packet of smoked salmon, two eggs, a slab of mature cheddar and half a lime – nothing exciting to tease her appetite. Not that she was hungry. Instead, she topped up her drink and sat on the window seat, sipping, and staring at the street below. It had been a busy day of commuting between GP surgeries and hospitals and her concentration span was on the wane. Lexie had work to do, but she knew her efforts would be futile. There were pressing emotional aspects to deal with, and as uncomfortable as they might seem, deal with them she must.

Her nature, she mused, was to face situations and deal with the consequences. Problems out in the open, in her opinion, helped one to move forward. So why let things smoulder? Fear of recrimination or rejection, perhaps?

Oliver and Pippa were more like family, especially since her parents moved away. Why then was she intent on destroying everything? Memories of the row surfaced again as the conversation echoed in her brain...

'How dare you undermine my career. I can't believe you said that. At least I can go out and converse with people. You are your bloody job. That's all you are. There's nothing else to you, is there?'

'You know, Pippa, you're such a supercilious bitch. What's happened to you? Where's my friend gone?'

'I am your only friend, Lexie, but the way I feel now, that's not going to be for much longer. Have you any idea how you've changed? You haven't got a clue, have you? You're a self-absorbed high-flyer with zero personality. That phone is your life. You're constantly checking it. You can't even have a conversation!'

'No, Pippa. You're the one who's changed. Since you've got involved with all this alternative stuff, you're like a different person. You need a reality check. I can't talk to you anymore.'

'That's just fine because I've got nothing left to say to you.'

Lexie remembered Pippa stalking from the wine bar, her eyes ablaze. But Pippa was right, she was her only friend. Pippa was the only person Lexie had allowed to get close. Should she call her? She glanced at the clock – too late now. How would she begin the conversation, anyway? Tomorrow was Saturday, and she had nothing much planned for the weekend, aside from popping to Waitrose or a session at the gym. It would drive her crazy having a little time on her hands for a change. But life was like that; when you needed space, a full schedule dictated, and when your mind tormented you, there was time to sit and brood.

To dispel her tormented thoughts, she opted for a soak in the bath and then retired to bed with a book.

Jeffery Deaver failed to distract her, so half an hour later she switched off the lamp and snuggled down under the duvet.

Tossing and turning, she punched the pillow in frustration, pulling the quilt over her head.

When sleep came, she was once again with Oliver, straddling him, grinding her hips, riding him. Alex stood in the corner, watching.

'What are you doing to my daddy, Auntie Lex?' he cried out.

She woke up with a start, sweating, her heart pounding. She leaned up on her elbow, switched on the lamp and looked at the time display on her mobile. Only 3am! She flopped back, trying to settle, tired and tormented.

Lexie made a decision: tomorrow, she would visit Pippa.

SIX

Pippa

Friday's clinic had not been busy, and by the time Pippa had fed, bathed and put Alexander to bed, it was almost time for the news broadcast; being a military wife, she was conditioned to watch.

Oliver's twelve-year period of service was nearly finished. Thankfully, he'd been lucky and remained unharmed.

Her excitement had been building and she couldn't wait to see him, even though this latest stint away had been shorter.

When she put the kettle on to make a chamomile tea, she breathed a contented sigh. One more day and she'd be in Oliver's arms, feeling complete again. She poured the boiling water over fresh chamomile in a strainer over the teapot. While she waited for the leaves to infuse, she picked up an orange from the fruit bowl and dug her thumb into its knobbly skin, causing the juice to burst through the air. She peeled it and sucked on a segment, the zesty tang waking up her taste buds. Once she'd finished, she disposed of the skin, washed her sticky hands and poured the tea.

Back in the lounge, she switched on the television, reducing the volume to avoid disturbing Alexander. She sat on the sofa, curling her legs beneath her, and reached for her briefcase at the side of the coffee table. She pulled out a plastic file.

Pippa flipped through the pages to familiarise herself with Charles's medical history, then drew a detailed timeline of vaccine dates and health issues. Studying the graph, Pippa checked if symptoms had tended to occur around times of vaccinations. Deep in concentration, she chewed the end of her pencil, absorbing the sequence of events, pausing to add to her notes.

When she glanced up at the clock, it was 9pm and her tea had gone cold. Pippa set the folder aside and relaxed into the cushion.

She frowned. Oliver should have phoned by now. The normal plan was to speak to Alexander before his bedtime. Alexander missed Oliver too, frequently asking for him.

When Oliver was at Brize Norton, it wasn't always possible to call at dusk if they were on night flight training. When he was out of the country, he relied on Skype.

She leaned forward for the remote control and increased the volume a touch. While listening to the reporter, her thoughts remained preoccupied.

Pippa heard the faint sound of a key in the lock at 9.20. Springing up, she ran through the hallway, straight into Oliver's arms.

'You're early. You're not due until tomorrow.' Pippa

beamed as she spoke. She wrapped herself around him, clinging tight.

'Are you complaining?' Oliver dropped his kitbag to the floor and lowered his lips to hers.

The hunger for one another locked them into a moment of oblivion until an excitable voice alerted them.

'Daddy, Daddy!' exclaimed Alexander, shouting from the landing. 'You're back!' As they looked up, Alexander scrambled down the stairs, clad in a pair of Batman pyjamas, his straw-coloured hair tousled from sleep.

'You should be asleep, young man.' Pippa stifled a smile, knowing there was no chance now Oliver was home. He jumped into his father's waiting arms, clinging to him like a limpet.

'Did you bring me a present?' His cornflower eyes were wide with excitement.

'Hmm, let me see… Has he been a good boy, Mummy?'

'Yes, yes! Haven't I, Mummy?' Alexander asked breathlessly. 'I've done my reading book and spellings and… and… everything.' His expectant eyes darted between their faces.

'OK then.' Oliver lowered his son to the floor, his grin displaying his pride. He reached for his bag and pulled out a parcel. 'But you can only open it tonight and play tomorrow. Is that a deal?'

Alexander nodded, his body fidgeting in anticipation.

'And,' Oliver added, handing the gift to him, 'you must go back to your room afterward, it's late.'

'K.' Alexander tore at the wrapping. His face lit up with delight. 'Wow, a Chinook! Thank you, Daddy,' he said, bouncing on his toes.

'You're welcome, son. Right, let's get you a glass of milk, and then sleep.' Oliver lifted him onto his back like a koala bear.

'Can I take my helicopter?'

'I'll put it beside your bed.' He turned, winked at Pippa, dropped a kiss on her forehead and headed for the kitchen.

'He's settled,' Oliver told Pippa a few minutes later as he joined her in the kitchen.

Pippa was uncorking a bottle of Rioja. 'Have you eaten?' she asked, glancing over her shoulder.

'Yes thanks. I had something earlier.'

'What did you eat? Anything exciting?'

'This casserole-type thing at the base,' he said, leafing through the post.

'Nothing there for you,' said Pippa, walking over and wrapping her arms around him. She rested her head on his back. 'I've missed you so much.'

He turned, and she stood on her tiptoes, raising her face.

Oliver bent to kiss her. 'Mm, I've missed you too, baby.' He squeezed her to his chest, curling his finger through her hair.

She gave a sigh of contentment. She enjoyed him playing with her hair.

'I could stay like this forever, but I'd better pour the wine.' She moved across to the oak worktop. 'Now, tell me,' she said, handing him a cut-crystal glass, 'how come you didn't tell me you were back?'

'I wanted to surprise you.' He gave her a lopsided grin. 'Have you missed me?'

Pippa's heart always melted at that particular expression.

He cocked his head further to one side, waiting for her answer.

'What do you think?' She chinked glasses. 'Cheers.'

It was their ritual, even at home. Oliver placed a firm palm on her buttocks, steering her into the lounge.

'Come on, let's get comfy.'

Once seated, he reached for her, drawing her closer. She snuggled into him, folding her arm around his waist. The sound of his heartbeat offered her a sense of security. He was back, and safe.

'You OK?' Pippa asked, after a few minutes. She felt Oliver tense, and she looked up searching his face, sensing a distinct shift in his mood.

'Just tired.' He bent and pecked her lips.

Dark half-moon rings sat beneath his eyes. He did look tired, thought Pippa.

'Not *too* tired I hope?' she said.

SEVEN

Lexie

The thirty-minute journey had passed too soon, thought Lexie as she pulled onto the drive of Primrose Cottage. It had been a while since she'd been here and the cottage looked beautiful, covered in deep purple wisteria, reminding her of the home she grew up in.

She sat for a moment, trying to still her hammering heart, before stepping out beside the front lawn. She moistened her lips and let out a slow breath. The birdsong didn't mask the sound of blood pounding through her ears.

The gable around the entrance had a blood-red rambling rose clinging to it, giving off a powerful, sweet fragrance. A queen bee buzzed around a rosebud to draw its nectar, and Lexie ducked, dodging it. At the door, she tapped the wrought-iron knocker and held her breath.

'Hi,' said Lexie as Pippa opened the door, her expression stunned.

'Oh... hello.' She moved aside to allow Lexie in. 'This is a surprise.'

Against Lexie's height, Pippa appeared even more petite. She was dressed in an ankle-length skirt adorned with a wide tan-coloured belt, and a gypsy-style top. An arty painted clip held her copper hair, though random curls escaped, framing her high cheekbones. Her feet were bare. She was the picture of innocence, which served to trigger Lexie's shame.

'I… erm, thought it time for a truce,' said Lexie, swallowing.

Pippa's warm smile dispelled the awkwardness. So far so good, Lexie thought.

'Coffee?' Pippa asked, moving into the kitchen.

'Please, if you're having one.'

Pippa poured water into the kettle from a filter jug and spooned coffee into a cafetière. Taking cups from the cupboard, she peered over her shoulder.

'Aren't you going to sit down?' She nodded towards the farmhouse oak table and chairs. The table was embellished with embroidered coasters, and a teapot vase of wild spring flowers stood in the middle.

'You've only just missed Oliver. He's taken Alexander to McDonald's.' Pippa shook her head in disapproval.

Lexie's stomach flipped at the mention of Oliver. She wondered if he'd told Pippa they'd met. If only he'd answered her text!

'All kids love McDonald's.' Lexie tried to focus.

'They're likely to, with such blatant marketing strategies.'

Lexie suppressed a sigh as she watched Pippa adding hot water and allowing the coffee to brew.

'More needs to be done about these mega companies making junk food appealing, don't you think?' Pippa brought the coffee and china to the table and sat down.

'They've reduced salt and sugar. And they are selling healthier choices at least.' Lexie chose her words with care. Pippa had a thing about children consuming too much sugar, and Lexie was in no mood to have a big debate. She needed to keep the conversation light. 'How is Alex?' she said, changing the subject.

Pippa pushed down the plunger, filled the cups and handed one to Lexie. It smelled appealing but tasted weak. Decaffeinated, she guessed.

'Alexander is well.'

Lexie didn't fail to notice that Pippa made a point of using the full name. She disliked shortened versions.

Lexie cast her mind back to when Pippa had chosen the name as a variant of her own. She'd been honoured. Pippa had informed her of the name's meaning: 'Defender of men', like his father. Tied even by name, Lexie mused in irony.

'That's good.'

'He's so excited having Oliver home.'

'I'll bet. What gift did he bring this time?'

'A Chinook helicopter. He was delighted. He even demanded to know if it was exactly the same kind of helicopter Oliver flies!'

Lexie imagined Alex's happy face as he opened the gift.

'I've missed him.'

'He's been asking for you.'

'And now I feel guilty.'

'Me too.' Pippa rested her chin on her hand, elbow on the table. 'Sometimes we don't consider how things affect those around us till afterwards, when it's too late.'

'And is it?'

'What?'

'Too late?' Lexie held her mug in both hands. She waited. Perhaps it was a mistake to come. Maybe severing them from her life was simpler. But looking at Pippa now, there was only warmth and comfort, and being with her felt right. She wished she'd come earlier. Then last night would never have happened.

'I'd better go,' she blurted out, crossing the room to rinse her cup in the Belfast sink. The room fell silent, the atmosphere loaded with uncertainty. The sound of running water and the soft whirring of the fridge were the only audible sounds.

'Alexander would love to see you,' said Pippa, breaking the silence. 'They shouldn't be too long now.'

Lexie's pulse sped up. It was difficult enough for her to be standing here now, at a loss for words, without them being all together in the same room.

'Maybe I could call one day and take him for a trip out?' Lexie's heart weighed heavy in her chest. She turned to face Pippa, who was rising from her chair.

Pippa met her eyes, not answering. Was she saying she couldn't? Or implying she wanted no further personal communication, but Alex could stay in touch? Had their gap grown too wide? Lexie didn't know what to say next, but the shrill of the telephone was a welcome intrusion.

'One second.' Pippa lifted the handset. 'Oh, hi, honey.' Her eyes widened. 'No thanks, I had muesli. Guess who's here?'

Lexie's heart jolted.

Pippa talked into the mouthpiece. 'Hmm, just what I said. Yes, I'll ask. I knew Alexander would be happy. Did he enjoy his junk food treat?'

Lexie needed to leave before they got back. She racked her frantic mind for an adequate excuse. When Pippa hung up, Lexie's brain was buzzing, but she tried to appear calm. Pippa was an expert at reading emotion. Lexie thought Pippa ought to have chosen a career in psychotherapy instead.

'Oliver asked if you'd be here when they get back. He said Alexander screamed with delight knowing you're here.'

'I… erm…' She was on the spot now. 'I suppose—'

'That's settled then.'

EIGHT

Pippa

A sensation in Pippa's gut told her something was wrong, and her instinct never failed her. Why had Lexie turned up? It was not like her to back down from an argument, and they'd had a few lately – the last one, awful. Pippa wondered if they'd ever get over it. Lexie appeared jittery, and that wasn't her. Something was amiss.

'You'll stay then?' Pippa saw a strange fleeting expression cross Lexie's face.

'I should get back.'

'Why? Do you have a more pressing engagement on a Saturday morning?'

'I need to catch up on reports.'

'Can't it wait? Have a day off. Besides, we've got catching up to do – if we can stay civil.' Pippa gave a light-hearted smile. 'And Oliver thought it a good idea too.'

'I'm sure you want family time. Oliver has only just got home,' Lexie said, making her way towards the front door. 'I can pop in another time.'

'Nonsense, we'll have plenty of time together,' said Pippa, wondering how Lexie knew Oliver had only just got home.

'I don't mind. I'll come back later.'

'What's up, Lexie?'

'Nothing. It's been a tough week, and I still have stuff to do.'

'So why come?'

'I thought—'

'Spit it out, Lexie. What's on your mind? You're never at a loss for words.'

'Look, there's nothing. I thought we needed... I wanted to see you.'

'You could have phoned.'

'As could you.'

'Well, you're here now, so why not stay a while?'

'Because... I don't want to end up arguing, again.'

'We won't.' Pippa felt more emotionally responsive towards her now. 'Things haven't been the same. It's ages since you've stayed over when Oliver's away. I've missed our midnight chats.'

Lexie's lips curled. 'Like our uni days.'

It reminded Pippa of when Lexie used to burn the candle at both ends, but still managed to finish her assignments on time and achieve a First.

She looked at her now, noticing a strained expression. Reaching out, she touched Lexie's arm. Lexie's muscle tensed in response.

'Come on, stay for lunch at least.'

'OK.' Lexie smiled but Pippa noticed the smile failed to reach her eyes.

They headed back to the kitchen and Pippa scanned the cupboards.

'I'll see what I can rustle up. Relax, I'll make another drink. I don't suppose you want herbal tea?' she asked, grinning.

'Caffeine's my fix. Flowers are for the garden.' Lexie laughed for the first time since she'd arrived.

'Better not use decaffeinated this time then.'

'Was I that obvious?'

'Your nose wrinkled. Sure you don't want to try a herbal? I'm partial to this one.' Pippa reached into the cupboard and pulled out a box. 'Ginseng and pomegranate.'

'I could think of nothing worse. Give me caffeine and alcohol any day.' They laughed, lifting the earlier atmosphere.

'Coffee it is then. Unless you'd prefer wine?'

Lexie's eyebrows lifted. 'At this time? Even I don't drink this early, though I've been drinking more lately.'

'Oh, why's that?'

'Usual stress at work. Still a man's world.' Lexie shook her head. 'They hate it when I beat their targets and they're pissed off if I don't. Whatever I do, they want more. Higher targets, new custom, more travel. There's no let-up.'

Pippa noticed Lexie looked exhausted, and she felt concerned, but she was too worried to pass any work-related comments. Things could get heated, like last time.

'Here's your caffeine fix.'

'Thanks.'

Pippa peered into the fridge. 'Now, what do you fancy for lunch? I have couscous with haricot beans, a nice leafy salad, or—'

'Don't you have real food?'

Pippa turned to Lexie who was shuddering exaggeratedly. Pippa raised a finger. 'I know, you want a nice, meat-filled sandwich, eh?'

'Sounds wonderful.'

'Chicken on granary?' Pippa asked, selecting the items. 'And salad, no onions.' It reminded her how well they knew one another.

Pippa busied herself with the task, glad to have her back to Lexie. There were many unanswered questions. What happened in their lives shaped who they'd become, and, despite everything, she missed her. Their friendship was stronger than opinions, wasn't it? They'd shared secrets and mutual understanding. So when did beliefs and emotions take over?

Placing the food on the table, Pippa joined Lexie to eat.

'Mm,' said Lexie, taking a small bite.

Pippa noticed Lexie nibbling, rather than eating and enjoying her food as she usually did. She stabbed a piece of tomato with her fork.

'Your salad looks appetising,' Lexie said, nodding at Pippa's plate. 'It reminds me when we first met at uni, remember?'

'And you were eating a huge slab of cake.' Pippa smiled. 'You thought I was studying art, and I thought you were studying law. It's funny how we make first impressions on people.'

'You looked like a healthy hippy,' said Lexie grinning. 'You still eat the same.'

'I adore salad. If it wasn't for Oliver's desire for meat, I'm not sure I'd buy it.'

'You're not a veggie now, are you?'

'No, though the more I discover what's injected into animals the less meat I eat.' Pippa saw Lexie's perfectly waxed eyebrows rise.

'If we worried about everything, I'm sure we wouldn't eat.' Her tone became tetchy.

'It has to affect our health. Think what they do to fatten pigs. Everything is hurried for faster production.' She picked up a spring onion and dipped it in hummus.

'Vegetables get sprayed, and you eat those,' Lexie challenged.

'I grow my own now or buy organic.'

'How about when you eat out?' Lexie set her sandwich down, sat back and crossed her arms. 'Do you ask the chef if everything on your plate's organic?'

'Now you're being pedantic.'

'No, Pippa, it's you. Must every conversation be a debate?' Lexie moved the plate away. 'Thanks for the sandwich but I've lost my appetite.'

Pippa saw the familiar nostril flare.

'I guessed this was a bad idea,' Lexie said.

'What is your problem?' Pippa said, with a slow disbelieving shake of her head. Only Lexie had the ability to trigger her. She felt her anger build.

Lexie rolled her eyes. 'My problem? My problem is you. You've changed so much. There is not a single topic we can discuss. You make me feel bad even when I'm trying to eat a fucking sandwich, for Christ's sake!'

Pippa felt a rush of blood to her cheeks. 'That's your paranoia. People can pass an opinion without worrying about causing offence, surely. What's the matter? Are you feeling guilty about marketing poisons?'

'Fuck you, Pippa!' Lexie raised her voice, eyes blazing. 'You're so sanctimonious. It's about time you lived in the real world. People die without drugs. And you're wrong, I've got nothing to feel guilty about.' She forced the chair back with her thighs, standing.

'Oh no? You work for these pharma giants, who use the media for their scaremonger tactics. Forcing statins on people, making them believe they'll prevent heart attacks. Promoting flu vaccines when they can't possibly know what strain of flu will strike!' Pippa's heart raced. 'Why do you think people are becoming sicker, despite the advances in medicine?'

Lexie glared at her. 'I'm not listening to this shit.' She stomped out of the kitchen, calling behind her, 'Don't bother to see me out.'

Pippa's chest heaved with rage. How dare Lexie come into her home, hurling foul-mouthed insults? She marched after her. 'Truth hurts doesn't—'

They halted as Oliver's key slid into the lock.

'Hi, honey,' Oliver said, stepping into the hallway. 'Hello, Lex.'

Pippa's eyes darted between them. Lexie looked at the floor. That was a stiff exchange, thought Pippa.

'Hellooo, Auntie Lexie. Look what I've got!' Alexander thrust an activity book into her hand.

'Hello. What's this then?'

'It's *Doodlepedia*. We had to go to another shop to get it, didn't we, son?' Oliver told them.

'But first, we had nuggets.' Alex looked up at Oliver. 'And I ate them all like a good boy, didn't I, Daddy?'

'Yes, you did.' Oliver grinned at him. 'We took a voucher

to WHSmith's in exchange for the book. That's why we were longer than I'd expected,' said Oliver. 'There's another one too, *Animal Antics*. I promised him that one next week if he's good, didn't I, son?' Oliver rubbed Alexander's hair.

Alexander nodded in agreement. 'Will you come too?'

'I'm sorry, darling, I've lots of work to do.' Lexie reached down to pick him up for a cuddle.

'I like your new book.'

Pippa scrutinised Lexie as she surveyed the book, flicking through the pages to appease Alexander. Lexie smiled at Alexander and passed it back.

'Is everything OK?' Oliver asked.

'Lexie was just leaving.'

'Oh nooo, you've only just come. I haven't seen you yet,' Alexander protested, screwing up his face, pouting his lips.

Lexie kissed his cheek and put him down. 'I know but—'

'Pleeease, Mummy, ask Auntie Lex to stay,' he pleaded, disappointment in his eyes.

'I'm afraid she has to go. She's got work to do and—'

'But I want her to stay.'

Pippa knelt beside him to hug him. 'Sometimes we have to do things we don't want, Alexander. Lexie's busy. She needs to collect medicines to make people better.' Her voice was laced with cynicism. 'Isn't that right?' she asked, tilting her face to Lexie.

'Mummy's right, darling. If I didn't, lots of people would get sick.' Lexie shot a look back at Pippa, her mouth set.

'Mummy makes people better too, don't you, Mummy?'

'I do. Now, Daddy will take you upstairs to fetch the crayons for your new book, OK?'

'K,' said Alexander, clutching his father's hand.

Pippa stared at Oliver, giving him the cue to leave, and held the door ajar for Lexie.

'Bye bye, Auntie. See you soon.'

'Bye, Alexander. Thank you for showing me your lovely book.' She turned to Oliver.

'Goodbye, Oli.'

'See you.'

Pippa watched their exchange intently. She wanted Lexie out of her home.

Alexander clambered up the stairs. Oliver followed, twisting around, his quizzical expression settling on Pippa.

Pippa's only concern was for Lexie to leave. As she opened the door wider, their gazes locked. Lexie shook her head and stepped outside.

Pippa fixed her stare on Lexie's rigid back as she marched to her car, climbed in and drove off without a backward glance. Pippa closed the door, leaned against the wall and heaved a juddering sigh. Tears of anger prickled, ready to spill. Closing her eyes to calm herself, she focused on stabilising her breathing for a moment.

Back in the kitchen, she cleared the table and disposed of the uneaten lunch. Then she filled the bowl with water, squeezed in detergent and washed the plates vigorously.

Her chest was still heaving. Lexie had enraged her, leaving her feeling sick. Why had she evoked so much fury in her today? This time, it had ended their relationship for sure. She never wanted to see her again. But more disturbing had been the look Lexie and Oliver exchanged. And her words, 'I'm sure you want family time, Oliver has only just got home.' Pippa hadn't mentioned to Lexie how long he'd been on leave so far. Just then, she felt Oliver's arms encircling her.

'What was all that about?'

Pippa stiffened and continued to rinse the plates.

'Hey, talk to me,' Oliver said, turning her around to face him.

She grabbed a towel to dry her hands, still in his arms but not meeting his eyes.

'Pippa,' he said, taking the towel and putting his finger under her chin to turn her face towards him.

'Where's Alexander?'

'He's playing. Are you going to tell me what's going on?'

'She's a bitch! I never want to see her again!' Her lips trembled, and she drew a deep shaky breath. She was glad when he tightened his arms around her, but she could no longer restrain the huge wave of sadness. Sobs burst from her as he stroked her hair.

'Shh… It will be OK. You'll work things out.' He kissed her head and held her, rocking her like a child.

She calmed, enjoying his comforting arms. Her thoughts reverted to the look, but she forced herself to push it to the back of her mind. He tilted her chin and brushed her lips with his own, his thumb stroking her damp cheeks.

'No more tears. Sit in the lounge and I'll bring you a cup of chamomile.'

Pippa did as he suggested, too emotionally spent to resist. When Oliver joined her, she peered up at him as he crossed the floor. Her pulse quickened. 'When were you going to tell me about Lexie?'

NINE

Oliver

Oliver froze in shock at Pippa's question. Her head tilted, as it invariably did when she was waiting for an answer. His jaw dropped and his brain fought to decipher her exact words.

'You're acting as though you've something to hide.' Her eyes were glued on him, with questioning suspicion.

'Tell you what?' His tone sounded defensive, even to his own ears.

'You tell me?' She folded her arms across her chest.

Oliver bent to set the cup on the coffee table, not wanting to meet her challenging stare. He was unaccustomed to lying to his wife. She was astute, and he feared she would be aware in an instant he did have something to hide. He sat down beside her and pulled her to him, trying to nestle her head on his shoulder.

'You're upset. Now, explain what's happened between you two.'

'Don't change the subject,' she said, pulling away, not allowing him to hide her face. 'Look at me, Oliver—'

'I don't know what you're talking about.' How much had Lexie said? He tried hard to look normal, but his nerve endings were jumping. Panic rose within him. 'Whatever's wrong with you two, don't vent your anger on me.' He bounced up. 'I'm fed up with this shit. I haven't come home for more conflict. There's enough at work, for fuck's sake!'

As he stormed from the room, he sensed her eyes boring into him. Attack first, he thought. Attack was always the best form of defence.

'Where are you going?' she shouted at his retreating back.

'Out. I need air.' Oliver needed to call Lexie to find out what she'd said. He grabbed his car keys and phone and left, Pippa's words still ringing in his ears.

Oliver needed a drink but drove past their local, not wanting to bump into anyone he knew. He continued farther to one he didn't normally frequent.

He pulled into the car park and made his way inside. It was quiet, and he was grateful for that. At the bar, he ordered a bottle of Beck's and sat on a rickety wooden stool, rubbing his brow. The barmaid handed him the beer and smiled.

'I haven't seen you in here before,' she said, leaning on her elbow, as though preparing for a long conversation. 'Are you from round these parts?'

'No,' he answered, taking a sip and picking at the label on the bottle. There was no one else waiting to be served, he noticed, glancing down the bar. Not in the mood for idle chit-chat, but not wanting to offend her either, he smiled back.

'Would you like a menu?' she asked, not taking his earlier monosyllabic answer as a hint. She smiled again as she polished a brass pump. 'We're renowned for our food, especially the steak and ale pie.'

'No thanks.' Oliver stood, placing a five-pound note down. 'Excuse me,' he said with a curt nod and left the bar to find a private seat in the corner. His agenda involved speaking to Lexie, and soon. He didn't think Pippa would call her first, judging by the exchange he'd witnessed earlier. At least, he hoped not.

Oliver pulled the phone out of his pocket and tapped the screen, scrolling through the list of contacts. Lexie's number selected, he waited. She answered after the first ring.

'What the fuck did you say to Pippa?' he growled into the mouthpiece. His jaw was rigid.

'Fuck you, Oliver. Don't you dare speak to me like that!'

The line went dead. Frustrated, he redialled, relief swamping him when she answered.

'Care to amend your tone?'

'I'm sorry, Lex… Please, just tell me.' His imagination was full of the image of Lexie easing her conscience to Pippa; he hoped and prayed that he was wrong. 'What happened?' he asked, his dread rising as he waited.

'I didn't tell her about us if that's what you mean.'

He closed his eyes and let out the breath he'd been unconsciously holding.

'Don't you worry, Oli. Far be it from me to come between you and the lovely Pippa,' she added. 'You're still safe to play happy families. You men make me sick, having your fucking cake and eating it!' Her bitterness was almost palpable, even at the end of the phone.

'Is that what you believe?' he asked, heavy-hearted. 'Lex—'

'Don't apologise, Oli. We're both grown-ups.'

He was lost for words. But what was he supposed to say? He couldn't explain his own feelings, let alone hers. His mind searched for a reason beyond his logic. It was an instinctive moral weakness. There was no explanation, except a gnawing fear he couldn't disclose to his wife. Maybe he'd needed to feel alive without the complication of deep love – love he only held for his wife? Or was it to channel his pent-up sexual demons? But why Lexie, and why now?

His personal mission as mediator had failed with drastic consequences. He'd fuelled the fire, big time!

'No regrets, remember?'

'Lexie, I—'

'I'm a big girl, Oli. I enjoyed myself as much as you did, so don't flatter yourself by assuming I need anything more from you. It was just sex.' Oliver recoiled at her directness. 'It shouldn't have happened, but it did, so move on.'

'What happened earlier?' Oliver asked, uncomfortable talking about their liaison.

'It doesn't matter, does it? As long as you two are OK.'

He heard her sigh and then there was an uneasy silence.

'Look, Oli, I've tried… and right now, I wouldn't care if I ever saw her again.'

'Don't *say* that.' He frowned and leaned his chin on his hand. 'It shouldn't be like this.' But as he uttered the words, he knew things would never be the same. How could it? 'You and Pip—'

'Are no more,' she interjected. 'Don't you see, Oli? There's no going back. It's over… for all of us.'

She was right, and on a selfish note, it was easier for him. Easier not having to face Lexie, and easier not having to worry about them all being together. He felt bad, but deep down, this was his get-out clause. He wouldn't risk losing his marriage or be divided from Alex; that would kill him.

'What will you do?'

'Survive… just like always.'

Despite her confident retort, her voice was thick, and Oliver realised she was trying not to cry.

'You sound defeated. I'm sorry, Lex.'

'So am I.' She ended the call.

Oliver gulped back his Beck's and visited the bar to order one more. Sitting down again, he rested his head against the fake leather seat. He took a sip, appreciating the taste of the chilled beer.

Even war service appeared more favourable than his state of anxiety right now. At least he was always prepared for the unexpected. This was way out of his comfort zone. What was wrong with his head?

His phone rang, interrupting his thoughts.

'Why did you think I'd told her?' Lexie asked.

'Just something she said. I didn't hang around to find out what she meant. I needed to speak to you first.'

'What did she say?'

'She said, "When were you going to tell me about Lexie?" and my brain flew into overdrive.' Pippa's words had stayed lodged in his brain.

'I wasn't sure myself if you'd said anything, either.'

'Why?'

'The way she kept looking at me. Kind of strange; you know the look she gives, when she knows something but doesn't tell you? And you didn't answer my text, so I didn't know if you told her we'd... erm, met. You know, to talk, before we—'

'You didn't wake me, so we hardly had time to discuss that, did we?' His mind filled with a fleeting picture of their passion. He cleared his throat. 'And I owe you for the room.' He tried to focus on her voice, not the playback in his head.

'I figured you wouldn't want the transaction on your statement.'

She was right. It could have been a disastrous mistake. That's what he admired about Lexie, her amazing foresight. But it still didn't sit right. 'I'll think of another way to pay you back.'

'Don't worry about it. We are in a world of equality. Don't be such a dinosaur.'

'I miss you already,' he said, meaning it for the right reasons.

'Me too... And Oli—'

'Yeah?'

'Make sure you delete my messages. She doesn't miss a trick.'

'Already have,' he said, wishing he could delete his infidelity.

On the way home, Oliver's dread lifted. He still didn't understand what Pippa had meant, but after talking to Lexie, decided there couldn't have been any incriminating evidence. Pippa must be bluffing, assuming he had called Lexie to persuade her to make it right between them. Thank God it was nothing more sinister.

He pulled onto the forecourt of a florist shop to pick up a vibrant bouquet of orange roses, freesias and alstroemeria, her favourites. Some men gave flowers to ease their guilt and Oliver understood why. He'd always bought them for his wife, just because she loved them. 'Flowers make a house a home,' she'd say. Pippa knew the meanings of most flowers, but he only remembered alstroemeria meant devotion, daffodils rebirth and renewal; he remembered this because Pippa mentioned something about the earliest buds to spring. Roses, of course, were for love, though even their colours held different meanings!

Farther into the journey, he stopped at the local wine merchant for a bottle of Beaujolais. He wanted to take her out for dinner, but she didn't like leaving Alex except for the odd occasion with his parents. Alexander was happy to be with them. Perhaps it would be a good idea for him to go later, to give them time alone?

When he arrived home, she wasn't there. His heart plummeted. As he entered the kitchen, he saw a note on the table.

Sorry for this morning, I was upset about Lexie. Gone to deliver remedies to Gillian and drop Alexander off at your parents' for the night. I hope that's OK with you. If you're reading this, you are home (hopefully) before me. Call me if you have other plans.

Love you. P xx

Oliver smiled, feeling the weight lift from his shoulders. He didn't call her in case she was driving; even with the hands-free option, it was still a distraction and Pippa hated using her mobile at the best of times, always concerned about radiation.

He was relieved there would be no more arguing. He'd had enough friction lately and didn't have the energy. She must have read his mind about Alexander – always so in tune with him. Oliver stood the flowers in the sink for her to arrange later and helped himself to a bottle of Beck's from the fridge.

Kicking off his shoes, he switched on the TV to watch the rugby. When Pippa got back, he would run her a nice bubble bath while she decided what she'd prefer to do for dinner. He assumed she would probably want to go out since she'd dropped Alexander off, though she might want a night at home free from interruption. That being the case, he would make their evening romantic and special. He would light scented candles and place them around the bath. Then, he'd pour her a glass of wine to relax with before soaping her all over. The thought of her naked body woke up his cock, and he felt the pressure tug at his jeans.

'Down boy,' he said, patting his groin. One part of his body was functioning well at least. A little too well, he thought guiltily.

TEN

Lexie

When Lexie ended the call with Oliver, she slumped in the chair, put her head between her hands and cried, letting out every bit of pent-up tension. Pippa had enraged her, and Oliver's abandonment stung. She brushed away her fat tears of dejection, frustrated at letting her guard down. It drained her, and she could not banish thoughts of either of them.

Had she provoked Pippa, venting her anger through jealousy? Pippa had tried to be civil, and Lexie had blown a fuse, guilt gnawing at her. As for Oliver, Lexie had introduced panic into his life, bringing uncertainty to his perfect, stable marriage. But he was a man, and like all men, a bastard!

If she was honest with herself, though, she knew he was different. But he'd aroused something new. An insatiable carnal instinct, as though only the two of them existed, connecting on a mysterious level.

In the moment, she hadn't seen Oliver as her friend, rather as the object of her desire. A pure, masculine Adonis, and she'd wanted him, abandoning all sense of right and wrong.

Lexie reached into her bag for a packet of tissues. It was unlike her to be in such a state, wallowing in self-pity, but she'd brought it on herself.

So, what drove her to such a sense of abandonment? Perhaps it was an underlying emotional hunger? Or the safety of knowing Oliver was unobtainable and so she could feed the need without the complications of a serious relationship? Or pleasure without strings? But there were strings and more complications. So why Oliver? There had been something in his expression that evening she couldn't fathom.

Now, the harsh reality was that she was once again alone. As her mind revisited events, Lexie was no more forward in the understanding of her lapse of judgment. In fact, she was more confused than ever.

Now, she could never put things right and she couldn't shake off the sadness. She was miserable and vulnerable, and she didn't do vulnerable. Exhausted, she drew her knees to her chest and slept.

The shrill ring of the phone made Lexie jump.

'Lexie darling, how are you?' Julian's chirpy voice asked. 'Fancy catching up with a cocktail later?'

Lexie tried hard to engage her foggy brain. She forced herself to respond, rubbing her arm, trying to stop the pins and needles caused by her awkward position. 'I… erm…'

'I won't listen to excuses. We've not caught up for ages.'

'Why do you sound so upbeat?'

'I've just got back, and I know you'll want to hear about the new proposals for Shanghai and Bangalore. So how about it?'

She didn't have the energy to protest, especially with Julian, who had an answer for everything and wasn't put off easily. That was one trait that made him successful, and the reason he was such a valuable asset to RestrilPharma. With his persuasive conversation, he made even the strongest-willed people surrender to his requests. He made people question their decision-making processes and come around to his way of thinking. And that meant more sales and more business taken from their competitors.

'OK, what time?'

'I'll pick you up at eight.'

Before she had time to reply, he'd ended the call.

'Oh God,' she said aloud, massaging her stiff neck and glancing at the clock, which said 6.30; she'd been sleeping a while. She must buck herself up and get ready for an evening out.

Under the shower, water bounced off her face, livening her drowsy state. She shampooed and conditioned her hair and soaped her body with Givenchy *Dahlia Noir*, her bathtime luxury. She inhaled its scent, feeling more refreshed.

Julian lifted her spirits, she mused, and she welcomed that. Her thoughts drifted to Sebastian's comment. She would ask him about Amelia later – not that it was any of her business now they were no longer a couple.

Lexie dried off and reached for the body lotion from the bathroom shelf, looking at the label. She gave a wry smile as she read *Guilty* by Gucci and replaced it, choosing Calvin Klein's *Escape* instead.

As she added a spray of antiperspirant, Pippa's comment jumped in her mind: '*You shouldn't use antiperspirants, the aluminium content causes breast cancer. Try a deodorising stone, it's far more natural.'*

There was evidence for that claim, but Pippa didn't wear under-wired bras either for the same reason. Lexie thought that was going too far and anyway, she required extra support for her 34E cup.

In the bedroom, she sat at the dresser. She applied concealer and a light dusting of make-up. Afterwards, she blow-dried her silky hair into a chic bob.

Feeling more human, she selected a simple black dress to match her mood and Jimmy Choo Abel nude shoes, another indulgent luxury. And why not? She worked hard enough to reward herself with a few designer items. Satisfied she looked presentable, Lexie sprayed matching perfume and titivated her hairstyle.

Once in the kitchen, she poured a large glass of Chardonnay to get her in the mood while she waited for Julian.

*

Julian had Lexie laughing with his infectious wit as soon as they reached the bistro-style bar. It was as though they'd never been apart, and she soon relaxed in his company.

His newly tanned face emphasised his aligned white teeth, through which he was currently sucking garlicky mussels. He was vibrant and captivating, his energy boundless.

'The project is set to start in the summer and there's much to be done over there.' He licked his lips, threw a shell into a bowl and dipped his fingers into his bowl of lemon water. 'I love the way you eat those,' he said, staring at her lips. 'They slide down nicely, eh?' His grin was mischievous. 'Talking of sliding.'

'Behave, Jules. Let me enjoy them in peace... without your sexual connotations.'

'Is that a "no" then? Not even for old times' sake? I mean, who needs Viagra when there are beautiful, tempting women like you?'

'Erectile dysfunction has many causes and—'

'I for one don't need Viagra. I can prove it if you like?' His nutmeg-coloured eyes lowered to his groin. 'No dysfunction, see?'

'You're incorrigible.'

'Simply displaying my admiration for my girl.'

He winked and Lexie smiled, despite herself. 'I'm ignoring you,' she said, dabbing her lip with a paper napkin. 'And I'm not your girl.'

'You know we're good together. You just won't admit it.'

'Were.' She took a long sip of gin and tonic.

'You're hurting my feelings,' Julian said, his hand tapping his firm chest.

He was right: they were good together, and she did miss him. Her emotions were already shot; she didn't need further complications.

Lexie couldn't resist. 'I'm sure Amelia is more than happy to oblige?'

'Amelia?'

'Don't tell me you didn't use the opportunity to get cosy in Shanghai?'

Julian's face was incredulous. 'You've got to be joking, right? I can't stand her. She's one conceited little bitch. If her brain size matched her tit size, she'd go far. It was all I could do to attend meetings with her.'

'Why?'

'She's so up her own arse she meets her teeth.'

Lexie burst into laughter; her drink splashed over the rim of her glass. Julian soaked up the spillage with a beer mat.

'And she thinks she knows it all,' he said, picking up a slice of garlic bread, munching on it. 'I asked for you and me to go on the trip,' he said between mouthfuls.

'It wasn't mentioned to me.'

'Rupert's sending you out there. "I'll be the one to accompany Lexie," he told me in his usual pompous way. My bet's he wants to have you to himself.'

'Don't even go there.' Lexie's expression expressed her horror.

'It's true.'

'I'll speak to him on Monday.'

'You don't believe me, do you? I'm serious.' He leaned back and sipped his drink. 'We all know he lusts after you.'

'Don't…'

'See, I'm a far better choice. Aren't you sorry you dumped me?'

'How is the charming Serena?'

'She's finally off my back, I hope.'

'Pulled in her talons then?'

'As soon as you and I finished.'

*

When Julian parked outside Lexie's home, he leaned over and pecked her cheek. 'Are you going to invite me in for a nightcap?'

'You're driving.'

'I've only had one pint.'

'And a glass of wine.'

'I could always have a cup of hot chocolate.'

'Am I supposed to believe that?'

'Why not? Besides, there's always your spare room,' he said, leaning closer. 'I miss you, Lex.' His voice took on a more serious tone. He raised his hand and traced her lips with his finger, then lifted her hand and kissed her palm.

'You miss the sex.' She weakened as his thumb brushed the back of her hand.

'No, I miss you. Things aren't the same since—'

'Don't get all serious on me. Let's go in for that drink, though I don't have any cocoa, you joker, coffee will have to do.' She bent down for her clutch bag and opened the car door, turning to look at him. 'Come on, before I come to my senses.'

An hour later, following two glasses of Remy Martin, they lay naked on the cashmere rug. Julian poured brandy over Lexie's nipples, making her gasp with excitement. He traced the alcohol with his tongue, sucking her nipples that stood proud and firm from the onslaught of the liquid. His hands explored her, reigniting the passion between them. There were no inhibitions with Julian; their passion held no secrets, just mutual chemistry and complete satiety.

As Julian's breathing settled into a sleepy rhythm, Lexie whispered, 'I've missed you too.'

ELEVEN

Pippa

Pippa looked at Oliver as he lay sleeping. Her eyes roamed his body, the body she knew so well. The quilt rested across his hips. One leg dangled out of the bed, exposing a muscular thigh peppered with fine, black curls. Her eyes moved up to his hipbone, then across his flat abdomen. Jet-black hair descended from his navel to the triangle of tight pubic curls.

She studied him, scanning his body upwards, from the taut muscles of his upper abdomen to his solid chest. The bulging bicep of one arm cushioned his head. Thick eyelashes fanned his cheeks – eyelashes the envy of any woman. Dark purple shadows sat beneath them. His sharp jaw defined masculine bone structure, and a small dimple dipped the centre of his chin. His soft lips were parted to reveal perfect even teeth. A small V of chest hair sat between his nipples and finished just short of a milky-white birthmark, a contrast to his bronze skin.

She watched the rise and fall of his chest. His breaths

were deep, his sleep heavy. His face was thinner, and pale, against the bronze shade of his body.

As she studied him, something disturbed her. His torso was leaner, and his pecs didn't look as pumped as when he was last home.

Oliver coughed, making her jump. He turned onto his side, pulling the quilt up to his chest, stirring, but not waking. He drew his leg up, revealing the gluteal muscles of his backside, rigid and firm, tapering to muscular thighs.

Pippa kissed his back and circled her arms around his waist, pulling him tighter towards her. Eventually, her breathing rhythm matched his, and she fell asleep.

When she woke, Oliver was still sleeping, but restless with the cough. Pippa didn't like its short, spasmodic sound. Her brain flipped into medical mode. What was it with coughs this week? Everyone appeared to have one. She'd seen four clients in the clinic, all of whom had coughs of different types.

Her brain registered the differences in her prescribing repertory. Oliver's cough symptoms were akin to those of one of her patients with advanced disease. She would check her remedy guide later, she decided, pushing away the uneasy thought creeping into her mind. Perhaps the tiredness was because the cough disturbed his sleep? And probably the cause of the shadows beneath his eyes too, she reasoned. Pippa slipped on her dressing gown and padded downstairs to put the kettle on.

It felt strange not having Alexander in the house, running around at dawn. It meant she and Oliver could indulge in a rare lie-in for a change. She rustled up breakfast and carried the tray upstairs.

As she re-entered the bedroom, he was sitting up in bed.

'Hello, sleepyhead,' she said, placing the tray on the bedside table. 'I was wondering if you—'

Oliver pulled her onto the bed, silencing her with his kiss. 'Morning, babe.' He wrapped his arms around her in a vice-like grip as she tried to resist. 'Oh no, you're not escaping that easy,' he said as she sought to wriggle from his grip.

'But I have your breakfast.'

'You're my breakfast.'

'Oliver, sit up and eat before I feed you myself.' Her face was serious.

He tickled her ribs, and she fell back chuckling, her body writhing. 'Stop it before—'

'Before… what?' He pecked her lips. 'Alexander's not here, and,' he said, drawing her closer, 'I could think of a far better use of our time.'

She felt him stiffen, his heat penetrating through the gap in her gown. She looked at him grinning.

'Didn't you have enough last night?'

'I could never have enough of you,' he said, clutching her tighter. 'Besides, there's lots of time to make up, all those weeks I'm away from home, having to suffer.'

She laughed. His eyes were twinkling with anticipatory desire. 'Ah, you poor, neglected baby.'

'Can you make me better?' His eyes narrowed, fleetingly. He gave a lopsided smile, released her and sat up. 'OK, you win… for now at least.' He reached for the tray and took a sip of coffee. 'Now, open wide,' he said, taking the granary toast and putting it to her lips. She took a bite, and he did the same.

'I thought I was going to feed you?' she said, chewing.

He wiped a crumb from her lip and popped it into his own mouth.

'Waste not, want not.' He licked his finger. 'This marmalade's good.'

'I got it from the farm shop. The farmer's wife makes it. I bought a tomato and chilli chutney too.' She sipped her tea. 'Maybe we should buy Christmas goodies there? It's all organic.'

'Christmas? You're planning ahead! It's only March.' Another look crossed his face, and Pippa felt a frisson of unease but dismissed it as her mind doing overtime.

'I'm organised, as you well know. And I'm excited you're at home this year.'

'Hopefully, but I'll still be on the base.' They were quiet, with the thought of his imminent departure. 'But I—'

'That's the reason for this short leave now. We might need to go back out to Afghanistan.'

'But not you though? You'll be out of the service next year... for good. And you've done your stints now,' she grumbled, crossing her arms across her chest like a petulant child.

Oliver stroked her hair and tucked a curl around her ear. 'Stop worrying and finish your toast.' He passed her a slice. 'Let's not worry and enjoy the time we've got... for now, at least.' He took a bite from the other end of the bread as she lifted it to her mouth.

When they'd finished eating, Pippa switched on the shower and stepped in. She heard the door open and felt Oliver's hands cupping her breasts. She turned to face him.

'Can't a girl get any peace around here?'

'Not when her husband's home.' He drew her to him. 'I thought you'd need a hand, to wash this gorgeous body.'

Oliver squeezed shower gel onto his palm and rubbed it across Pippa's hips and over her breasts. He groaned when her nipple hardened to his touch. 'You're gorgeous, baby.' He kissed her as the water trickled over their faces and his tongue slipped deeper into the depths of her mouth, meeting with hers. His palm moved down between her thighs. His other hand played with the copper curls stretching down her back with the weight of the water. Oliver kissed her neck and growled when her soapy hand found him.

'Two can play that game,' she said, moaning at his touch.

Their lovemaking was tender and profound as rivulets of soapy water ran over their bodies. It was steady and romantic, not urgent and lusty.

They sat on the shower cubicle floor for a while, each in their private thoughts as sharp needles of water bounced off them.

Pippa lifted her head from his shoulder. 'I love you.'

'I love you more.' He stood and pulled Pippa to her feet. 'Now, where were we?' he asked, squeezing shampoo into his hand.

'I was about to wash, before being so rudely disturbed.'

Oliver smiled and rubbed her hair, massaging her scalp.

'I didn't see you protesting.' He grinned, wiping suds from her face and moistening his own head with the rest of the shampoo. She gave him a playful pat on his buttocks. 'Now, now, you wouldn't like me to punish you for that, would you?'

'Promises, promises.' Standing on her tiptoes Pippa kissed his lips, finding him again.

'It's just as well we have our son to pick up then, isn't it?' he said, moving her hand. 'Or I just might have to show you your punishment and we'd have to spend the whole day in bed, wouldn't we?'

'Ah, trying to distract me? What's the matter, I'm too much for you to handle? It's not like you to turn down a second helping. You're showing your age.'

'Don't tempt me, baby,' he threatened. 'Or we will be late.'

*

On the journey, Oliver sat with one hand on the wheel, the other on Pippa's thigh. She stole a sidelong glance at his profile and her heart swelled with pride, watching him as he manoeuvred the Discovery with skill and precision. He steered it through the country lanes, one hand on the wheel, only moving his other hand to change gear as he negotiated the bends.

That Oliver was oblivious of his good looks made him even more appealing. He was sexy in whatever he wore. Today jeans moulded to his thighs like a second skin. She watched his muscles contract as he changed gear. Her stomach lurched in appreciation. She felt a tiny twinge between her thighs. He had the power to excite her by observation alone. He raised a fist to his mouth, covering it as he coughed.

'How long have you had that cough?'

'About three weeks,' he said, distracted as he waved his hand to allow a motorist to pull out from a side road.

'Three weeks! And I don't suppose you've had the medics check you over?'

'No need. It's just a cough. Besides, I've got my own medic.' He squeezed her thigh. 'Probably just a flu thing.'

'Your immune system must be run down. I'll give you a remedy when we get home. Your constitution needs strengthening.'

'I'm strong enough to handle you, baby.'

'I don't doubt it,' she said, troubled now. That was a long time for a cough. Oliver could be vague with the truth. It might have been longer. She wouldn't ask too many questions. She didn't want to worry him. Not that he ever worried.

Pippa gazed through the window, marvelling at the beauty of the scenery. The trees were a beautiful sight in their new shades of green. She loved the season of spring, though nothing could top the turn of spectacular autumnal colours of rusty red, gold and orange leaves. Glorious shades dominated hillsides and fields just before trees shed their foliage to prepare for winter where once again, nature would bring a drastic change to the landscape, with bright red berries and blackberries lining the hedgerows, adding a different dimension to the mixed shades of flora in spring.

Lambs bleated, chasing the ewes for food. The visual impact soothed her mind. Autumn might be her favourite, but spring was the time of rebirth and new life.

Pippa lowered the window, breathing deeply, filling her lungs with the country air. She tilted her head back on the headrest and closed her eyes for the briefest moment. She heard crows squawking in the background and looked up to see them circling the treetops.

As they travelled along the lanes past more fields, a tractor trundled in a distant field, spreading manure and changing the odour of the air, bringing a memory of her childhood as she recalled her father saying, 'Now *that's* the smell of the countryside.' Pippa felt a pang of sorrow, missing her parents and wondering how they were. Not that they bothered to keep in touch much. 'You know what cruising is like, dear,' her mother would say, defending their failure to communicate. At least she could rely on Oliver's parents, James and Gabrielle. She was thankful they had, unlike her own parents, such a good relationship with Alexander.

When they drove through the wrought-iron gates of the grounds of Oliver's parents' house, Pippa noticed the Labradors roaming in the distance. Alert to the sound of the opening gates and the crunching of gravel as the car neared, they pricked their ears, bounding to greet them.

'Hello, Bailey. Hello, Jasper,' said Oliver, getting out of the car and bending to ruffle their coats. The dogs ran to Pippa, wagging their tails, and barked for attention. She reached into the door compartment and pulled out the mini gravy bones. She closed the door, and both dogs sat, expecting their treat.

'Gently now,' she said, handing out the biscuits which they gulped with gusto. Pippa laughed as they sat wagging their tails, staring up at her dolefully. 'Only one more.' She gave each of them another.

'You spoil them,' said Gabrielle, opening the heavy oak door of the Cotswold-stone residence. The sun's rays lit up the coloured panels in the upper portion of stained glass, casting colour on the Victorian monochrome floor tiles.

'I can't resist their faces when they look at me like that.' The Labradors followed as Pippa met Oliver's mother with a hug. She stood aside.

'Darling,' Gabrielle said, turning her attention to Oliver. Gabrielle oozed class, in her confident posture and style. She looked elegant, wearing a cream tailored blouse and a knee-length, two-tone linen tweed skirt. Her hair was styled in an asymmetrical short bob with a wispy fringe. Fine-framed glasses balanced the style, making her face appear more youthful. She wore a platinum necklace with a single pearl pendant and earrings to match. 'Good to have you home, if only for a short visit.' She kissed his cheek and stood back, holding him at arm's length, scanning him. A frown formed across her brow. 'Don't they feed you in the Royal Air Force? You're looking on the lean side. Come through and I'll get Margaret to fatten you up with her charming lemon drizzle cake.' She didn't wait for a response as she turned on her heels and led the way.

Oliver raised his eyebrows and grinned at Pippa as he closed the door, leaving the dogs outside to roam.

'Where's Alexander? We expected an exciting welcome,' Oliver said.

'He's down at the stables with your father, tending to the horses. It makes a nice change for your father to have company. He's a bit lost since Ronnie died.' Gabrielle peered out of the side window in the hall, looking across at the outbuildings. 'Losing his only sibling has hit him hard. They'll be up in a moment, I imagine.'

'It's a good thing Alexander is keeping him company then,' said Oliver, remembering his uncle's sad demise from cancer.

They took seats in the drawing room, and it wasn't long before the housekeeper appeared with a selection of cakes on a Royal Doulton stand.

Oliver said, 'Mm, those look delicious, Margaret. Mother mentioned a slice of lemon drizzle, but I can see at least two more of your specialties.'

Margaret placed the tray of refreshments on the rubber-wood coffee table and beamed at Oliver.

'I thought a choice would be nice.' She brushed her apron. 'And there's a pot of tea, and fruit teas with a separate jug of hot water.' She directed a knowing smile at Pippa and left the room.

'I don't know how those hippy teas appeal at all.' Gabrielle wrinkled her sharp nose. The action pushed up her tortoiseshell spectacles. 'I must say I prefer a nice Earl Grey.'

'You are traditional in your choices, Mother.' Oliver turned to Pippa, throwing her a reassuring smile.

'Nonsense, dear. Daddy and I went out for dinner at the new, expensive Gurkha restaurant and experienced a Nepalese curry dish of some sort.'

Pippa struggled to stifle a smile.

'And how was it?' Oliver asked, giving a secret wink to Pippa when he passed her tea.

'Daddy appeared to appreciate it, but I spent the whole time blowing my nose and I can't tell you the effect it had on my stomach. I suffered horrific indigestion for the duration of the evening!' She positioned a napkin over her skirt and straightened out imaginary creases. 'Do you enjoy spicy food, dear?' she asked Pippa, breaking off a small piece of cake with a fork and nibbling it.

'Not if it's too hot, though I cook with a wide range of spices. Oliver brings different varieties from other countries. The hotter the better for him,' she said, picking up her cup and saucer, avoiding eye contact with Oliver. 'He brought a wonderful selection back from Morocco.'

'Oh… are they safe? I mean, you don't know what harm might befall you eating produce from those types of places.'

Oliver burst into laughter. 'Oh, Mother. What do you suppose we eat when we are stationed in those types of places?' He mimicked inverted commas in the air.

'I dread to think, dear. Is it any wonder you're so lean? Those people have tapeworm and a whole myriad of undesirable diseases, I expect. I trust you have regular health checks?'

'Rest assured, Mother. The Royal Air Force takes superb care of us.'

'It must be a different story for those poor squaddies in the army,' said Gabrielle, picking up a bone-china cup and tilting it to her lips. Her little finger stood erect in the air as she sipped Earl Grey, leaving a peach lipstick half-moon at the rim of the cup.

It was a welcome relief to Pippa when Alexander burst into the room, followed closely behind by James.

'Mummy, Daddy! Granddad said one day I can have a horse.' He jumped onto Oliver's lap, his face beaming, showing a gap in his teeth.

'Hey, fella, what happened to your tooth?'

'It was loose, Daddy, and it fell out. Grandma said you were only five when your first one dropped, but I'm six already. A fairy took it. See what she left for me.' Alexander searched in his pocket and thrust a coin at Oliver.

'My, oh my, a two-pound coin! Inflation, eh?' Oliver grinned at his father. 'The fairy used to leave me a shiny fifty-pence piece.'

'Look, Mummy.' Alexander shook the coin.

'We must put it into your money box when we get home, mustn't we?'

'Can I buy a horse when I've saved some more coins?'

'You'll need a good few of those,' said James, smiling down at his grandson and shaking Oliver's hand. He leaned over and pecked Pippa's cheek. 'Hello, dear. I'll bet you two had a peaceful night last night, without this little live wire?' He ruffled Alexander's hair. Oliver peeped at Pippa with a gleam in his eye. She suppressed a smile, guessing his thoughts.

'Yes, we did, and this morning I got breakfast in bed.' Oliver covered a grin with his fist.

'Can't be bad, eh?'

Pippa observed the similarities in them. James's features were distinguished and handsome, despite his advancing years. His pewter hair was short, with white roots. His face creased into a kind smile as he watched Alexander. Even the mannerism of ruffling Alexander's hair was the same.

'Are we going now, so I can play with my helicopter?'

'In a while, once we've chatted with Granny and Grandpa,' said Oliver.

'Can I play outside with Bailey and Jasper then?'

'Come on, I'll come with you and leave the grown-ups to have a chat,' said Pippa, standing and holding out her hand. Alexander jumped off Oliver's lap and grasped his mother's hand.

'Is it OK if we take the dogs for a walk, Gabrielle?'

'Of course, they'll be delighted.'

'Come on then, young man. Let's get our raincoats on. It's getting rather blustery out there,' she said, nodding at the window.

'You know where the leads are,' said Gabrielle.

Pippa was glad of the excuse to leave. Gabrielle was a little trying, and she'd spent time with her and James yesterday, when she'd dropped off Alexander. It would be nice for Oliver to catch up with his parents, she mused, without Alexander's interruptions.

She peeped into the kitchen where Margaret was busy peeling potatoes into a colander.

'I don't suppose you've got a basket please, Margaret? Alexander and I are going for a walk with the dogs, and I thought we'd pick spring flowers. It's a good opportunity to get country air into his lungs too.'

'Certainly.' She looked up, wiped her hands and waddled across the flagstone floor, to a huge pantry-style cupboard. 'I use this to collect the garden herbs.' She handed her a chestnut-wood trug with a handle.

'Thank you. This should keep him occupied. I hope the rain holds off.'

Margaret peered through the window. 'The sky looks heavy. There may be a shower, but I'm sure you'll be back before then.'

Alexander tugged at her sleeve.

'Come on, please, Mummy. Jasper and Bailey are waiting.'

'I'm coming. Thanks again, Margaret for the tea.'

'You're welcome. Have a nice walk now.'

'We will,' said Pippa, slipping on Alexander's mac and heading for the door.

TWELVE

Oliver

Oliver needed someone to confide in. He wondered if he should talk to his father about his fears, but his mother remained close, and in a few days, his leave would be finished.

Aware of his deteriorating health, he feared something sinister. People had noticed his weight loss and this damn cough had lasted weeks. More worrying was his decline in energy, becoming clear to him during sex.

It was his norm to be able to go all night, all the more so after the long months away from Pippa, 3,500 miles away, at Camp Bastian.

It took time to settle after the tempo, buzz and adrenaline of being on the front line. It was human nature to take a while and reconnect. But usually after settling into a routine, they couldn't get enough of one another, once he'd adjusted psychologically after his decompression period. Leaving a war zone required that length of time, but he'd been at Odiham followed by Brize Norton before returning this time.

Last night he was relieved Pippa was sated and content after only making love once. He couldn't summon the strength for more, despite their usual for two, even three times in quick succession. He was glad they'd arranged to collect Alex early because he didn't have extra energy for more and Pippa was hungry for him. It stunned him when he couldn't hold her up in the shower, and she was tiny, unlike Lexie, whose legs were almost as long as his.

The other night, he'd moved Lexie from the wall to the bed because his knees almost buckled. Another wave of guilt...

'Are you all right, dear? You're pensive. What are you thinking about?'

'Nothing important, Mother.' He coughed and cleared his throat, almost laughing out loud. God forbid if she could read his thoughts!

'About?'

'About retiring from the RAF.' The truth would make his mother's hair curl, but he was still uncomfortable with the lie.

'Won't be long now, son. What are your plans then?'

'Maybe I'll have a month or so off to take Pippa and Alexander somewhere exotic, then possibly doing private chartering.'

'Haven't you had a sufficiency of flying, dear?'

'Being a pilot is all I desire, Mother, you know that. I can't imagine doing anything else.' He rubbed his chin. 'It will be good to fly something other than the Chinook. It's a big machine, though nothing like the C-17 that transports it.' He smiled with pride. 'That's a monster cargo plane.'

'The Chinook's vital, though, for navigating that

uninhabitable terrain.' James shook his head. 'And airlifting troops and moving loads. Not to forget evacuating casualties.'

'It's a costly hunk of machinery, but I couldn't imagine desert warfare operations without it.'

'Speaking of which, do you have another stretch, son?'

'Hopefully not... I'll be at Odiham for a while, then Brize, though nothing's ever certain.'

'I'll be so happy when you come home for good,' said Gabrielle, holding a hand to her neck. 'I do worry so.'

'Now, now, don't upset yourself,' James soothed. 'Why don't you go for more tea, my dear?'

'All right.'

When she'd left the room, James turned toward Oliver. 'What's really on your mind, son?'

Oliver raked his cropped hair, stood up and walked to the French doors. He pushed his hands into his pockets and leaned against the frame, looking across the lawn, his eyes focusing on the fountain in the centre.

What should he say? He turned to face James, conscious of his familiar, knowing expression. There wasn't much his father missed. He was the silent observer who said little but absorbed everything.

'Are you going to tell me what's troubling you?' James prompted, moving across the room. He laid a hand on Oliver's shoulder, patting it twice. 'Come on, son, out with it.'

Oliver sighed. 'I don't know, Dad... it may be something and nothing?' He shook his head, his brows furrowing.

'Have you been up to no good? You understand what I mean?' His father was astute, but Lexie wasn't who he needed to talk about. 'It's difficult being away for long stints, but—'

'War kinda kills the appetite, Dad. Last month we winched up a young girl, only about twelve years old. She'd been used as a decoy and came into contact with an explosive.' Oliver remembered the girl's raven curls matted with blood and recalling her piercing scream as they lifted her small body for transfer. Her scream had haunted him ever since. 'She'd lost an arm, but we got her to the medics. She survived the blast, miraculously. After that, all I craved was to get home and hold Alexander in my arms.'

'The poor child. May God help her. Such atrocities have a huge impact. Part of being human is to help, and you're doing that. I'm proud of you, son. Promise me, never bottle things up.' James pulled Oliver into a man hug. 'I can only imagine the horror you see out there, and by God, that's distressing enough.'

'War's not pleasant. People die, that's the harsh reality, but it eats at me when it's a defenceless child.'

'You've made the right decision, you know. You've served enough time out there.' His father shook his head. 'We worry constantly. Every repatriation ceremony on the news, we're relieved it's not you, son. I know it sounds awful to admit, and our hearts go out to the families, but it's true.'

Oliver was not used to his father being so truthful and so tactile. He felt humbled. James was of the generation where men were too reserved for such displays of emotion.

'Over forty dead servicemen and women brought home from overseas, since Brize took over the ceremonies from Lyneham.'

'Only since 2011 then?'

'Yeah... twenty-one ceremonies, and all that's heard on the base is the sombre silence of the C-17's engine taxiing, bringing them home.' Oliver sighed.

'It's the Union Jack covering the coffin. It gets me, every time,' James answered, his lips drawn into a line of pity. He tapped Oliver's arm and shook his head. 'Next year can't come soon enough.'

James had mellowed over the years and watching him with Alexander epitomised it. Oliver wanted to spend precious time with his son, especially now.

The sooner he was out, the better. He needed his family, now more than ever. Gabrielle returned to the room and the moment to confide in James was lost. There would not be another opportunity for Oliver to talk privately with his father.

'I've instructed Margaret to set the tea on the terrace. Oh, I hadn't given it a thought,' she said looking out. 'Perhaps it's a little too breezy?'

'Don't worry about tea, Mother. I expect Pippa will want to get Alexander home.'

'Nonsense, darling. We'll share a pot before you go.' She linked her arm in his and James opened the French doors. 'Besides, knowing Pippa, she'll use the opportunity to take in the air and enjoy the hounds. I imagine they will be a while yet.'

'You're right, I suppose,' Oliver conceded. 'It will exhaust Alexander trying to keep up with them. At least he'll sleep well tonight.'

'He certainly will,' James agreed.

'Do you need a shawl, Mother?' Oliver asked, hoping for a few private minutes.

'Not for the moment,' she answered, taking a seat. 'The sun is shining now. So much for the predicted showers; not a cloud in the sky.'

*

An hour later, Pippa and Alexander returned with two not-so-lively Labradors, who rehydrated themselves from their water bowls and flaked out on the turf.

Alexander ran across the lawn to the terrace with a huge bunch of mixed flowers dangling from his small hand. Pippa followed behind. Her face was alive with a beaming smile fixed upon their son. She emanated a radiance that melted his heart, her cheeks now tinged with the healthy colour only nature brought, and the sun highlighted her long hair's coppery tones. She reminded him of a beautiful gypsy, as wild as the flowers she carried in the basket.

She was his wild gypsy.

'For you, Grandma,' Alexander panted, cocking his head to one side looking pleased with himself. 'I got some for Mummy and Mrs Margaret too.' He turned and pointed to the larger selection in Pippa's care.

'What a lovely surprise, thank you, Alexander.' Gabrielle received his offering and tapped his crown. 'Let's get a vase.' She rose and took his hand. 'These are in need of a drink.'

'Nice walk, honey?' Oliver rose and kissed Pippa's cheek. 'I can see Alexander enjoyed it.'

'Wonderful, the dogs enjoyed it too. Alexander asked for a puppy again.'

'You two will give in eventually,' said James. 'I can see it coming.' A knowing smile tugged the edges of his mouth.

THIRTEEN

Lexie

Lexie woke the next morning to find Julian flaked out in her bed. She rose to make coffee. Soon, the pungent aroma of brewed beans filled the air, sparking a memory. According to her mother, ground coffee and home-baked bread were the essences of selling houses. Lexie smiled to herself, thinking of her mother's practicalities. Their home had sold within days, so she had a point. Lexie found it hard to believe they had been gone for eleven months already. Time passed so quickly, or was that a sign of getting older? She would call her later. There hadn't been the time to chat this week, and Lexie felt a pang of guilt.

As Lexie filled two mugs, she thought about Hugo's desire for coffee. His consumption was restricted; caffeine increased his hyperactivity. Warmth radiated through her when she pictured Hugo in her mind's eye. Lexie had missed him more than she expected, and though it broke her heart when they left, she'd known France would be good for all of them.

Lexie smiled to herself remembering the farewell party at Château Impney, a nineteenth-century hotel in Worcestershire. It was one of her parents' favourite places. Her mother told her of its history; it had been built in classic French château style by a wealthy man who had travelled to France and fallen in love with a beautiful French governess. He used his wealth to build the grandest house in the county with sixty-three acres of land. He had been so charmed by Versailles and the châteaux of the Loire Valley, that they had influenced the design of the château. Sadly, the love story was ill-fated, and his wife moved to Wales; she never liked the château. He remained there alone until he opened it to the public. Love was a mystery and relationships complex, thought Lexie, who had spent months alone and now had had two lovers in a matter of days, something she never would have predicted, just as the owner of the château hadn't.

On that night at Château Impney, her father had persuaded Lexie to play the grand piano that stood in the hotel lobby, and a small crowd had gathered to listen. At first, she was a little embarrassed, but soon got lost in her music and realised how much she missed playing. She couldn't deny such thoughts had her yearning to see her family, to be with them as a whole unit, but she pushed them to the back of her mind and concentrated on the present. She picked up the drinks and padded through to the bedroom.

'Wake up, Romeo.' She nudged Julian with her elbow.

He stretched his arms above his head and yawned. 'Mm, coffee.'

Lexie handed him a mug and sat on the side of the bed.

'Fancy getting back in?' He patted the mattress, giving

her a cheeky lopsided smile. 'Or am I too much for you to handle?'

'No contest, but I have more important things to do. Now drink.'

'Ah, but what shall I do about this?' He pointed to the elevated wigwam of the sheet across his hips.

'That,' she said, nodding her head at his groin, 'will be hosed down with cold water if you don't get up.'

'I'm happy to get up.'

'You know what I mean, up and out of this bed. You've got five minutes!' Lexie grinned at him, happy he'd stayed the night. She'd missed his outrageous cheek and his awful jokes. But most of all, she missed having someone around, occasionally. Looking at him now, with his thick chestnut hair ruffled from sleep and his morning stubble, gave her a comforting glow. She was used to seeing him clean-shaven and immaculate, dressed in Armani suits, ready for corporate action. There were talks about him moving permanently to India, to negotiate deals for the planned medicine manufacturing unit. The thought of a total separation from him didn't sit comfortably with her, however much her brave dismissal implied the opposite.

'If you're really good, I'll make you breakfast, though it is a bit Mother Hubbard's out there.'

'A full English will suffice. And don't forget the fried bread.'

She hurled the pillow at him and stood. 'You're pushing your luck.' She left the room and called over her shoulder, 'You'll be lucky if I find an egg.'

*

After breakfast, Julian left; she'd promised to see him again, soon. She poured more coffee and sat on the sofa, her legs folded beneath her ready for a lengthy chat. She reached for her phone.

'Hi, Mum. How are you?'

'Lexie darling, we're all fine. I was about to call but you've beaten me to it.' Warmth filled Lexie, hearing her mother's voice.

'And Hugo?'

'Much more settled now. Still talks of Chipping Norton and misses you. He's constantly asking for you.' Lexie grimaced and bit her lower lip. She hadn't been over in weeks. Her mother always managed to instil guilt.

'I miss him too. I miss you all. You know I do.'

Her mother couldn't possibly comprehend her schedule. The coming weeks would be manic too. Maybe she could juggle things and take a few days' leave in between? She cleared her throat. 'Is he OK… other than that though?'

'He cherishes the open fields. We spend much more time walking. Fresh air would do you some good too, driving those polluted motorways all the time.'

'I'm sorry. I promised him, I know, but work's been unrelenting.'

She picked up the mug, wrapped her fingers through the handle and hugged it to her chest.

'Then you need to look at your work-life balance.'

'Come on, Mum. I have to make sacrifices if I aim to be National Sales Manager. I'm on target for the promotion too.'

'Prioritising work tasks is one thing, but balance it with other areas in your life, Lex. You can't allow work to take over everything.'

Lexie felt a wave of disappointment when her mother failed to praise her. Miriam had adopted a different attitude to what was important in life. And she did have a point, but Lexie enjoyed every aspect of her job, except perhaps the travel and her non-existent social life. Dinner with Oliver had been her first evening out in ages.

Oliver…

She groaned inwardly, tipping her head backward, closing her eyes for a split second.

Perhaps gaining distance from Oliver would be perfect and everyone would be happy. 'How about I check my diary, Mum, to see if I can grab a couple of days to visit?' She reached for her MacBook and opened up the planner.

'That would be splendid. I'll tell your father. He'll be so pleased, and Hugo will be delighted. Though don't promise if you can't make it. I couldn't bear Hugo's disappointment.'

'I wouldn't do that to him.' Lexie studied the screen, and her heart sank at the enormous list of tasks to complete. Deciding she'd go over it later, she closed the lid. How on earth could she fit in the break?

'I know, darling. I'm sorry. It's my default over-protectiveness.'

Lexie smiled. At least her mother admitted it now.

'It sounds awfully quiet there.' The absence of background noise confirmed Hugo must be out. He would shout with excitement until Lexie spoke with him. Only then would he settle and let them talk in peace.

'They've gone to the boulangerie. Talking of food, are you eating properly?'

'Yes.'

'Hmm.'

'Mum… I'm an adult.'

'Sorry, how is work anyway?'

'Busy. The CEO has been in talks about setting up a medicine manufacturing unit in India. It will create 250 new jobs.'

'Good for the workforce. Whereabout?'

'Bangalore will most likely be the lead site. It's exciting stuff at the minute, especially after the disappointment of that second-stage drug trial.'

'I remember you telling me. For heart failure, wasn't it?'

'Predominantly atherosclerosis, you know, hardening of the arteries.' Lexie was impressed. Usually, this sort of thing went over Miriam's head, so she didn't bother talking of the ins and outs, or what the FTSE analysts were predicting. It triggered no enthusiasm in her mother. Her only interest was in drugs which could help autism spectrum disorder.

New research had to happen, and Lexie was passionate about that area too. They still needed drugs to normalise crucial brain functions. Commonplace ones only eased symptoms, helping with sleep patterns and attention deficit disorders. Thinking about this, she asked, 'How's Hugo's behaviour been?'

'Much better, and calmer. Goodness, we assumed he would never settle at first. How's Pippa, by the way?'

'I'll fill you in when I come over.' Lexie had a flash of irritation at the mention of Pippa.

'You two haven't fallen out again?'

'I saw her on Saturday,' said Lexie, misleading her. 'How's Dad doing with his vegetable garden?'

'He's taken to it with such passion. He harvested some wonderful spinach and herbs, and he's been planting potatoes this week… last years were gorgeous.' She sounded proud. 'When you come, I'll make dinner and you can taste them.'

'I can't wait. Send my love, and I'll call you when I get a date fixed.'

'All right. I'll look forward to it.'

'Me too. Bye for now, Mum.'

'Bye, darling… and remember, slow down. Life's too short and that company won't worry if you end up ill. No one is indispensable.'

'Well, I will be over for a couple of days to rest soon, won't I? And I'm sure your French cuisine will boost my health.'

'Absolutely. I'm well aware you need rest and you're probably living on fast food junk with the hours you work; that's if you find any time to eat at all.'

'Mum, I'm fine, really I am.' But as she ended the call, she recognised how fatigued she indeed was.

*

Lexie forced herself not to focus on negativity and tidied the apartment. She sorted laundry: one pile to go to the dry cleaners and the other to load in the washing machine. Securing her iPhone into the dock, she chose Pink as the vocalist to uplift her mood.

Music was her passion; it filled her soul and kept her company during the lonely hours commuting.

Tunes blasted from the speakers and Lexie burst into song, harmonising with Pink, swaying as she cleaned. It had been a long time since she'd danced. There was irony in the lyrics; as Pink sang about the flame of desire, she couldn't help but think of her situation with Oliver. She switched to Vivaldi.

Once the chores were finished, she poured more coffee and sat with her laptop to prepare presentations. Even Sundays were busy! She was deep in concentration when the phone rang.

'Lexie, oh darling, we're at the hospital!' Miriam was crying. 'There's been an accident and—'

Lexie's heart plummeted.

'What?' She jumped up. 'What's happened?'

'It was while they were out,' she blurted. 'And, and—'

Lexie's gut clenched in fear as she tried to make sense of what her mother was telling her. 'Who is hurt, Mum? Listen, try to calm down and tell me!'

'Hugo! He was having one of his meltdowns… and it was a shock because he's been much calmer, as I said. Now he's injured his arm.'

Lexie let out a long breath, relieved it was only minor in the grand scheme of things. Then her brain switched to details.

'How badly? What's he done? When you say injured—'

'He's in theatre now. There may be irreparable tendon damage to his hand and…' She cried louder. 'How will he cope? My God what if they have to amputate his fingers?' she said between sobs. 'He'll never—'

'Mum, *breathe*. Where's Dad?'

'Gone for coffee from the machine, while we wait for news.'

'OK, listen to me, Mum. I'm going to come over, don't worry. I'll call you back in a moment. Where are you?'

'Bordeaux.'

'Give me a few minutes.' Lexie ended the call and loaded Google to search for flights, then checked her diary.

'Shit, shit, shit!'

There was stuff that would wait, but she had a seminar to teach and appointments booked. Tomorrow would be hectic, but the rest of the week's events could be rearranged. She hit Julian's contact.

'Hey, honey, missing me already?'

'Listen, Julian. Something has happened and I—'

'Lex... Are you OK?'

'Yes, no, I mean... I need to fly to Bordeaux. Hugo's been in an accident and—'

'Gosh! Is he all right?'

'He's in theatre having surgery. He's damaged his hand, but I'm not too sure of the details yet as Mum's half hysterical. You know how she is with Hugo. It sounds bad though because she mentioned tendon damage and amputation of his fingers and...' Her voice trembled and her eyes smarted.

'Look, I'll come over.'

The line went dead, and Lexie sat down and allowed her tears to fall. She'd cried more in these past few days than ever before. One minute she was singing and happy, the next crying. She'd experienced a whole plethora of emotions: loneliness, guilt, anger, shame, ecstasy, fleeting happiness and now shock and fear.

By the time Julian arrived, Lexie had already thrown clothes into a suitcase. 'Hiya,' he said, putting his arms around her, rubbing her shoulders.

'I'll need your help if that's OK?'

'Sure, what do you want me to do?'

Scrolling through her phone organiser, she made a mental note of what could and couldn't be rescheduled. 'Work stuff mainly.'

'Typical,' he said, raising his eyebrows, trying to make light of the situation. 'And here's me thinking you wanted this.' He lifted her chin and kissed her. It was a kiss of comfort, not passion. 'Now then, what delights do you propose?' Julian's calming effect brought her back to reality, and once they sat and got down to business, Lexie's agitation settled.

She questioned herself for breaking up with him. Was it the competitive side of her that had been causing the friction between them? Or because he got too close, making her panic?

Their relationship had been easy at first. Julian was a fellow workaholic. He understood the need to put the job first. Being out of town wasn't an issue because when they met, the sex was great, their relationship never stale.

But Julian having been newly separated complicated things, and Lexie's barriers were up. Julian's ex-wife, Serena, didn't want to let go of her comfortable lifestyle and was so scorned when she learned Julian had started dating Lexie, she screwed him over financially as punishment.

The added tension had caused pressure, as if work demands weren't bad enough.

As she looked at him now, she realised how much she missed him, and she was grateful to him for coming to her rescue.

'Right, we've agreed you must be there tomorrow. But the rest of the week, we can get covered.' He rubbed a pen through his thick, unruly hair. 'So, airport next. What are the flight times looking like?'

'There's a late one, Monday from Gatwick, or an early one Tuesday morning.'

'I'll drop you tomorrow night if you want?'

'It will depend on how the day works out. You know what Mondays are like. I'll go for the early one on Tuesday.'

'Then you must leave your car because I can take you and pick you up when you get back. Decide in a minute once you've thought it through. Have you checked out Hertz yet?'

'I'll do that now.'

'I can check for you. You call your mum for an update.' Lexie was glad that Julian was taking control, and for once, she didn't mind.

Later in the evening, they sat on the sofa eating a Cantonese takeaway meal, accompanied by two large Merlots.

'Eat, don't push it around your plate,' said Julian, sucking up a noodle. 'This is hot, don't you think?'

'You asked for extra chillies.'

'Eat,' he repeated, nodding at her food. 'You've hardly touched yours.'

'I've lost my appetite,' said Lexie, setting her plate down.

'Stop worrying. He's in the right place and your parents are with him. Eat your food.' He picked up her plate and balanced it on her lap. 'Otherwise, I'll take you to your room and give you a spanking!' He grinned, twisting his noodles on his fork. 'I'm waiting…'

'All right, all right, I'm eating!' She stabbed a king prawn and smiled. He always cheered her up.

Once they finished, he cleared the plates, and she heard him loading the dishwasher. She sipped her wine, placed it down and rested her head back, expelling a sigh.

She closed her eyes and allowed her brain to switch off for the briefest moment…

Lexie woke up with a start; it was 2am. She was on the sofa with a throw covering her. She sat up disorientated, rubbing her eyes.

'Julian?' she called, glancing around. There was no answer. She spied a note on the table, saddened he'd gone. A familiar emptiness gnawed at her. She took it and read:

Didn't want to wake you – tempted to undress you and have my wicked way with you though. Call you tomorrow. Sweet dreams.

Jules x

She laughed aloud and picked up the bottle of Evian he'd left with a glass next to it. Ignoring the glass, she drank thirstily from the bottle and moved to the bathroom before flopping into bed. Her last waking thought was of how thoughtful Julian was.

FOURTEEN

Oliver

Oliver drained the parboiled potatoes, then drizzled olive oil and Himalayan rock salt over them. He slid them into the oven to roast in their skins. Next, he took out chicken breasts, wrapped in Parma ham and filled with Gorgonzola and pine nuts, and sprinkled garlic breadcrumbs on top. The fine green beans and Chantenay carrots were steaming in a pan.

Oliver enjoyed cooking but rarely had the opportunity. When he did, he experimented. Tonight, he was confident with the meal.

While he was busy making dinner, Pippa bathed Alexander, who'd already eaten a light meal. Oliver set the table and moved to the bottom of the stairs.

'Dinner's almost ready, honey.'

He heard the whizzing of the hairdryer, indicating bathtime was over.

'I'll be down soon, we're almost done,' Pippa shouted over the noise. 'I will read our little man a quick story first.'

'OK, I'll be up to tuck him in.'

He returned to the kitchen and busied himself with the final touches. The aroma of garlic made his mouth water; he was starving! He pricked the beans and carrots with a fork. Satisfied they were cooked, he replaced the lid of the steamer and switched off the hob.

Pleased things were under control with the food, Oliver popped upstairs. He stood in the doorframe and watched his wife and child, unobserved for a moment. His heart swelled at the sight.

Pippa was sitting cross-legged on the bed with *The Hungry Caterpillar* book perched on her lap. Her hair was damp from Alex's water play and she was tucking a strand behind her ears. She looked almost juvenile herself, being so petite. Alexander pointed at the book as she turned the page, his face filled with joy as Pippa read aloud in a silly voice.

'I'm as hungry as the caterpillar,' said Oliver, interrupting them.

'Daddy!' Alexander exclaimed, sitting up. 'Have you come to listen to the story?'

'I'm here to say night night.' Oliver planted a kiss on top of his head. 'I'm cooking Mummy's dinner because she's hungry too. Goodnight, buddy.'

'Night, Daddy.' Alex rested his head on his Batman pillow and yawned.

'I'll be serving up soon.' Oliver gave Pippa a wink.

'Mm, can't wait.'

Oliver left Pippa to conclude the story with Alexander. As he went down the stairs, a sudden wooziness hit him. His hand reached out to clutch the balustrade for support.

He pressed his eyelids open and shut for clarity, dispelling the blur, and proceeded with caution down the remainder of the stairs.

In the kitchen, he poured water from the filter tap and drank, leaning against the sink. He rested for a few seconds, conscious of his sporadic breaths. He closed his eyes and concentrated on regulating the flow. His palms were hot and clammy. The coolness of the glass dissipated the heat. He set it aside and washed his hands. What the hell was wrong with him? Maybe it was time to research his symptoms? That way, no one needed to know, but being faced with possible answers gave him a feeling of dread. Not wanting to dwell on any of it, he continued with the task in hand and returned to the stove to warm the plates.

'Something smells good.' Pippa appeared behind him. He looked over his shoulder.

'I aim to please.' Oliver still felt light-headed and was glad to have his back to her.

'Anything I can do?'

'You could uncork the wine, please.'

'The tell-tale sign you are home,' she remarked with a chuckle. 'The empty wine bottles are stacking up. I rarely drink when you're away.'

'I don't know about that. You and Lex—' He stopped mid-sentence, annoyed. They'd had such a nice day, so far. He cringed, berating himself.

'Let's change the subject, shall we?'

Oliver heard the pop of the cork and the familiar *glug, glug* sound of the wine as she poured. He retrieved the warmed plates from the oven and arranged the food.

She walked over to him and put her arms around him.

'I don't want to discuss her,' she said, breaking the silence. 'It makes me tense thinking of her. She's a legalised drug-pusher, with too much opinion.'

Oliver turned to face her. 'That's a bit harsh, Pip.'

'Oh, sticking up for her now?'

'Don't be ridiculous.' Why had he raised the subject to give her more ammunition when what he needed was to placate her? He reached down and gave her a perfunctory kiss. 'Let's forget about her and eat.' He spun her around, giving her a gentle push towards the table. 'You'll be so impressed. Sit down and I'll serve you, Madam.'

Pippa giggled as Oliver draped a napkin across her lap and set a plate before her. He'd arranged the food to precision.

'Cheers,' she said, chinking her glass against his, sipping, then setting the wine aside. 'I'm impressed.' She stared at her plate. 'And I haven't even sampled it yet.' She picked up her utensils and sliced through the chicken breast. It revealed softened cheese, packed in the centre. She put a piece into her mouth, allowing her taste buds to savour it. 'Gosh it's so tender. I love the cheese with the chicken, and do I detect a hint of garlic?'

'Yeah… it's in the breadcrumbs.'

'It complements it. You should be called Jamie Oliver, it's so good.'

He smiled, watching her as she nibbled on a bean. Fuck, she even aroused him when she ate! He imagined her mouth around him; he was getting hard. Whatever was wrong with him, his sex drive wasn't affected, for sure. Trying to divert his horny thoughts, he stabbed pieces of carrot, bean, potato and chicken, all lined up together on his fork.

Pippa's eyes widened.

'What?'

'I can't believe the amount you put on your fork.'

He pushed it into his mouth, chewed and swallowed. 'You know I like to taste everything together.'

'But surely you can't taste individual flavours?'

'Food's food; it all goes down the same way.' He laughed and repeated the process.

'Why are you laughing?'

'Because… you always tell me that whenever I eat.'

Oliver searched his wife's face. She was beautiful. He loved everything about her, from the fine freckles over her nose, to the tiny mole on her big toe. She was his sexy Romany he could scoop into his arms and carry with ease.

Her heart was as big as the planet, and it got her into trouble. His wife wanted to heal the world. She couldn't bear to see pain or suffering. That was the one reason not to let her keep him from his duty. She was aware he made a difference, and placed herself at the bottom of the list, aware of his responsibilities. Oliver didn't tend to mention the sights he witnessed, for it would break her heart and play on her mind. 'How's work?'

'Good, though I'm concerned about Gillian. She didn't look well when I dropped off her remedies. There's conflict with her daughter too. Mainly over her choices.'

'You can't worry about everyone, Pip.' Oliver worried she'd burn out and constantly reminded her of the fact. 'You always do your best. Sometimes things are out of our control, babe. You need to switch off sometimes.'

He pleaded with her to put herself first, but she wouldn't hear of it. In Pippa's opinion, if you could help, then you should, no matter what. She was so unselfish, giving her own time too freely, especially to the less fortunate. Before being blessed with Alexander, Pippa had worked with travelling homeopaths, delivering medicines to people who couldn't finance their own care.

She had also worked for the Big Issue, helping drug addicts and alcoholics, much to his mother's horror!

'You know I love my work, Oliver. I'm duty-bound to help people understand they can help themselves to heal naturally. I'm there to give them a catalyst, and time, that's all.' She blew him a kiss across the table. 'Besides, I have hours to fill when you are away.'

'Just don't get too involved with Gillian, please. Or anybody else for that matter.'

Oliver had seen Pippa's successful cures through her expert prescribing and wondered if he should mention his own symptoms. But he knew she'd worry, and he didn't want her to fret while he was away. He believed the conventional route was not the answer, either. In his opinion, too many people popped drugs into their bodies, without a thought for the long-term effects.

'Yes, sir!' Pippa saluted, and Oliver grinned. 'Talking of work, how's Josh?'

'He's OK, I guess. I think he spends too much time at work. I was thinking actually,' said Oliver, fork suspended in the air, 'perhaps he could come to dinner one evening?'

'Sounds good to me. He needs to get a social life.'

'He needs a good woman like you.' Oliver pushed his plate away and laced his fingers behind his head, studying his wife as she tasted every morsel of food delicately, pausing briefly to sip her wine. She was delicate, though strong, he mused.

She had a strong belief in karma too, though the thought of retributive justice didn't sit comfortably with him now, after his escapade with Lexie.

'You've gone quiet. What are you thinking about?'

'Getting you to bed and making mad passionate love to you.'

'But you'll scream and wake Alexander,' Pippa said.

They burst into laughter.

Her witty sense of humour was another quality he admired in her. He raised silent prayers to the heavens, hoping there was nothing seriously wrong with him.

FIFTEEN

Lexie

Miriam was sitting by Hugo's bedside when Lexie arrived. Unlike some hospital wards at home, the room smelled of disinfectant and the shiny linoleum floor gleamed. Lexie could see Hugo, with his bandaged arm raised in a sling, hooked up to a frame. It gave her a pang to see her brother so vulnerable.

'Lexie!' Her mother jumped up as she entered the room. 'I'm so glad you're here.' She embraced her daughter and stood back, looking at her. 'You look wonderful, though a little tired. But you're in better shape than your poor brother,' she added, moving to the bed. 'They are keeping him sedated, for a head start on the hand healing. We can't allow him to thrash around so soon after surgery.'

'He looks peaceful, doesn't he?' Lexie bent and stroked Hugo's face with the back of her fingertips. 'How did the surgery go?'

'Better than they initially thought it would. The doctor

prepared us for the probability of him losing a finger.' Tears brimmed.

Lexie hugged her mother. 'Shh… he's fine now. He's over the worst, so let's be positive, eh?'

'It was such a shock. They'd only gone for bread… and the next thing, we ended up here.'

'So, what happened?'

'He wanted to carry the bread and strode ahead on his own, in the usual direction. Your father coaxed him back to a safer route. They're building on the wasteland, you see. Then, he had one of his tantrums and threw himself against the railings near the site.' Miriam frowned. 'His signet ring got caught on a spike and… Oh—'

'It's OK, Mum. Where's Dad now?' Lexie noticed how her salt-and-pepper hair aged her mother. She'd obviously gone natural. Yet Miriam was fit, and her body was still well toned for her age.

'He's gone home to fetch a few bits for Hugo – toiletries and things. I've been little use on that front. I just sit here, waiting.'

'Have you eaten anything, Mum?'

'Yes, I had a bite to eat earlier. Dad got me a baguette, but I have had no appetite late—'

'Hello, my darling!' Lexie turned at the sound of her father's voice. Edward crossed the floor with quick strides. He kissed Lexie's cheeks, before pulling her to his chest in a bear hug. 'How lovely to see you, darling.'

'Hi, Dad, you're getting well into the French style, aren't you?'

'Of course, but at least I kiss skin and not the air, like the French. When did you get here? You look wonderful.'

'Only arrived a few minutes ago. Mum's been telling me about the accident.' Edward looked at his sleeping son and back to Lexie, his expression sad.

'He's been so amenable lately. We've even been able to reduce his medication. In this episode, he was out of control.' Edward shook his head. 'He thrashed about and tried to climb a fence. That's when he caught his hand. I don't know. It is a strain sometimes, isn't it, dear?' He moved to Miriam and pecked her forehead. 'Your mother has barely slept since the accident. She won't leave his side.'

'I want to be here when he wakes. You know what he's like with strangers. It will be bad enough for him as it is.' Miriam brushed Hugo's hand with the side of her thumb, looking at him lovingly. 'What a shame, he'll be out of action now. He was just enjoying learning a new craft at the respite centre.'

'Oh, what's he doing?'

'Mosaicking. He's good too. He's making a pair of mosaic covers for our bedside tables.' Miriam's face lit up with pride when she talked of Hugo's achievements.

'How lovely. You must show me when they're finished.'

A nurse entered the room. 'Bonne après-midi,' she said with a smile before washing her hands. She pressed a few buttons on the monitor and inflated a cuff on Hugo's arm. She noted down the results on his chart. 'Beaucoup mieux,' she said to Miriam. 'A tout à l'heure.'

'What did she say?' Lexie asked when the nurse left.

'That he's much better and she'll be back later.'

'Your mother's French is improving.'

'Only the basics, but I manage.'

'How's the hospital care?' Lexie glanced from one to the other.

'Good,' they answered in unison.

'They're very attentive,' Miriam told her. 'Mind you, now Hugo's sedated, they can do their job. When we arrived, it was a different story. I don't think they understood the autism. We couldn't get through at first. Some of the staff speak English well, though, so that helps.'

'How long is he likely to be here?'

'Depends on how well the surgery went. Hopefully, there won't be any infection, though that's always a worry, apparently, but his temperature's fine. They took blood this morning.' Miriam stroked Hugo's hand again. 'The consultant came in earlier and he's pleased with the progress so far.' Her face brightened as she straightened the pristine sheet covering him.

'Why don't you go home and get some sleep now, Mum? I'll stay with Hugo.' Lexie noticed fine lines around Miriam's eyes and dark, taut skin straining beneath them. It was clear she hadn't slept in a while.

'I couldn't possibly, no! You go with your father, settle in and eat dinner. You can return later if you wish.' She fiddled with a strand of bandage fabric peeping out from under the base of the sling.

'Told you,' Edward said to Lexie, then focused his attention back to Miriam. 'Come home for a couple of hours to freshen up, dear,' he reasoned.

'I'm fine. You two go. You must be tired after that flight and long drive.'

'The flight is short, Mum, and the drive was OK. It only took me fifty minutes; traffic wasn't bad. I'm happy to stay with Hugo. It is the reason I came.'

After long deliberation, Miriam agreed and left with

Edward. Lexie sat looking down at Hugo. He looked so defenceless. His long eyelashes fanned cheeks with heightened colour, in stark contrast to the white sheet. His auburn hair felt damp at his forehead and Lexie touched his skin, hoping he wouldn't brew a fever, but he was cool to the touch. She leaned over and kissed his cheek.

She had missed him, and now she realised just how much.

He might be twenty-four, but he was her baby brother. There had been an eight-year gap after her birth before her mother's pregnancy with Hugo. When he was a baby, everything had seemed normal. Then, on becoming a toddler, he showed a fascination for certain things and wouldn't be distracted from them.

The health visitor and teachers assumed he had behavioural issues when he started nursery, but her parents wouldn't accept that. He started to display repetitive movements, like flapping his hands and rocking; stimming was the term used, as they were to learn later. His speech was delayed too, and despite speech therapy, Hugo didn't talk. After seeing multiple specialists, they had finally been given a diagnosis of autism spectrum disorder, together with attention deficit hyperactivity disorder.

Lexie stroked his uninjured hand for what seemed an age, casting her mind back to when he always stacked his toys with precision in a particular order. Certain colours would set him off into irrational behaviour. Hugo had had repetitive routines and clumsy dexterity. Lexie found his idiosyncrasies amusing until they developed into a problem. How would her mother cope when he woke? He'd be bound to throw a tantrum and be unbearable, his lack of linguistic skills proving difficult with staff and adding to the language barrier difficulty.

Her mother was the only one who could manage to keep Hugo stable. She'd devoted her life to him, sacrificing her own needs.

In turn, Lexie had spent countless hours researching potential drug treatments for him, but some only eased the symptoms and that frustrated her.

Lexie felt sure now that she would go to America, possibly next year, to visit the research centres doing the drug trials into ASD. It would be an opportunity to help Hugo and make progress with her career. If such research made further advances, it could change lives.

She let go of Hugo's hand and chose a different position. She'd been in the same position for over an hour, only moving when the nurse came in. Her back ached and her body felt stiff. She rolled her shoulders and sat back for a while, watching the rhythm of his breathing. She'd never seen him so still. He was normally restless, even in sleep.

The heat of the room was making Lexie drowsy. She stretched and picked up her bag to locate her phone. She could catch up with emails while she waited and add notes to her organiser. As she tapped the screen, she saw a picture message from Julian. He'd taken a selfie – not something he ever did – his bare chest boasting solid muscle, his jeans sitting snugly across his hips, exposing the top band of his boxers. His hair was damp from the shower. He was holding up a bottle of beer, making the pretence of relaxing, but his MacBook was on the table beside him, next to a mound of paperwork. She knew he'd been working late, just like always. The caption read:

Missing you already. Come back soon… I'm lonely without you. x

Lexie's lips curled into a smile. She texted a kiss and a smiley face, then scrolled to the organiser, trying to get the image of Julian's hunky body out of her mind. Blissful memories surfaced of their early days, when their relationship was new and they hungered for each other, especially after periods of working away. Their intimacy was intoxicating, stealing moments of passion, in sometimes shocking places, where thankfully, they'd never been caught. But all good things had to come to an end, she thought, when Serena put a dampener on their happiness, constantly whingeing in the background and creating non-existent problems regarding the sale of their home, among other things. Thankfully they didn't have children, or her nagging would never have come to an end!

Miriam came rushing into the room. 'How's he been?' she asked, breaking Lexie's reverie. 'Has there been any change?' She instantly checked Hugo in dread of something catastrophic having occurred in her absence.

'He's slept the entire time, Mum. The nurse came back in to do his blood pressure again and he stirred, so she topped up his medication.' Lexie nodded at the syringe-driver. 'I expect he'll stay sedated for a while longer.' She ran her fingers through his hair, pushing it off his forehead. 'Did you eat any proper food?'

'She spent the whole time fretting over the cats!' said Edward, who'd followed Miriam in. 'Your mother nurtures everything and everybody – always the same.'

'They are my babies too.' Miriam kissed Edward's nose.

'Not when they bring mice in though, eh, dear?'

'Hugo loves them.'

'When did you get cats?'

'I thought I told you. They were feral, and I was feeding them at first but now they're tamer and come as far as the kitchen.'

'Not daft, are they? Not when it's food time,' Edward interjected. 'She allowed herself a few minutes for a shower and change, at least.'

'And I ate.'

'Oh, I forgot, an appetising omelette. That's substantial, isn't it?' He raised his eyebrows and shook his head. A mannerism Lexie smirked at; it was his *I will never win* expression.

'Mum, you ought to take care of yourself. You're always so caring. Who will look after you?'

'Your father's my rock.' Miriam smiled up at Edward. 'And he's all I need.' She clutched his arm and put her cheek on his shoulder before pulling up an armchair next to the bed. She stroked Hugo's forehead. 'Mum's back, darling,' she whispered into his ear. Then she turned to Lexie. 'Right, I'm refreshed and ready for the night, Lex. You go with your father. There's plenty of food, but I'm afraid you must help yourself.'

'OK, Mum, if you're sure? I could always stay with you and keep you company?'

'I wouldn't hear of it! No, you've already helped, sitting with Hugo while I freshened up. I have a book with me, so I'll be fine and Dad's packed munchies and drinks.'

Lexie knew she couldn't dissuade her mother, so she bade her goodbye and left with Edward, looking forward to having a snack and getting into bed.

By the time she was on the road to Saint-Magne-de-Castillon, her body was jaded, her vision drowsy as she followed the trailing taillights of her father's car. It seemed strange to be driving on the right-hand side. She needed to be extra vigilant and more aware than normal, not driving mostly on autopilot as she did at home. She felt hypnotised by the rhythm of the wipers clearing light rain from the windscreen, and her eyelids drooped.

The blast of a car horn alerted her as she veered towards the middle of the road. She opened the window for fresh air. The fine rain abated, and she flicked off the wiper blades.

Lexie rubbed her forehead, pounding in protest again. Sleep could not come soon enough. When they finally reached 'Beauvoir', Lexie sighed with gratitude. She stepped out of the hired Fiat Punto and stretched her arms above her head, briefly glancing around at the woodland, home to wild boar. The grounds looked different at night and somewhat eerie. It was black, except for two garden lamplights at the side and back of the barn where mosquitoes whined underneath. What a stark contrast it was to the city lighting.

As she took a deep breath of pure air, peace enveloped her. An owl hooted in the distance, breaking the silence.

Her father was observing her. 'Tranquil, isn't it?'

'Being caught up in the rat race distances you from nature, sometimes. I forgot how beautiful this place is.'

'We're happy. The Cotswolds are truly beautiful too, but life is at a much slower pace here in Aquitaine.'

'I'm a little envious,' said Lexie, wondering for the first time if perhaps she could make such a huge lifestyle change? At that moment, with tiredness engulfing her, it seemed appealing. But in reality, she knew she couldn't exist without the frenetic schedule of her working life in the fast lane.

She craved a large glass of wine to help her wind down, and then, a conversational catch-up, followed by a night of undisturbed slumber.

'I'll just have a snack if that's OK?' Lexie joined her father in the kitchen.

'It's no trouble, darling. I *can* cook, you know.'

'Thank you, but I fancy something simple, like a small piece of baguette.'

'With some pâté?'

'Perfect.'

'We have some foie gras if you prefer?'

'No thanks. It's a bit rich for supper.'

'Coming straight up,' said Edward, washing his hands at the sink. 'There's a bottle of Beaujolais on the table if you'd like to pour?'

Once supper was finished, Edward refilled Lexie's glass and sat beside her on the patio. The night air was fresher, thanks to the light rain shower, and cooler than the earlier heat of the sun. She wouldn't be sitting outside at this hour back home.

'Lovely.' She took a drink and glanced around.

'The wine or the view?'

'Both.' She breathed a sigh of gratification. 'How's Mum been?' Lexie thought about her mother, sitting at Hugo's bedside in the hospital ward. She felt a little guilty relaxing with a glass of wine, peering out at the raw charm of the French landscape. The moon had cast its shadow across the treetops and sparkling stars dotted the sky. It had been a long time since Lexie had paused long enough to appreciate nature's stillness.

'You know your mother, darling… hard to change her now. Since the accident, she's become even more obsessive over Hugo.' Edward shook his head and sighed.

'I noticed, but that's her coping strategy.'

He smiled. 'You're right of course. At least the worst is over. My concern was the surgery. That went well. I just hope he recovers quickly. It's a lot of strain on your mother. I worry about her.'

'She always copes well, considering. I noticed a canvas. She's been painting again, so that's optimistic.'

'Yes, she has. Hugo had been making great progress before the accident, and she's had more time. She insists it is to do with Pippa's magic pills. I must admit, he's been much better.'

This took her by surprise. 'I didn't realise they were in touch. How long has Hugo been taking those? His improvement has nothing to do with remedies, I can assure you.' Miriam could be so gullible at times.

Edward's brow creased. 'I wouldn't let Pippa hear you say that, or your mother. It wouldn't go down too well.'

If only he knew, thought Lexie.

'There's no science behind homeopathy, Father. It's all placebo.' She swallowed, struggling to hide her disappointment. What irked her more, was her mother's trust in Pippa. What Hugo needed was better medication, not empty sugar pills.

'It is popular here in France. Many swear by it.'

Lexie couldn't muster up a reply without the sound of resentment in her tone. She didn't want her father to sense anything or get into a further debate. She rubbed the stem of her glass and stared into the distance.

'What time for the hospital tomorrow?'

'I'm going early to pick your mother up. Would you stay with Hugo a while?'

'Do you think Mother will leave his side?'

'She must, for a few hours at least, anyhow.'

'Why?'

Edward bowed his head.

'Dad?'

'We've got an appointment.'

'Can't you reschedule? She's hardly likely to leave Hugo.'

'I will insist.'

Lexie laughed, but her father's mouth set into a grim line.

'Is everything OK?'

'Nothing we can't deal with.' Edward tapped the back of Lexie's hand.

'Dad, what is it?' Lexie put down her glass and faced her father. He frowned in obvious turmoil. 'Come on, tell me. There's something else on your mind.'

'It's just... well, I worry about her. I wish you were here, with us, together, as a family again. I know your job is demanding, but we see little of you.'

'Dad, what's brought this on? Is it the accident?'

Edward stared into his glass and Lexie saw it was already half empty – unusual for her father who didn't drink much. Lexie pushed her irritation to the back of her mind. He looked up at her, tilting his head.

'Are you happy, Lexie darling? Really happy, I mean?'

'Yes, Dad. What's this all about?'

'Pay no attention. I'm a silly old fool.' He refilled his glass and topped up hers. 'I'm missing my girl, that's all.

I miss our chats. I miss your piano playing. I miss your crazy laugh. But most of all, I miss our camaraderie.' His face took on an expression of solemnity, for the slightest second. He squeezed her hand and chortled. 'I can't win any battles with your mother, now you're not here to back me.'

'It's not like you to be melancholy,' said Lexie, scrutinising her father's face. 'I miss you too,' she said, but she wasn't fooled by his sudden change of tactics. His mood was pensive, despite his cheerful conversation. 'Sometimes I wish we were together too, but…' Feeling suddenly emotional, she looked away and scanned the barn and the forest below. 'Your lifestyle here seems much better, I have to admit. Mother tells me you made a vegetable garden.'

'Yes, and Hugo's been helping to dig, in a fashion!' He smiled. 'Homegrown is all good. It is a different way of living here. Most people grow their own produce. It's been a great distraction since giving up architecture. Though I may have a little project seeding in my mind.'

'What?'

His lips twitched in a knowing grin.

'Tell me.'

'Maybe another separate addition to the barn, somewhere for you, on this estate. There's enough land,' he said, swinging his arm to indicate the expanse of the grounds. 'Then, one day, when you're bored with your high-flying career, there will be a place for you, here, in France.'

Lexie grinned at her father. 'That's going to the extreme isn't it, Dad? You'll do anything to make me take on your chores, won't you?'

Edward clasped his chin. 'I'm serious. I've created the

drawings. Think about it. It doesn't have to be permanent, just your own space.'

'There's enough room in the barn, with you. I don't need my own place.'

'But when Hugo's home, you get no peace and I want us to provide for you.'

'Dad, I'm thirty-two years old. I have a great career and earn an incredible salary. I can fend for myself. I don't need you to make provision for me. There's enough to consider with Hugo.'

'You're also headstrong and too independent.' Edward lit a cigar and sucked in deeply.

'Dad, I don't mean to sound ungrateful. It's just that—'

'It's our fault, I suppose, giving all our attention to Hugo.'

'That's not true.'

'Be honest, Lexie. Sometimes it must have been unbearable for you.' His head bowed. 'It's the hand we were dealt. There's nothing we could do. And… you lost friends because Hugo was different. You had to grow up fast and—'

'Dad, stop this regret. What's this soul-searching all about?'

Edward turned to face her. 'I want you near, that's all. I know that sounds selfish, but I'm being honest. Besides, you admitted sometimes you feel like moving here.'

'Not literally. I'm under pressure occasionally and have the need for escape, that's all.'

'You work too hard. Life has a habit of creeping up on you. One day you'll wonder where the years have gone.'

'I suppose Hugo's accident has been a catalyst for all this talk of mortality,' she said as she watched her father's expression change again. He drew on his cigar, then drained his glass.

'I expect so,' he replied unconvincingly.

'Dad, talk to me. There's something else. What's this appointment?'

'You always were astute.' Edward puffed out his cheeks in defeat. He stubbed out his cigar and stood. 'Come on, let's go inside, it is getting chilly out here.'

'Now you're playing for time. Just tell me.'

'Your mother discovered a lump in her breast.'

*

After a restless night, Lexie showered and dressed, feeling the worse for wear. The extra glasses of wine hadn't helped, but it was the shocking news that had had her tossing and turning. Edward had made her promise not to mention anything to Miriam and, under duress, she'd agreed.

When they walked onto the ward, Miriam looked exhausted, strain and worry etched on her fine-boned features.

'Hi, Mum, how's Hugo been?' Lexie tried to sound upbeat as she kissed Miriam's cheek.

'They're going to reduce his sedation later this afternoon, so that's good news.'

'Brilliant! He looks peaceful, doesn't he?' Lexie made her way over to Hugo's bedside and leaned over to kiss him. She had to bite her tongue regarding her mother's pending investigation, and it was proving difficult. 'You go and get some rest now and I'll stay.'

Miriam yawned and looked at Edward with a puzzled frown.

'Come on, my love. Let Lexie have some time alone with her brother. After all, you can't have him all to yourself. And she has to go back tomorrow.' Edward gave Lexie a knowing look as Miriam bent to kiss Hugo.

'I'll be a couple of hours. Will that be all right, Lex?'

'Take as long as you need, Mum.'

*

The following morning, Lexie bade a tearful goodbye and left for the airport. As she boarded the plane, she wondered if she was doing the right thing. Edward had insisted she stick to the plan, or her mother would suspect. He promised to call her if more tests were needed. So far, she'd had a scan and a needle biopsy, according to her father, who knew little about the procedures. He'd repeated what Miriam had told him, and Lexie understood. Now it was a waiting game.

Lexie fastened her seatbelt and stared out of the window of the aircraft as it taxied to the runway. She did not bother watching the in-flight safety procedure; she was too distracted, worrying about her mother.

The news had come as a bolt out of the blue. One minute she was digesting the impact of Hugo's accident, the next, even more shocking news.

Why had her mother not mentioned the breast lump to her? Did she think Lexie was too busy? Lexie felt full of remorse, allowing her work to dominate her life to such a degree she was oblivious to her family's needs.

Her father must be living in fear, and now, she was too. How would he cope? How would any of them?

Her mother was the altruistic one, never complaining.

And yet, their lives were not as perfect as her mother led her to believe. And to add to their toils, they had the daunting possibility of a cancer diagnosis haunting them.

For now, at least, Hugo was recovering well. It was ironic, on the outbound flight she had been so anxious about Hugo; on the inbound she had these new fears.

She switched her phone to airplane mode and pushed her handbag beneath the seat in front of her, preparing for take-off. Resting her head back, she shut her eyes, but her brain didn't give her the satisfaction of switching off. Instead, it fired up with scenarios of her mother's dilemma.

What if it were cancer? And if so, what if it had spread to lymph nodes or wasn't curable? It might be too late for drugs. Lexie pushed the possibility from her mind.

She would get the best for her mother, she thought.

But it might not come to that. It could be a cyst or a deep-tissue injury, after all; she was always bumping into things, rushing around, and if Hugo was having one of his major meltdowns, it was possible.

Her anxiety built, the more she envisaged a negative outcome. She swallowed, but her mouth was dry.

'Excuse me.' Lexie signalled to a petite air hostess as she passed. She halted in the aisle and leaned towards Lexie's seat. Her pungent perfume wafting up Lexie's nose made her feel nauseous.

'May I have a glass of water, please?'

'We'll serve refreshments soon, Madam.' Her flawless makeup made her appear more like a candidate for a cosmetics advert. There wasn't a hair straying out of place from her tight chignon, and her navy dress fitted her figure perfectly, highlighting her tiny waist beneath a scarlet belt.

'I'd like one now, please. Not soon, I need to take a pill.'

'I'll be right back.' Her saccharine smile didn't please Lexie as she watched her glide with ease down the aisle, wearing matching navy shoes with heels that would make any woman's feet ache, standing all day.

Lexie cursed herself for not buying water at the airport.

The captain's voice over the tannoy made her jump. She needed to calm her jangling nerves. It was time to be positive. There was no genetic history of cancer in the family, as far as she was aware, and treatments had come a long way, with continuing positive research. Her brain buzzed, trying to recall what current drug trials were going on.

Her mother was a strong lady, and whatever the outcome of the test, they would deal with it.

SIXTEEN

Oliver

'Alexander, look who's here!' Oliver placed the tongs down and closed the lid of the barbecue.

'Uncle Josh!' Alexander ran to the garden gate to greet him, and Josh scooped him up.

'Hello, fella. Look what I've got for you.'

'Not sweeties, I hope,' said Pippa, walking out through the French doors, armed with a bowl of salad and a jug of iced water. She set them down on the cast-iron garden table and met Josh on the lawn. Josh leaned in to peck her cheek while Alexander fidgeted in his arms.

'Good to see you, Pippa.'

'What have you got for me, Uncle Josh?' Alexander demanded.

'Well, I know Mummy doesn't like you having sweets, but I'm sure she won't mind me giving you some just this once.' Josh set Alexander down and fished inside the pocket of his denim jacket. 'Here you are, but you can't eat them until after dinner. Is that a deal?'

Alexander took the big paper bag containing Pick n Mix and peered inside. 'Wow, thank you!' He scrunched the bag closed and ran to the table. 'Where's my dinner, Mummy? I need it now!'

'That's one way to get him to eat his dinner,' said Oliver, joining them and meeting Josh's handshake. 'Beer?'

'Thanks, mate. You picked a good day for it.'

'It's been fantastic weather the past few weeks,' said Pippa. 'But the great thing is that we can still be outside these days, even if it rains, now we've got this extra area under cover. I can spend more time out in the garden with Alexander.'

Josh looked around at the bespoke pergola, designed with solar-powered lighting and decorated with a variety of trailing plants. 'It looks great!'

'Oliver had to spend a bit of time getting it right.'

'Well, I missed the upheaval, thanks to having to go up north last year, but I can see it was worth the effort,' said Josh, accepting the bottle of Beck's Oliver held out. 'You can do more than pilot a plane, eh?'

'I've been known to assemble things before.'

'Yeah, Lego and Airfix,' said Josh, aiming a cheeky grin at Oliver.

'It's a work of art if I say so myself.' Oliver eyed his landscaped project proudly. 'I even laid the paving around the pond and put in a water feature at the bottom.' He pointed to the end of the garden.

'And he made that seat around the tree,' said Pippa, looking at Oliver with pride. 'On a nice day, I sit there with a book.'

'Even though it's a textbook,' Oliver said, a smile playing around his lips.

'Seriously, you've done an impressive job, mate.'

'Mummy, where's my dinner?' said Alexander, tugging at his mother's sleeve.

'Daddy's cooking it today, remember?'

'Where's my sausage, Daddy?'

'Coming right up,' Oliver said, crossing the garden to the barbecue and inspecting the meat. 'And,' he said, lifting a sizzling sausage on a fork and turning, 'this one's ready, especially for my soldier.'

Oliver watched Pippa pick up a plastic plate from the table and approach him. She looked beautiful even when wearing casual shorts, a crop top and white pumps. Her hair was in a ponytail, which bounced from side to side as she walked.

'Smells delicious!' she said, looking down at the grill.

'Do you mean you're actually going to have meat again?'

'Oh, the thought of joining the carnivores!'

'So, do you fancy a sausage?' Oliver raised an eyebrow.

Pippa laughed. 'Give me Alexander's sausage and behave yourself.'

'I've been careful not to put any onions near it,' he said, dropping the sausage onto the plate. 'And I bought veggie burgers from M&S for you.'

'You're so thoughtful.' Pippa stood on tiptoe to kiss his cheek. 'I'm not ready yet. I'll get your steaks out of the fridge in a minute.'

Oliver's heart lurched yet again at the thought of leaving her. He stood back, observing the three of them now at the table. He needed a quiet word with Josh, so he joined them. 'Another beer, Josh?'

'No thanks, I'm driving.'

'Are you sure?' Pippa asked, slicing through a bread roll. 'Can't you stay over?'

'I'd love to, but I've got business up north tomorrow. Besides, the next tour starts again soon, so I won't encroach on your time together.'

'Don't even mention that,' said Pippa, looking sad.

'We could pop out and get some alcohol-free if you like?' Oliver said, thinking this might give them a chance to talk.

'I'm all good, thanks, mate.'

'Ketchup, Mummy, please.'

'OK, darling, I'll fetch you some.'

When Pippa went inside, Oliver said, 'I need a quick chat in private.'

'What's up?'

'Daddy, I don't like this,' Alexander interrupted, dangling a piece of lettuce.

'OK, leave it on the side of your plate and eat the sausage.'

'I need ketchup!'

Pippa returned with the bottle. 'Here it is,' she said, squirting some along the bun. 'I'll fetch the steak now.' She headed back into the kitchen.

'Come over to the barbecue. OK?' Oliver said.

Josh nodded. When Pippa came back, he stood up. 'I'll take those. I can't have him cremating mine.'

'Great, you can cook your own then.' Oliver got up too, grateful for Josh's diversion. 'Or you can supervise and watch a master at work?'

'You two, honestly, always in competition.' Pippa smiled up at them. 'Such alpha males.' She shook her head as they walked off.

'What's up?' Josh asked, as they reached the barbecue and Oliver set about plonking two sirloins on the grill.

Oliver glanced over to the table. 'I want you to promise me something.'

'What's this about? You look serious. Are you in trouble?'

Oliver moved the steaks to a hotter part of the grill. Fat began to sizzle and spit. 'No, of course not. I just need—'

'Oliver, what's going on?'

'I want you to promise you'll always look out for them.'

'What *are* you talking about?'

Oliver looked up, his gaze intense. 'Just promise me! Can you do that?'

Josh stepped back, hands out. 'All right. Chill. I promise. What's eating you?'

Oliver turned back to the grill. Neither man spoke as he flipped the steaks in turn, Alexander's happy laughter coming to them across the lawn.

'So, who's the best chef then?' Pippa asked, coming over with the plates a few minutes later.

Oliver was grateful for the interruption this time. He didn't want to answer more questions from Josh. He'd got his answer, though he knew in his heart he hadn't needed to ask. Oliver picked up one of the steaks with the tongs and held it in the air for their inspection. 'Say no more,' he said, resting it on the plate Pippa held out for him. 'I think Josh has to agree that he's looking at perfection.'

*

Of course, Oliver was accustomed to leaving. That came with the job. The anguish when being deployed was normal, especially for military spouses. It was normal for couples to argue as the time approached, but military people were conditioned to deal with the diverse periods of the emotional cycle, because there was a job to be done. With pre-deployment came detachment, withdrawal and sometimes even a sense of loss. But this time…

Intense loneliness and fear brewed, haunting Oliver differently. There was constant underlying anxiety, the sense of being out of control. Oliver was a man used to being in control. Something organic was going on inside him. He knew it. He *felt* it.

'What were you boys talking about?' Pippa asked, entering the lounge after putting Alexander to bed.

'Oh, just chit-chat.'

'You don't do chit-chat, Oliver. And… you two looked very serious over at the barbecue earlier, and I'm sure it wasn't only a discussion about how rare you like your steak.'

'We were just talking about work.'

'Is there something you're not telling me?'

'No. Now come here.' Oliver pulled Pippa onto his lap and silenced her with a kiss. Her mouth was hungry as his tongue found hers. She twisted and straddled him on the sofa, not pausing for breath. He groaned as she rubbed herself against him. Their lips briefly parted as Pippa pulled Oliver's T-shirt over his head. All previous thoughts were erased as Pippa took complete control of him.

SEVENTEEN

Pippa

Pippa was missing Oliver already. She felt a huge void when he'd gone, but at least it wasn't to Camp Bastian this time. He was on the base in Oxfordshire, so that was something, at least. The worry remained though, despite this. She recalled the recent shooting of a soldier in broad daylight. He was killed as he was returning to his barracks. It seemed nobody was safe. She shuddered at the notion.

She'd dropped Alexander off at school and was at the Riverside Holistic Clinic early, wanting to do some research before her client appointments. Pippa was in the communal kitchen putting her lunch in the fridge when Sandy came in to join her.

'Hi, Pip, you're early.'

'Kettle's boiled.'

'Great.' Sandy fished in her rucksack and brought out a lemon, setting it down. 'Any particular reason?' She quartered it, put a piece into a mug and added boiling water.

'Not really, Sandy. You know what I'm like when Oliver leaves. I get restless, so I thought I'd put my time to good use and catch up with notes. It takes my mind off things and gets me organised into the bargain.'

Pippa leaned against the surface and sipped green tea. 'How about you? Do you have a full clinic today?'

Sandy squeezed the lemon against the side of her mug and added a teaspoon of honey. Pippa frowned as she watched her. 'You aren't coming down with anything are you?' she asked, nodding at the honey.

'This? Oh no, I'm trying to give my liver a detox.' Sandy grinned. 'I know, I'm not supposed to add honey, but it's so bitter without. I tell my clients about detoxing and here am I breaking the rules.' She bent to put the remaining lemon in the fridge. 'I've got three this morning and one of those is Matt. You remember me telling you about him, don't you?'

'The whiplash injury?'

'Yeah. I'm trying to realign his spine, but it's hard keeping a professional distance. His body is to die for! I have to keep chanting inwardly, *skin, bones, muscle*, while I'm working, instead of seeing his body as an object of desire. That body!' Sandy stuck out her studded tongue, mimicking a panting dog, begging with his paws. Her long ginger plait swung as she wriggled her hips.

Pippa almost choked on her tea. 'You're married!'

'A girl can dream, can't she? There's nothing wrong with a little eye candy. Seriously though, he's a nice guy. Sceptical about osteopathy until he tried it. It should be his final session today,' she said, her mouth pouting sorrowfully. 'But he's so happy, he's referred his friend.' She smiled. 'So, I've got another client.'

'That's great, but you are superb at your job... when you keep it professional.' Pippa looked down her nose in mock chastisement. 'What time's your first?'

'Nine-thirty. Matt's my last one thankfully. I'll be all hot and bothered by the time I've finished with him. I wonder what his friend's like?'

'You're terrible!'

'But you haven't seen his torso.' Sandy put a hand to her brow. 'Mind you, Oliver's body should be more than enough. All six-pack and ripped, I suppose. I bet he's never out of shape. Not like my Nathan; he's getting a proper pouch. I must put him on a diet.'

'Nathan? You're joking. He loves his carbs, doesn't he?'

'He won't even notice. I'm good at disguising healthy food. I'm not sure about his beer though, he'd have a right strop.' Sandy shook her head. 'Oh well, I'd better set up, see you later.'

'Yeah, me too.' Pippa followed her, heading for her own room. She glanced over her shoulder. 'And please, keep your mind on the anatomy.'

'I'll try.' Sandy's chuckle echoed as she closed the door.

Sandy was a breath of fresh air, full of life and never serious. Unlike Lexie, who obsessed about targets, competing with the big boys. Lexie always strived for perfection. Pippa didn't want to think about her. Instead, she sat and centred herself in a brief meditation to clear her mind.

Suitably composed, she got out the notes for her first client of the day and refreshed herself once more with her detailed notes. Gillian was battling ovarian cancer and only wanted homeopathic treatment. Her family, however, lived in dread of her impending death and had urged her to have chemotherapy. Pippa read a chart to update her on the last prescription. When she flipped through the pages, she worked out which support remedies she would prescribe to help with the side effects of the chemotherapy. Then she went out into the waiting area. Gillian had arrived and was sitting alone, with her now familiar red bandanna on her head.

'Hi, Gill, come through and have a seat.' Pippa pulled up a comfy chair for her. Gillian's skin was sallow, her cheeks sunken. She was breathless but smiled such an undefeated smile.

'How have you been?'

'Oh, you know, Pippa, up and down. As you know, I have my good days and my bad. I can handle the physical stuff, but emotionally... let's just say things are taking their toll on all of us.'

'I noticed that when I called to see you at home,' said Pippa, pulling up a chair to sit beside her. 'Want to talk about it? Get your breath back first.'

'It's the same old battle.' Gillian gave a juddering sigh. 'They don't want me to contradict the doctor's word. The physician is God as far as they're all concerned, and his word is law. Woe betide if I have an opinion of my own.' Her breathing settled into a better rhythm. 'I didn't want this other lot of chemo. I feel awful. They're terrified, I know, but so am I. Sometimes it's like I'm the one supporting them, so I go through with it.' A tear escaped and slid down her cheek. She wiped it away in frustration. 'I'm sorry about Debbie calling you.'

'No worries. I understand her concerns.' Pippa passed

Gillian a tissue, getting emotional herself. 'We had a lengthy conversation. She's scared, naturally.'

Gillian had become more of a friend than a client. Pippa found it hard to keep a professional distance and not have her judgement clouded by personal emotions and opinions.

'They worry, I know. However, you must be able to choose for yourself too.' Pippa tapped Gillian's forearm, understanding her dilemma. 'I can prescribe a remedy for your side effects and, for this frustration. First, let's go through things systematically and you can tell me how you've been since your last visit.' Pippa stroked her hand. 'Any more constipation since reducing the painkillers?'

'No, I've gone the other way now since contracting C. difficile in hospital.'

'That will be the strong antibiotics.' Gillian's resilience amazed Pippa. So far, she had defied the odds and the seriousness of the superbug. It was a condition capable of causing death in far healthier people. 'Are you still juicing the raw vegetables?'

'I am and I've upped my intake.'

Gillian had researched her own condition. She had devised a strict dietary regime involving raw foods. Pippa found her ideas of interest. Gillian was a very determined lady who believed the universe would give one all the answers if one asked. She invested her time in her spiritual growth and loved crystal healing, yoga and all things natural. She was fascinated by American Indian culture too. She'd painted a picture of a Native American chief for Pippa. 'That's your spiritual guide,' she'd told her. The painting took pride of place above Pippa's desk.

Pippa took notes as they chatted, going over new

symptoms. She was perturbed about Gillian's psychological state, more so than her physical symptoms, because if she was balanced in her mind, she would cope better with the physical manifestations.

After a lengthy case review, Pippa talked Gillian through the prescription regime and helped her out to the car where her husband, David, was waiting for her.

'I was about to come in to see if you'd finished,' he said, jumping out of the car, ready to help Gillian into her seat. 'You've been longer than usual today.' When he closed the door, he whispered in Pippa's ear while Gillian was distracted, making herself comfortable. 'She's been talking a lot about dying. I think she's giving up,' he said, his eyes full of tears.

'You must allow her to express her feelings, David,' Pippa answered, rubbing his shoulder for comfort. 'I know it's difficult for you all but hang on in there. It's not all doom and gloom, despite what we're all led to believe by the medics sometimes. Gillian has her faith and is exploring lots of other avenues—'

Gillian opened her window. 'What are you two chatting about?'

'Nothing, dear,' said David, smiling down at her. 'You have a very suspicious mind.'

He looked up at Pippa and rolled his eyes. 'See you next week then.' He walked round to the driver's side and got behind the wheel. Gillian looked up at Pippa, her mouth set. Fear sat behind her eyes and Pippa's heart sank with sorrow. She wished she could do more to help her. She leaned into the car and rubbed her arm.

'You can call me at any time. Even if you just want to chat.'

'Thanks, I will,' said Gillian, squeezing Pippa's hand.

When they drove off, Pippa swallowed hard. The disease was clearly at its end stage and any course of treatment now would only be palliative.

*

Back in her office, Pippa sat at her desk with her head in her hands, frustrated with her inability to change things. She thought it was unfair that Gillian was an exceptional wife and mother who put her family first, even above her own survival, whereas her own mother had little time for anyone but herself. She barely took the time to call her. Her parents' lives in Virginia were too socially busy.

Being the other side of the pond, as her father called the geographical distance, meant she rarely saw them, and they were always too wrapped up in one another to give much thought to her. It was no wonder she was an only child. They had not denied her the material things in life, but that wasn't what she had needed, or wanted.

She'd wanted to be part of a close, loving family, but though she couldn't deny they loved her, they did not notice she was on the outside of their unit.

Probably this was why she was so skilful when it came to determining someone else's need for love. And, on some deeper level, that was why she had related so well to Lexie.

Oliver told her she couldn't save the world, and that she took too much to heart, but it was who she was.

She picked up a book on homeopathic prescribing in cancer cases and thumbed through the pages to confirm that she'd prescribed as well as she possibly could for Gillian and had missed nothing. Satisfied, she sighed and replaced the book on the shelf with a heavy heart. She selected the next set of notes and prepared herself for the rest of the morning's clients.

*

By the end of the day, Pippa was exhausted. She'd read to Alexander and tucked him up in bed. Now, she lay in the bath, surrounded by scented candles, indulging in a little relaxation. The bath was filled to the top and the bubbles popped as they reached up to her neck. She enjoyed the buoyancy of the water as she soaked her body. Her muscles eased, though her mind did not share the same benefit.

She closed her eyes. Something troubled her and she couldn't dispel it. In her gut was the lurking sensation something drastic was going to happen. And it nagged at her. Perhaps it was all the negativity with some of her clients now?

Maybe she was feeling low about Lexie, and she missed her friendship? Or was it the thought of Gillian dying? But she knew in her heart it was something more.

There were the constant thoughts of Oliver and the way he'd looked. Something wasn't right. She had the sudden urge to speak to him, but she resisted the temptation. They'd already chatted, and she didn't want him to think her needy, so she forced herself to relax.

After a while, she stepped out and towelled herself dry.

She checked Alexander. He slept peacefully, looking like a cherub. He made everything worthwhile, and he brought joy into their lives. She crept into the room and covered him with the quilt, then kissed him gently before pulling the door nearly closed, leaving it slightly ajar.

In her bedroom, she removed her towel and slipped on a nightie, before getting into bed and snuggling under the duvet. It wasn't the same in an empty bed and she tossed and turned, trying to find sleep.

Feeling frustrated, she went downstairs and made a chamomile tea, taking it to her bedroom. She picked up a book by Jodi Picoult to visit a world of fiction and dissipate her negative thoughts. But her mind was tormented, and she still had an overwhelming sensation of pure dread. A sensation so profound, it was hard to deny.

EIGHTEEN

Lexie

When Lexie caught up with some of her workload the following week, she was thrilled to learn the company wanted her to attend a research seminar on psychotherapeutic medications and their role in neurodevelopmental disorders. Her only wish was that she didn't have the worry of her mother's results looming.

Her father had told her the date of Miriam's next appointment for the needle biopsy results; she had an early morning clinic appointment on Friday. Lexie had scarcely slept since her return from France, despite her exhausting schedule. There were only two more days to wait.

After an evening meal with Julian, Lexie needed her bed. Julian had an early start too, with appointments in Bristol, Stroud and Gloucester, so he dropped her home and left, much to his disappointment.

As much as she was enjoying him, Lexie needed some mind-clearing space. She felt peopled out and longed for emotional solitude. She couldn't even use Serena's aimless loquacity as an excuse now. Since Julian had given Serena a handsome settlement – and received a hefty solicitor's bill into the bargain – Serena had found a new use for her time: frequent spa breaks at luxury hotels, 'to get over the stress', she'd told Julian. The woman didn't know the meaning of stress!

As Lexie flopped into bed, she couldn't resist scanning the seminar programme for the following day. She was thrilled at the prospect of a new development into ASD, and as she drifted into sleep, her thoughts were of Hugo.

*

'I hear you're off to China with the boss?' said Sebastian, seating himself next to Lexie. She was sitting behind a table at the Centre for Pharmaceutical Medicine Research in King's College London. 'Careful your sales don't drop in your absence.'

'I have no worries on that score, I can assure you, Sebastian. I have an excellent team. So why not concentrate on your own figures? I hear they're in need of improvement.'

The thought of going to Shanghai with Rupert filled Lexie with dread, following Julian's comments. She pushed the impending trip from her mind and leaned down to take her computer out of her briefcase. She preferred to type notes directly, instead of transcribing them later from a notepad. For Lexie, all time-saving solutions were essential and something she advocated to her recruits.

Lexie opened up her MacBook and turned her face away, wrinkling her nose. A pungent smell of body odour emanated from Sebastian's underarm as he slipped off his suit jacket, exposing grey half-circles of sweat stains on his creased white shirt. Lexie stifled a gag and shifted slightly. Despite his expensively tailored suits, Sebastian always looked slovenly, from his tousled mop of mousy hair down to his unpolished shoes. She wondered how he got any sales at all, and more to the point, why Rupert didn't say anything about his unkempt appearance.

'Right, let's get started,' said Amin Khan, the lead of neurodevelopmental research in pharmacology. 'We have a full day with lots to get through. Before we start, I'll go through the order of the day, after the usual housekeeping rules of the building, fire exits, etc, which I'm sure most of you know already.'

'Blah, blah, blah,' whispered Sebastian in Lexie's ear.

'If you're going to interrupt, I suggest you move elsewhere. I, for one, want to listen.' Lexie glared at him.

Sebastian shrugged his shoulders. 'Touchy.'

'Why are you even here?'

'Same reason as you, though product research bores the arse off me. I'd rather be on the road,' said Sebastian, fishing in his trouser pocket and pulling out a roll of mints. 'Want one?' He popped one into his mouth, sucking noisily.

'No thank you.' Lexie suppressed her irritation and turned to face the speaker as he continued.

'Later this afternoon we'll be joined by Ingrid Karlsson, an analytical chemist from Brighton. She's involved in the research of a new product, specifically addressing the psychological symptoms of anxiety and repetitive motions of ASD, rather than the multiple antipsychotics, SSRIs, etc, that can cause fundamental changes in brain chemistry.'

Lexie couldn't wait for Ingrid's session. She felt a bubble of excitement and her mood changed. Today would be a good day, she mused, and she would not allow Sebastian's presence to spoil it. For a few hours at least, her mind would be distracted from her feelings of trepidation at the possibility that tomorrow could bring more distressing news.

*

The rain bounced off the windscreen, giving Lexie a sense of comfort. It had been another relentless week with highs and lows, but today, Lexie had taken a leap of faith.

She leaned back into the seat and sighed with relief after fearing the worst. Her heart rate slowed to a normal rhythm.

She'd just pulled over into a lane, to give full attention to the phone call she'd been waiting nervously for. Her father had promised to ring whatever the outcome, but when Miriam's number lit up the screen, Lexie held her breath, thinking it must be good news. And it was. The breast lump was a large cyst, and she was waiting to have it drained.

Her eyes filled with tears of relief. That rare feeling of exhilaration was a welcome change from the past few weeks of worry and stress. Her mother hadn't been happy when Edward blurted out in delight that he must call Lexie to put her mind at rest. Miriam expressed her disapproval of Edward's betrayal of confidence, but Lexie insisted, as her daughter, she had a right to know and not to keep secrets, to which Miriam had replied:

'Always remember: what you don't know, can't hurt you.' Lexie smiled to herself at her mother's words of wisdom. She looked out across the fields and allowed herself to sit and appreciate the joy of nature. Sheep grazed and cattle clattered over an iron grid, on their way for milking. The animals didn't appear to be bothered by the rain. Life could be so simple sometimes. It was people who made it complicated.

Lexie remained there for ten minutes more to wallow in her gratitude, before firing up the engine of the Audi, to continue with her hospital visits. The weekend couldn't come soon enough.

NINETEEN

Oliver

Oliver woke in the middle of the night, disorientated and covered in sweat. His heart rammed against his ribs. He sat up and tried to settle the dizziness before he stood. His body was on fire, so he staggered into the shower and turned it on full force, switching the dial to the cool setting. He shuddered at the onslaught of the water.

His symptoms had worsened over the past few weeks. Somehow, he had to get through the next stint of service abroad.

He glanced down at his body. It was losing muscle mass fast, and when he'd looked in the mirror to shave that morning, he saw a likeness of his Uncle Ronnie's face staring back.

Oliver remembered Ronnie's emaciated body and his protuberant eyes. Oliver's own cheeks were showing signs of dipping, and the pallor to his skin was a sure sign of disease. He could no longer deny the seriousness of the situation.

The water bounced hard off his upturned face, and he allowed the torrent to assault him as Josh's words echoed in his brain: 'For Christ's sake, Oli, see the medics! You're sick and it's affecting your work. And that can't happen!'

Oliver had told Josh to get off his back and he hadn't raised the subject since. Things were becoming tense between them, so Oliver stayed in his room, away from everyone. All he wanted was to go home. He needed to be with his family, but the enormous fear of the acceptance of his illness held him back.

Pippa would know how sick he was as soon as she saw him. While he was away, he could save her the torment for at least a little while longer. He couldn't bear the thought of her worry. He would do the worrying for both instead. It was his duty to protect all his family for as long as he could. He would not burden them with his disease. He had guessed what was wrong with him. He didn't need a medic to tell him. And he didn't need a label. After all, ignorance was bliss, wasn't it? And for now, he would finish out his term and only then, reunite with his wife and son.

Oliver didn't bother drying himself. Instead, he positioned the towel on his bed and lay naked on top, with his hands behind his head, staring into the darkness.

It broke him to think about Alexander. Oliver knew now that he would not see his son grow into a man. He felt sure his time was limited. He didn't need an examination to confirm what his own body told him.

He felt bad arguing with Josh; he was his best mate and deserved more. Oliver decided, once morning broke, it would be time to talk.

TWENTY

Lexie

On Monday morning, Lexie knocked on Rupert's office door and stepped inside. He wasn't seated at his grand walnut desk, which was empty of his paraphernalia. Instead, he was staring out of the window, shoulders slumped.

'Rupert?'

'Shanghai has to be postponed,' Rupert said, keeping his back to her.

'Why?'

'I have family business,' he answered, turning. He didn't make eye contact, he just stared at his empty desk. 'I'm leaving for Sussex. Not sure when I'll be back.'

'Do they know?' Lexie fought to hide her inner gratitude for this unexpected gift of time. The thought of not having to be in Rupert's close company resulted in a welcome release of her pent-up tension. But it wasn't good for business, and she wanted to know more. As if sensing her need, he spoke.

'My father's dead. Died suddenly in the night.' His voice

was flat. He raised his face. 'I can't believe he's gone… just like that!'

Lexie didn't know how to respond. Should she close the distance between them and offer support?

'What an awful shock for you. I'm so, so sorry.'

'I'll call when I have more news. Can I leave you to explain and rearrange?'

'Of course, don't worry, I'll handle it. Just be with your family,' she replied, noticing a vulnerability in him she'd never seen before. 'I'll do it immediately.' She turned to leave. 'I'll wait to hear from you. Please pass on my condolences.' He didn't reply, his expression blank. She closed the door softly behind her.

Lexie settled in her own office, feeling stunned. A frisson of guilt ran through her as she remembered her selfish thoughts of freedom, while Rupert was processing devastating news.

Five minutes later, he hurried past her window. He was speaking into his phone, tucked between his left ear and shoulder, while shrugging his free arm into the sleeve of his jacket. For the first time, she was sorry for him and didn't envy what he'd face in Sussex.

She shuddered at the thought of losing a parent, her mind revisiting her fear when she first heard the news of her mother's breast lump. The outcome could have been so different. She felt immensely grateful.

For now, at least, she could relieve Rupert of his most pressing business tasks. She called the chief executive to explain, assuring him he'd receive an update as soon as possible.

That done, she relaxed into her leather chair and

allowed herself a few minutes to reflect. Maybe some good could come out of the situation? It was too late for Rupert to be with his father, but at least he could spend some long overdue time with the rest of his family, albeit for a sombre reason. Rupert's entire existence revolved around RestrilPharma. And as she'd discovered recently, life could change in the blink of an eye.

Thinking about that, she was mindful of the danger of slipping back into the work trap herself. Maybe this was an opportune moment for her too? Her diary was free, and she could concentrate on other business. Before, that's precisely what she would have done. But was this yet another sign? She had leave to use up; it made sense to take it. She could conduct her calls from home or France, and after all, she had promised her parents she'd return for a few days.

Perhaps a surprise visit would cheer Hugo up following his accident? She'd spent so little time with him on the previous trip, apart from when he was lying unconscious. No time for bonding, there.

She knew he'd asked multiple times for her since, listening to her voice only on the phone or seeing her via the occasional Skype connection.

Feeling a tinge of excitement, Lexie reached for her diary. Plenty of things needed her attention and she toyed with clearing them, but dismissed the fleeting thought and phoned her mother instead.

By the end of the afternoon, Lexie was satisfied with what she had accomplished, including booking a flight to Bordeaux. When she left the building, she felt a rare sense of liberation. It felt good. Except it didn't last because her daily subconscious thoughts still tainted her happiness... Oliver!

She must banish thoughts of him and Pippa and concentrate on a future without them. But a future without Alexander too? A frown creased her brow. Did godparents have any legal rights? As she unlocked her car and sat behind the wheel, she pondered this question. She concluded that none was the most likely answer; she wondered if Pippa would allow her to see him. And would there be a contact arrangement if so?

To dispel all such thoughts on her commute, Lexie selected her new playlist, music with no memory links to either Oliver or Pippa. She was determined to clear her brain of negativity and look forward to the days ahead, visiting her own family.

TWENTY-ONE

Lexie

Two days later, Julian dropped Lexie at the airport before leaving on a business trip to Manchester. It was a treat to be chauffeured around. The weekly miles she covered exhausted her, and she wouldn't need a car on this visit because her father had arranged to pick her up in Bordeaux. She intended to relax for a change.

The flight took just under an hour, and after disembarking from the plane and passing through passport control, Lexie messaged Julian to tell him she'd landed. She waited to retrieve her suitcase from the designated carousel in the crowded baggage claim area. It didn't take long, and as soon as she walked outside, she spotted her father sprinting along the pavement to meet her. His wide smile as he approached filled her with joy.

'What a sight for sore eyes!' Edward almost knocked Lexie off her feet as he embraced her before reaching down for her suitcase. 'Welcome back, darling. We've missed you.'

'I've missed you too, but it hasn't been that long this time,' Lexie said, dropping into step with Edward as they headed toward the car park.

'It's always too long!' Edward wheeled the case through lines of parked cars. 'I'm just there,' he said, pointing to his Land Rover Discovery at the end of the row. 'I'm looking forward to an uninterrupted chat on the journey.'

'How is Hugo?'

'Doing much better, thankfully. Though he's hyper, so be prepared!' Edward pressed the key fob and placed the bags in the boot.

'And Mum?'

'She's busy trying to make everything perfect for your stay. You know what she's like. They're both excited, so we'd better get going!'

*

When they arrived at 'Beauvoir', Lexie followed Edward inside. They left her luggage in the hallway before making their way to the lounge. Lexie wished she could surprise her brother, but a sudden appearance would overstimulate him, so Miriam would have prepared him.

When Lexie eased the door open, Hugo turned his head and jumped to his feet. He bounced up and down and flapped his hand. His eyes grew wider, the more excited he became.

'Hi, Hugo. Hello, Mum.'

'Le, Le, Le,' he chanted as he charged across the room and hugged her.

'So, you're pleased to see me then?' Lexie laughed as he

blinked rapidly and rocked from one foot to the other, his stims a sign of his joy.

'He's missed you,' said Miriam, looking at her son. 'You've been asking for Lexie, haven't you, Hugo?' She turned to Lexie. 'He's been pointing to your photograph.' She nodded to a gilt-framed photo on the wall.

'Aww, I've missed you too.'

'I'll get the kettle on,' said Edward, watching the exchange fondly.

'I'll do it, darling. You've just come from the airport.'

Miriam hugged Lexie, but as she did, Hugo wedged himself between them, forcing Miriam aside.

'All right. I know you want your sister to yourself,' she said with a chuckle. 'Remember, be careful with your arm. It's healing well. You don't want to hurt yourself again, do you?' Hugo grasped Lexie's hand in a tight grip and turned his back on his mother.

'Wow! There's nothing wrong with your other hand, is there, Hugo?' Lexie couldn't believe his physical strength, marvelling at how her petite mother coped with him.

'It's wonderful to see you, Lex,' Miriam said. 'What would you like to drink?'

'Coffee, please, Mum.'

'Tea for me, please,' said Edward.

The momentary pause was enough to alter Hugo's attention span, and he slapped Lexie. Knowing his sensory needs, she recognised it as his happy slap, as they all referred to it.

'OK, let's see what you want,' she said, giving him her undivided attention. Hugo gestured towards a table holding craft materials.

'He wants to show you his mosaic,' said Edward. 'Hugo, show Lexie what you made for Mum.'

Bending down, Lexie looked at the items and studied them intently. 'These are amazing. You're so clever.'

Hugo rocked back and forth, delighted while Lexie spent time observing each piece.

'He has a natural artistic ability, it seems. Obviously gets it from your mother.'

'What's from me?' Miriam asked, entering the room with a tray of steaming beverages.

'His artistic ability.'

'He loves doing them, don't you, Hugo? It's the only time he's still for a few minutes,' Miriam said, setting the drinks down on the coffee table. 'The only problem is how determined he is to complete a piece when it's bedtime, so we're working on monitoring his session times to avoid his meltdowns.'

Hugo tugged at Lexie's sleeve and pointed to a square-shaped piece of his work.

'This one? Is this for me? What pretty colours.'

Excitement had him bouncing.

'Oh, thank you! I love it.' Lexie examined the multicoloured coaster as she turned it over in her hands. As she examined the intricate details, she fought to hold back her emotions.

Hugo directed her to make use of her gift by pointing to the mug beside the cafetière. Miriam promptly pushed down the plunger and poured some coffee. With a swift movement, Hugo grasped Lexie's arm and pulled her towards the coffee table.

'One minute, Mum,' Lexie said, setting the coaster down in readiness.

Hugo sounded his familiar happy-voice stim and wrapped himself around Lexie, holding her close, squeezing her ribs. Lexie smiled and hugged him.

'Can I sit down now?' she asked, after kissing the top of his head.

'Hugo, let Lexie drink her coffee. Come sit with me,' said Edward, patting the sofa next to him. 'Mum's going to make dinner soon. I'll bet you're hungry, aren't you?'

Hugo grabbed a handful of grapes from the fruit bowl as he passed.

'Not too many,' said Miriam, 'or you'll spoil your dinner.'

His lips turned down in disapproval. He bowed his head and stomped to the sofa. He sat, looked at his father and frowned.

'I know you want more, son, but dinner won't be long.'

'I see his appetite hasn't changed,' said Lexie. She took a sip of her drink, then set her mug down. 'What are you cooking, Mum? Something smells delicious.'

'One of your favourites, beef bourguignon, or *bœuf bourguignon*, to be correct.'

'Listen to you,' Lexie smiled with pride. 'Your French is coming on!'

'And she's perfected the dish too,' said Edward, smiling up at his wife.

'Mm, I can't wait to eat it. I get to try your veg too, Dad.' Lexie's tongue skimmed her top lip.

*

Before dinner, Edward was settling Hugo earlier than usual. Lexie's visit had triggered his hyperactivity, prompting

Edward to take him up to bed once he'd finished his cheese and potato pie with baked beans.

Miriam was engrossed in the kitchen, fussing over the stove.

'Mum, come sit at the table and enjoy a glass of wine with me. You've been non-stop since I got here.'

'I'll just warm the plates and—'

'Mum! Sit!'

Miriam raised her hand as Lexie poured wine. 'Not too much for me. I need a clear head.'

'Oh, Mother, one glass won't hurt. Now come and join me.'

'OK.' Miriam couldn't resist a quick peer into the oven. She lowered the temperature, hung up the oven gloves and sat beside her daughter. '*Santé*,' she said, picking up her glass.

'*Santé!*' They chinked glasses and sipped.

'So, how have you been, Mum?'

'Fine, and you?'

'That's your usual response. Now... you've been through a lot lately, so I'll ask again, how've you been?'

As Miriam straightened a napkin, Lexie reached across and stilled her hand.

'Relax. I know you find it difficult, but everything is under control. The food's in the oven. You can serve it in a little while. We rarely get time to sit together for uninterrupted conversation.'

'How's work? I know you filled me in about China, but—'

'Mum, you're digressing again. I'd like a conversation about you! You've not spoken to me about your feelings since your scare. Have you been taking more time to look after yourself?'

Miriam faced Lexie and sighed. 'If I'm being honest, I was worried. More so about your father, and Hugo. Sometimes we get a wake-up call, like a message… to put things in order, just in case.' Miriam stroked the back of Lexie's hand with her thumb. 'I questioned whether coming to France was the right decision.'

'Why?'

'Because you're there, and we're all here. It doesn't seem right. It's not just about missing you. I don't mean to be selfish, but it got me thinking about how your father would handle Hugo alone if the news was different.'

'Mum, that's so typical of you. What about worrying about yourself?'

'I feel thankful for my life. The relief I felt when I found out it wasn't cancer was overwhelming. It meant I had time to reassess.'

'And?'

'Have you thought any more about your father's suggestion?'

'To live here?'

'Yes… I know that look of exasperation. Please don't dismiss the idea, darling. Your job is important to you, but remember there are pharma companies here too.'

'Oh, Mum…'

'Just think about it. Please?'

Lexie raised her glass to her lips and took a sip of wine. Her mother could read her every expression and she didn't want her to see disappointment, especially after all she had been through. How could she glorify her own career now?

'Mum, I would never leave Dad to manage on his own. That's one fear you can dismiss.' The relief that crossed her mother's face confirmed how concerned she'd been.

'I'm not pleading with you to come here to replace me if the worst should happen. We long for you to be here with us. If it's not possible, then at least spend more time visiting us. You're my daughter and I love you. I'm hoping we'll have some quality time to make precious memories together.'

'And we will, Mum. I promise.'

'I need a large wine,' said Edward, entering the kitchen and seating himself opposite Lexie.

'Has he settled?' Miriam asked as she stood up from the chair.

'Yes, he's sound asleep. Relax, sit down and enjoy the wine.'

Lexie nodded in agreement. 'Now you've heard it from the boss.'

Edward let out a chuckle. 'If only,' he said as he filled a glass.

'You two are so bossy when you're together.'

'We have to team up, Mum.'

Miriam filled three glasses with water, attempting to keep a straight face. She lifted one and drank from it.

'One sip of wine, followed by one sip of water. Can't be too careful, eh, Mum? You make me laugh.'

'It's called pacing yourself.'

'After one sip!' Lexie couldn't help but laugh aloud.

'Well, you'd better serve dinner, my love. We don't want you to be too merry,' Edward said.

'Cheeky!'

*

As always with her mother's cooking, the meal was delicious, and after a pleasant evening catching up, they all retired to bed. Lexie's head sank into the duck down pillow, and she revelled in its softness. The day had been tiring, but she allowed contentment to wash over her while she lay nestled in a comfy bed with her family around her.

She closed her eyes, but her brain remained active. Work wasn't occupying her thoughts. Instead, she pictured the pleasure on Hugo's face, feeling a surge of pride. She had a deep love for her brother. He was so special; to her, his autism only made him more so. It annoyed her how people could dismiss him and frown upon him, as if he were less of a human being. They didn't have a clue! Being confined to a different world by autism did not make him inferior. The opposite was true, in fact. His brain functioned at an advanced level, but with a unique programming. He had a heightened sensibility. You could almost sense his neurons firing when he made physical contact. He had a greater level of awareness on contact. Hugo's fingertips traced every detail of her features, bringing to mind someone without sight. Without uttering a word, he communicated a pivotal message by investigating deep into her soul with his eyes.

All his senses were acute; when he tasted food, she envisioned an explosion of flavour on his taste buds. Hugo savoured every mouthful he ate. Hearing sounds, he analysed every pitch, and his expression would transform itself. From her research, she knew he was someone who noticed intricate details, rather than the bigger picture. It had astounded Lexie to learn that in a forest, an autistic person would focus upon a magnified raindrop balanced on a leaf, whereas most would see only the tree.

There was silence and darkness now. It was too quiet to sleep. Back home, streetlights and traffic distinguished the night-time experience. Here, sturdy stone walls blocked out the noise. There was no audible sign of the heating boiler starting up, or the gentle humming of the fridge. In some hotels she frequented, the muffled snoring of others and the rare, discourteous, alcohol-fuelled guest had often disturbed her slumber.

Despite the solid granite keeping the bedroom cool, Lexie craved some fresh air. She rose from the bed and padded across the room. Opening the window, she took a deep breath. She sat on the cushioned window seat and stretched her legs out across the wooden sill. The stars twinkled brightly, and a full moon cast its glow across the cornfields. The gentle night breeze lifted tendrils of hair, which she tucked behind her ears. Reclining, she closed her eyes and simply breathed, savouring the purity of clean air flushing out her lungs. The distant hoot of an owl broke the silence, bringing with it a memory of Pippa.

'It's a sign of death,' Pippa had once proclaimed at which Lexie had laughed. 'Believe me, it's true. The closer the sound, the closer the connection – like a friend or a relative.' Lexie had dismissed it as nonsense. But Pippa insisted on talking about her research into American Indians, and their belief in the signs of nature.

The screech of the owl grew louder and closer. Had it flown to a nearer location, and if so, did that mean death was imminent? Lexie chastised herself for even thinking such nonsense. She closed the window and returned to bed. She knew one thing for certain: Pippa was never far from her thoughts.

*

At 6.20am the bedroom door burst open, startling Lexie. 'What the… Oh!'

Hugo jumped on the bed and snuggled up to her.

'Sorry, darling, he was too excited to wait and ran to your room before I could stop him,' Miriam apologised, following close behind.

'It's fine, Mum.' Lexie rubbed her eyes and smiled. 'Morning, Hugo.'

He yanked her arm.

'Oh, you want me to get up, do you?'

'Come on, Hugo,' said Miriam firmly. 'Let Lexie take a shower and get dressed and she'll be down soon.'

He lay next to Lexie, pulling pillows and cushions around them, forming a barricade, which he did when he refused to move, or needed security.

'Do you want to sleep some more?' Lexie teased. Hugo dragged the sheet over his face.

'Dad's making waffles,' Miriam coaxed.

He pushed away the sheet and pillows and got up.

Miriam chuckled as he rushed past her. 'I'll make coffee.'

'Who needs a jolt of caffeine to wake you when Hugo's around?'

'Or an alarm clock!'

'I'll grab a quick shower and be down. Thanks, Mum.'

*

'Mm, the enticing scent of maple syrup. There's nothing quite like it,' said Lexie, walking into the kitchen, ready for the day.

'Good morning, sweetheart,' said Edward, carrying a plate of warm waffles to the table. 'Coffee?'

'Yes, please. Those look tempting. Since when did you cook breakfast, Dad?'

'Since I retired to France. Wonders never cease, eh? I did tell you this on your last visit, but you didn't believe me.'

Lexie took a seat next to her brother, who was licking syrup from his waffle.

'No more, Hugo,' said Miriam, moving the syrup out of his reach. 'We thought he could have a treat as you were here, but as you can see, he's tipped more on.' Miriam rolled her eyes. 'This is the second plate of waffles your father has made. Hugo's already eaten some. It's a good thing we didn't move to America!'

'Are they tasty, Hugo?' asked Lexie.

He nodded, eating with gusto. He didn't waste time before taking another bite.

'There's granola and fruit if you'd like some first,' Miriam said to her. 'And juice. Oh, I forgot the glasses – just a minute.'

'Mum, you're fussing again. Sit down for breakfast.'

'Yes, I have everything under control, dear. Look, I've even timed your poached eggs to perfection.' Edward set a plate of eggs on a placemat. 'And,' he said, turning at the sound of the toaster ejecting the bread, 'toast... timed to precision.'

She flashed a smile. '*Merci beaucoup. Très bien, mon ami.*'

Edward planted a soft kiss on Miriam's cheek, peeled off his apron and sat opposite her. 'Now, let's tuck into these waffles,' he said, smiling at Hugo. 'That's if you haven't eaten them all, son.' Edward helped himself to two from the pile and spooned some berries onto his plate. 'I'd better have some fruit, or your mother will curse me for indulging in the unhealthy option, won't you, dear?' He granted Miriam a roguish wink.

'I'm guessing we'll have around five more minutes before Hugo's done, and then he'll either grab your waffles or he'll be off. So I'd eat up if I were you,' Miriam laughed, turning to Lexie. 'I'm safe. Hugo doesn't like eggs.'

'He has my sweet tooth, unfortunately,' said Edward, looking at his son. 'Isn't that right, son?'

In a flash, Hugo snatched a piece of waffle from Lexie's plate. Their laughter echoed throughout the kitchen. Hugo covered his ears, pushed his chair back with his thighs and ran from the room.

'I'll go,' said Edward, following him. 'You two enjoy your breakfast in peace.'

After breakfast, Lexie tried to load the dishwasher, but Miriam insisted on washing the dishes by hand.

'Oh, Mum, why don't you save precious time and energy? What's the use of having a dishwasher if it's never used?'

Miriam was engaged in piling the washed plates on the drainer. 'It's quicker. There are only a few dishes and in the time it would take to load it, I'll have them finished.'

It was pointless carrying on with the conversation, so Lexie cleared the table instead.

'Do you fancy a trip out, or would you rather relax here?' Miriam asked, spraying anti-bac on the worktops.

'Relax? With Hugo around?'

They shared a knowing smile. It was so good to be with her family.

*

After an energetic week with Hugo and another emotional farewell, Lexie was home once more. She set her suitcase down and closed the door behind her.

The apartment appeared spartan and uninviting after she'd spent a week in the warmth of her family's home. Lexie glanced around, taking in the pristine setting before her. It was a show home. Nothing out of place, no aroma of homely cooking, no sign of presence and, surprisingly, no sense of belonging.

The quality time shared with her family had emphasised how much she missed them. Hugo's presence brought her joy, and she knew how fortunate she was to have him in her life.

Memories flooded back, of the terror she'd felt after hearing the news of his accident and her complete helplessness because they were so far apart. On the visit this time, he had nearly been back to perfect health. Lexie had relished every moment, but she couldn't change the fact that there would be fallout now. Her stomach tightened as she thought about the meltdowns he'd have, his routine disrupted. Hugo would have to adjust to being without her again. Her parents would have their work cut out, trying to pacify him and keep him calm.

Guilt obliterated her earlier appetite, so she settled for an early nightcap of brandy instead of supper. She'd only been home an hour, but she was missing them already. Shaking off her sentimental thoughts, she opened her MacBook. Time for work.

PART TWO

Six Months Later

TWENTY-TWO

Pippa

Pippa wrung cool water from the flannel and mopped Oliver's brow. His fever had reached forty degrees. He'd been delirious, thrashing around in their bed, and she'd remained by his side for days.

Pneumonia had taken its toll. He was weaker by the day. His face was sallow, the bones protruding through the fine veil of skin. The hollows of his eye sockets were deep, encasing sunken eyeballs that resembled marbles enclosed by a paper, veined membrane. She dabbed gingerly at the side of them now, for fear of ripping his delicate skin.

An odour hung heavy in their bedroom, despite the open window. It was the odour of decomposition and impending death, a smell which could not be wiped out, no matter the effort.

It choked her to see Oliver's deterioration, his strong athletic body now robbed of body mass, gaunt and emaciated. The sheet covering him didn't conceal his skeletal frame.

He looked nothing like the man she loved; he was frail and broken. Every breath he drew proved an ordeal for him. Her heart was breaking as she watched him daily, slipping away from her towards another place. It sat like a boulder, deep in her core. She existed on pure willpower as she nursed him devotedly, day by day. The exhaustion was nothing she could have imagined. Her gritty eyes stung from night-watching and lack of sleep, but she couldn't, and wouldn't, close them for a minute, for fear of missing a single breath her husband took. Their time together now was so precious. It would only be days, if not hours, before she lost Oliver forever. Pippa could not contemplate a life without her soulmate. She felt so alone.

They would be left behind, and she couldn't bear to think of life without Oliver. But in fact, it was a reality; she'd already lost the person he was. Her vibrant, energetic, loving companion was now almost a marble shell, devoid of real consciousness, strength, or human life.

He murmured in his sleep, his speech a mumble, trying to escape from the depths of his voice box. He moved in and out of awareness, and his rambling was incoherent.

James opened the bedroom door. 'How is he doing?'

'His temperature is down somewhat, but he's restless.'

'Why don't you lie down for a while? You're exhausted.' Her father-in-law rested a caring hand on her shoulder. 'You need food and rest, otherwise you'll be ill yourself.' He handed her a cup of tea. She didn't want it, but she took it, anyway.

'Thank you. I'll be fine, honestly.'

'He's not going anywhere yet, is he? Get some sleep before you keel over. Your body can't go on like this, day in and day out.' He stared down at his son. 'It's not supposed to be like this, is it?'

James's emotional state was as fragile as her own. His hand reached down to touch his son's hair, then he felt Oliver's brow with the back of his hand.

'He doesn't seem as hot now.' James lowered himself onto the bed, perching beside his son. 'You know, when he was a lad, all he ever wanted was to be a pilot; always fascinated with planes. I used to buy Airfix models, and we'd make them together.' He stared at Oliver, reminiscing. 'Gabrielle used to complain he wasted too much time doing them and that his attention should be on more academic topics. So she bought him a stamp album, insisting it would help his geography.' He smiled at the memory. 'The thought of being a philatelist horrified Oliver, but he didn't want to upset his mother, so I ended up doing it for him. It was our little secret. At least that's what we thought. But Gabrielle, being Gabrielle, knew all along that while I was sticking in stamps, Oliver went on building his planes.' His eyes lit up as his smile reached them. 'He has quite a collection. We've still got them, boxed up in the loft. Perhaps Alexander would like them?' He looked from Pippa to Oliver. 'What do you think, son?' he asked, looking down at his son's sleeping face. 'They're no good up there gathering dust, are they?'

Pippa smiled, imagining Oliver as a child. An only child, he hadn't been spoilt, like some only children. He'd experienced a solid, disciplined upbringing, balanced with love. He'd been close to his uncle, Ronnie, a bachelor, and spent many days staying with him during school holidays. It devastated him when Ronnie died from lung cancer after a long struggle; even after having chemotherapy, radiotherapy and surgery, Ronnie still lost the battle to survive.

'I'd never go through all that if it were me. You die in the end anyway, no matter how much chemo and shit they pump into you. I swear if I had it, I would let nature take its course,' Oliver told her at Ronnie's funeral only a year ago.

Pippa's heart was shattered, her body barely able to contain her anguish as she bit her cheek constantly, trying to summon the energy to think straight and respond to James's question. He would be reliving his own private memories of Ronnie too, no doubt.

'I'm sure Alexander will treasure them.' She watched James tenderly stroking his son.

He was right, it wasn't supposed to be like this, and she was indignant. Parents shouldn't have to sit and watch their children suffer death. Death came hard enough, but to see your child slip away had to be the ultimate cross to bear.

Her heart threatened to burst through the wall of her chest, her throat constricted with sorrow for James and Gabrielle, about to lose their only child. It was not any easier to accept given that Oliver was a grown man, either. Your child was always your child, no matter their age.

Pippa could see James's internal conflict and she agonised for him too. Losing his son would only be the beginning.

How would he comfort Gabrielle? She was overwrought and been given diazepam by the doctor. James had taken her home for a few hours, to be in the care of her sister, Elizabeth, who was supporting her.

Pippa felt consumed with the burden of everyone else's despair, though she was barely functioning herself. It had proved an ever-increasing strain, continuing to keep life as normal as feasible for Alexander's sake.

TWENTY-THREE

Oliver

Oliver knew now he wasn't long for this world. He knew it deep inside his soul. His body was weak, his mind tormented and tortured. His chest burned with every breath he drew, and it felt as though a constant weight sat on his ribs. Each breath was like hauling up the gym weights. His face grimaced in pain as he coughed. It was akin to a thousand hot needles pricking at his skin while his lungs fought for the intake of oxygen. Even lifting his arm to put his hand to his mouth was a tremendous effort; the sheer weight exhausted him.

His mouth was parched again. His tongue was furred up like sandpaper, sticking against his teeth and the roof of his mouth. His eyes were heavy and gritty with tiredness he could not believe as he strained to keep them open for even the briefest of periods.

He wasn't a quitter, but he'd had enough existing like this. His exhausted body was hot and uncomfortable, and sweat plastered his hair to his head.

Oliver drifted off to sleep and once again, his dreams haunted him.

He was levitating in the air looking down at Pippa, Alexander and Lexie squatting around a campfire toasting marshmallows on long sticks, laughing, when suddenly, Pippa and Lexie started to fight.

Alexander shouted, 'No! Leave my mummy alone!'

But they continued to fight and roll near to the flames. Alexander was shrieking and calling out, 'You're going to die, Mummy. Please don't die.'

Pippa was shouting, 'Leave my husband alone!'

'No. No. Noooo!' Oliver cried out, thrashing around in the bed. He heard a faint voice in the distance, getting louder.

'Oliver, wake up. You're having a bad dream.' Pippa stood over him, mopping his brow. 'Shh, it was just a dream.'

The cool cloth took the heat from his forehead. His heart beat a loud tattoo in his chest, resounding in his ears. All his senses were on red alert as adrenaline pumped through his veins. His breathing settled as Pippa's voice soothed him.

A tear escaped and ran down his face. He wondered briefly about Lexie and the long friendship they'd lost, but there was no time left for regrets. All he'd ever wanted was his wife and he didn't want to leave her, but he knew he was dying. The time had come.

Pippa's lips delicately kissed his face, and he sensed the silent sobs in her chest. A tear dropped onto his cheek, warm, mingling with his own.

'I love you so much,' Pippa whispered.

He wanted to tell her he loved her too.

'Let go, honey. It's OK to let go. There's a beautiful place waiting for you where you'll feel good again and all your pain and suffering will be gone, I promise.'

She was giving him permission to leave them. A blockage formed deep within his throat. He was losing his battle. Something probed his mouth. The moisture was a welcome relief. Oliver wished his eyelids weren't so heavy and he could lift them to see his wife one more time. He drifted off again.

In his dream this time, he levitated above a field full of daffodils, yellow all around him, bright and fragrant. Pippa and Alexander were walking, cutting the stalks of the flowers and placing them into a long basket. She stopped and picked Alexander up, swinging him around, and he giggled. A Labrador puppy jumped at their legs, barking, wanting to join in their fun.

'Down, Mindy,' Pippa was saying, bending to ruffle the pup's ears. 'You've got sharp claws, little girly.' She picked up the puppy and cuddled her close to her chest. 'You are a beauty, aren't you? Here, have a treat.' She reached into her pocket and gave her a small piece of dried sausage, laughing. 'Your teeth are like needles.' She set her down again.

Alexander lay on his tummy next to Mindy, watching her chewing. He was filled with joy as he studied her. Pippa was watching them, wearing a huge grin. The sun was beaming down, lighting up her face, and it shone through her white cotton dress as it flapped at her ankles in the gentle breeze. The copper highlights in her hair caught the rays of sunshine. She was a vision of beauty. And as she stood in the golden field, she looked happy, vibrant and full of life.

It was a picture he clung to as everything else faded.

TWENTY-FOUR

Pippa

Pippa wasn't sure how, but she'd fallen asleep, her head lolling to one side. She jumped and wiped the dribble from her mouth as she sat up alarmed. James must have covered her with a blanket.

Oliver!

She checked him but he was sleeping peacefully. She glanced at the clock. Only an hour had passed. She'd slept so deep it felt later, somehow.

Standing up, she stretched her body. There was a distant echo of voices downstairs. Creeping out of the bedroom, she saw James and Sandy chatting in the hallway.

'I've just popped in for a pair of pyjamas for Alexander.' Sandy looked up at Pippa. 'James didn't want to disturb you when I phoned earlier.'

'Where's Alexander?' asked Pippa, feeling disorientated, tiptoeing down the stairs.

'He's at ours with the guys. He's having a great time

watching a film, chomping popcorn, so don't you fret about him.'

Pippa ran her hand through her dishevelled hair and undid the bobble. She bundled escaped tendrils together and secured them into a ponytail. 'I must look a sight,' she said, patting her cheeks to liven herself up. 'Isn't he asking for me?'

'Afraid not, he's having too much fun. Anyway, a change of routine will do him good and take some pressure off you. He's safe with us, so don't bother screwing your face up.' Sandy's eyes dropped to a bag in her hand and then to James. 'We've managed between the two of us to get Alexander an overnight bag, haven't we, James?'

'Yes, though I can't promise the clothes I've chosen for tomorrow will be right. I only packed fresh underwear, socks, a sweater and jeans. I didn't figure he'd need anything else until Sandy pointed out about his pyjamas.' He shook his head. 'I forgot those!'

'You did just fine.' Sandy smiled at James and turned to Pippa. 'I've left you some chilli in the kitchen for later, and before you protest, it's a mixed bean, so there's no excuse for not eating it.'

'I'll get her to eat something, Sandy, don't worry. Come on, Pippa, let's make you a nice cup of tea.' He looked at her enquiringly. 'I'll bet you could do with one?'

'Yes, please.' Pippa reached out and hugged Sandy. 'Are you sure about Alexander?'

'Of course! He hasn't even asked for you.' Sandy gave a teasing smile. 'And you can wipe the petulant expression from your face too, it doesn't suit you.'

With that, she moved to the front door, turning with a smile of reassurance. 'I'll come over at any hour, remember.

If you need me, call. You don't have to do this alone.' Tears shone in her eyes.

'Thanks,' said Pippa. 'Get Alexander to call me before he settles down for the night, will you?'

'Will do, I promise.'

Pippa heard Oliver cry out.

'I've got to go!'

She mounted the stairs two at a time and hurried into the room.

'Shh. Everything's fine now, it's just a bad dream.' She bent to soothe him and sprinkled a few drops of Rescue Remedy onto a pink sponge stick and popped it into his mouth. Gently, she moved it over his furred tongue. His mouth was dry, but he wasn't drinking, so she did her best to moisten it. 'Sleep now, my darling. I'm right beside you.' James came in and put a cup of tea on the bedside cabinet.

'Do you want me to do anything before I go, Pippa?' He stooped to kiss Oliver's head. He stared at his son for the longest time, in a trance-like state.

'No... thank you, James.'

He looked at her with a knowing expression. A vertical crease between his eyebrows showed he wanted to say more but perhaps couldn't trust himself with the words. Instead, he drew her into his arms and held her closely, before turning to leave.

'Will you call, if...' The words weren't necessary. They both knew what it meant.

'Of... of course,' she responded, desperately struggling to force down the volcano of grief waiting to burst free.

James left quietly, closing the door behind him with a soft click.

Pippa comforted Oliver as he stirred. He was still dreaming, but now there was a smile on his face. A lone tear fell down the side of his cheek, escaping from beneath his closed eyelid, leaving behind a salt-stained trail. As she bent over to kiss him, her own tears splashed on his face and she knew, in the depths of her soul, only hours remained.

Oliver was slipping away.

'I love you, so much,' she whispered, choking on her words. 'Let go, honey. It's OK to let go. There's a beautiful place waiting for you where you'll feel good again and all your pain and suffering will be gone, I promise.'

Pippa lay by Oliver's side and put her arm around him, listening to his irregular breaths growing further apart. She held him, remembering their precious times together with a desperation that was shattering her heart into a million pieces.

She was frightened and felt so alone. But for this final moment in time, he belonged solely to her. Oliver, her soulmate, the love of her life dying in her arms, and there was nothing she could do about it.

Grief burned through her like molten fire, and she wanted to die with him, not be left behind without him. Their separation was inconceivable. Nature had bound them together as one.

How could she exist without Oliver by her side?

She lifted Oliver's hand to place over her heart and held it, stroking it tenderly with the back of her thumb, pausing to twist his wedding ring, which had grown loose on his finger. She raised his finger to her lips and kissed it.

Then, she clasped their hands together and waited.

TWENTY-FIVE

Pippa

Pippa sat on the bed, sniffing Oliver's T-shirt. She breathed in and out with frantic urgency, inhaling his scent until she had well-nigh hyperventilated. She craved his unique aroma to permeate her body, to penetrate every cell so he could still be with her.

After she calmed, she drifted around the bedroom, feeling as though her body didn't belong to her – a vessel which went through the daily motions.

Picking up a bottle of Paco Rabanne, she sprayed it onto her breast, reliving him. The memory choked her, and she fell to her knees, heaving mammoth sobs of heartbreak.

Pippa didn't recognise the wail that reverberated through the air, bursting from deep within her. She rocked back and forth, arms wrapped around herself, gripping the T-shirt so tight, her knuckles showed white.

She would never inhale his scent again. Never see him in this T-shirt. Never run her fingers through his hair. Never be with him... ever again!

Pippa wept so hard her body went limp. She lay on the carpet spent and rolled onto her back, hugging the T-shirt.

She stared up at the ceiling, through her raw, puffy eyes, focusing on the chipped paint around the ceiling rose where Oliver had secured a new chrome light fitting.

'I'll touch it up, I promise. It will only take a small paint job.' His voice was almost audible to her now.

Sometimes they stared up at it after making love, and he insisted he would, one day, get around to dealing with it. Now, there were no days, and it would not be finished. She would allow nobody else to do it either. It was a precious memory between them.

Pippa dozed fitfully on the bedroom floor. After a short while, she woke up feeling cold. At first, disorientation fogged her brain. And then, cold, harsh reality hit her like a ton of stone. She got up, rubbing her spine and twisting her body to ease the ache. But nothing could ease the ache in her heart or fill the huge void Oliver had left.

Oliver's slippers swamped her tiny feet as she padded down the stairs. She wore his dressing gown, wrapped tightly around her.

The house was silent, except for the gentle humming of the refrigerator, which she opened to retrieve a carton of milk. She heated the milk on the stove and made cocoa, then moved to the lounge and huddled on the sofa.

Nerves jolted her body. She was shivering as if cold, but it was the shock that made her shake.

It was the middle of the night, but she didn't switch on the lamp. She sat in the dark, staring into space, sipping the hot chocolate but not tasting it, its only function as a lubricant to soothe her raw throat.

Her thoughts were irrational, clouded by grief; her fuzzy brain refused to function.

Pippa was frozen with indecision about her future. She craved Oliver so strongly it shook her faith in life. It was only her and Alexander now. And, though she idolised her son, she felt ashamed to admit that even her obsessive love for him might not be enough to help her through.

Her negative thoughts frightened her. She didn't know what she might be capable of, to escape her daily torture.

She needed Oliver, desperately. Their family was broken, never to be fixed, shattered into pieces like delicate porcelain.

Pippa relived the hours of Oliver's death. His soul had left his body at 4am, before his heart failed to beat. She knew this because there was the tiniest movement and then, a distinct change. It was her belief that his spirit was leaving. She opened the window, to give his soul freedom, and took in the garden's stillness. There was not the slightest breeze. Oliver's words were etched in her brain, on one of their final conversations during a moment of lucidity.

'When the trees are still, with not the movement of a leaf, it will be my time.'

He was right.

Pippa lay beside him even when his body was turning cold. Blood left his fingers and toes, turning them bluish at the tips. She covered him to keep him warm. In his remaining hours, she'd constantly checked the soles of his feet to discover if they were warm. She knew one of the signs of the body shutting down, was when the feet went cold, because blood left the extremities first.

After his death, she imagined breaths still came from

his chest, and Pippa fixed her eyes to his ribcage, only to be left bereft when his lungs remained still.

Later, his body was mottled in hypostasis, where blood pooled in areas of contact with the bed.

The very thought of anyone taking him filled her with horror, and she lay with her arms gripping him, her head on his chest. The undertaker's arrival meant finality, closure and abandonment.

They would not have him.

When James let himself in and found them, he took control and called the doctor to certify Oliver's death.

When the undertaker arrived, Pippa had to be prised from his body.

*

When daylight broke the following day, Pippa woke to the sound of the dawn chorus. She closed her heavy eyes for a moment and tried to concentrate on the sounds, knowing it was just another day for most people. Life would carry on without consequence or interruption. People would go about their daily business as normal. But for her, time was still. There was no normal now.

Pippa fought to restore her body into some kind of functioning state. She must arrange Oliver's funeral, and that would prove difficult. The RAF would want full regimental regalia, a service drawing many. Pippa wanted a private family burial.

Oliver had requested to be laid to rest in a woodland burial, as would she when her time came.

They had purchased their plots following Ronnie's

death. She had considered it odd at the time, yet now, it was one less detail for her to think about. Oliver expressed his views quite adamantly: 'Pippa, this is important. I know you don't enjoy discussing death, but we need to make matters straight. Clarify our wishes... just in case.'

She thought of the conversation now. Did he have an intimation he was ill? Or was Ronnie's death the trigger for an increased awareness of his own mortality? He was no stranger to death with his chosen career though, either.

Something was wrong. Deep inside her, she felt as though there was more devastation for her to face. How irrational! Was she going mad? Sleep deprivation must have something to do with it, she mused, getting to her feet like a robot and going to empty her bladder.

Pippa went through the basic functions of ablutions. She didn't care what she dressed in, or how she looked. None of it mattered, and she didn't have the strength to care if it did. She didn't look in the mirror when she cleaned her teeth, she didn't want to see the empty shell reflecting back. She wasn't whole anymore. As she dabbed her mouth with the towel, she thought about one of their last lucid conversations, when Oliver's haunted eyes had pleaded with her to face his end.

'Pippa we must talk.'

'I know, Oliver, just not now. You need to rest.'

Oliver sighed deeply. 'We must discuss this, Pippa, you can't keep avoiding it. There's no time. You know I'm—'

'Don't!' Pippa placed two fingers over his lips. 'We've still got time to get you treated at the hospital.'

'No, we've been through—' Oliver's coughing halted his words. Pippa tapped his back and gave him water.

'Just lie back and rest now. I'm going downstairs to call Dr Kerr. You need something for that chest, Oliver.'

'Your remedies,' he said through short bursts of breath.

'Antibiotics.'

'But you—'

'There are times when certain medicines are needed, Oliver, and this is one of them and if you refuse to be admitted, then at least see the GP.'

She watched him close his eyes and she swallowed back the huge lump of emotion that blocked her throat. She stroked his hair with slow tender fingers. He pushed out another weak breath, nodding in agreement, the very effort exhausting him. His hand moved to hers and he opened his eyes.

'Promise me, Pippa… that I can die here… in my own bed.'

Pippa kissed his lips gently to silence him. She refused to hear words of death. Oliver was strong. He could get through this. He had to. 'Shh.'

'Promise? I know it's a lot to ask of you.' He tried to lift his head and his eyes were glazed in defeat.

'If that time ever comes, then yes, I promise, but it won't.'

Once dressed, she crossed the landing to Alexander's room. The house was quiet without him. But losing Oliver had meant her loneliness affected her in a way no solitude ever could. She tried to imagine a world without Alexander and the thought terrified her. She had to be strong, for him. That was where her priorities must lie. She had to buck herself up for his sake.

But for now, at least, he was in the care of Gabrielle and James. They'd been insistent, to allow her time to grieve, sparing him having to witness her raw despair. Reluctantly, she'd agreed.

When she peered in, the toy Chinook helicopter was on his pillow. Pippa could see them in her mind's eye, twirling around together in the hallway. Tears burst from her once again, bringing a nausea that forced her stomach to retch. She covered her mouth and rushed to the bathroom, but she didn't vomit; her stomach was empty. Pippa splashed cold water over her face and moved downstairs to get a remedy from her home pharmacy: ignatia for acute grief. She popped a pill beneath her tongue to dissolve.

She had to pull herself together, and soon.

TWENTY-SIX

Lexie

Lexie's energy was depleted by the end of the week. The afternoon meeting at the headquarters of RestrilPharma had gone on and on about clinical research and development.

It might have been obvious to the other delegates that she couldn't focus properly, but by then she didn't care. Lexie pushed back her seat to stand as soon as the team leader switched off the projector.

'Gosh, Lexie, I've never seen you move so fast. You've been clock-watching and fidgeting through the entire meeting.' Marianne Stone was new to the company and thought she knew it all. As Sebastian's pharmaceutical assistant, she had a lot to learn, and the pecking order was one such lesson.

'If you've been observing me, then your concentration's as bad as mine.' Marianne reminded her of Amelia, who'd since left the company and moved to China, to marry a diplomat she'd met there. She had seen women like them come and go, all legs and fluttering lashes. Marianne's unctuous demeanour got on Lexie's nerves; she stopped at nothing to gain brownie points. She should try *learning* the role instead, thought Lexie, then she'd gain far more respect.

Today, Lexie couldn't be bothered to challenge her, so she picked up her phone and her Armani briefcase and left.

Lexie had no intention of staying behind today, and Marianne was right about one thing: Lexie couldn't wait to leave at the close of the meeting.

Finally arriving at her apartment in Charlbury after a two-hour commute, Lexie dropped her briefcase, not bothering to empty it. Her MacBook could remain inside for tonight; she'd had enough, for today at least.

Opting for a drink instead, she opened the cabinet, selected a tall crystal glass then filled it with a large gin and tonic over ice. As she sliced a lime, her phone rang. She blew out a long irritable breath at the intrusion and reached for it. Focusing on the screen, her brows knitted into a frown, bewildered.

'Josh?'

'Hello, Lexie. Is this a good time to talk?'

'Erm, yeah, give me a second,' she said, grabbing her drink and taking a seat. 'To what do I owe this pleasure?' She felt a knot of apprehension in her gut. She hadn't seen Josh for ages, especially since her estrangement from Oliver.

'Lexie, are you alone? I was wondering if I could see you.'

'Why?' Lexie was puzzled by his request. She hadn't heard from Oliver or Pippa for months, so what did Josh want with her? 'Tonight's not a good time. I've had a rough week. Can we make it some other time?'

'No. Not really. I need to talk to you.' His voice was soft.

Now she was intrigued. The sound of him clearing his

throat made her skin prickle; this could only be negative news. A pulse throbbed at the side of her throat. Were Oliver and Pippa OK? Had their marriage broken down? Did Pippa know? Why was Josh calling her? Questions fired across the synapses of her brain.

'What's this about, Josh? I don't mean to be rude, but as I said I—'

'Lexie—'

'It's not that we can't meet, Josh, just not tonight, that's all. I'm tired and need an early night. I'm sorry. I'll call you.' Lexie ended the call, but all the same, her brain went into overdrive. She rubbed her temples. What was so important it couldn't wait? He must know about the fling she had had with Oliver! Dread replaced her curiosity, and she took a huge gulp of gin, the alcohol tingling on her taste buds.

When the intercom buzzed, her shoulders tensed. She sprang from the chair and peeped through the blinds. Josh stood on the pavement, dressed in his green flying suit. He looked up, catching her eye. How the hell did he arrive so quickly? Her heart pounded. This was the last thing she needed.

Biting her lip, she had no option but to let him in. Trying to calm her breathing, she released the outside door and leaned in the doorway of the apartment, waiting. When he approached her front door and stood next to her, his powerful frame towered above her, and there weren't many people who did.

'What is this, Josh? What's so urgent and how did you get here so fast? I told you, I'm in no mood for company, yet you're here anyway.'

'I was already outside and saw you arrive. I was waiting for you to get home.'

'You're lucky I'm not abroad.'

'I've been parked up for an hour.'

Lexie turned her back on him and went through the open-plan lounge to the kitchen.

'Something to drink? If you've been outside for that long, you're in need of one.'

'No thanks. Lexie, this isn't a social visit.' Josh pushed his hands into his pockets. 'I didn't come here for that.'

Lexie turned and looked hard at the unreadable expression on his face.

'So… why did you come?'

'I'm here about Oliver.'

Lexie's heart raced. So he'd told Josh? Why else would he be here, in her kitchen? Lexie turned and picked up the kettle. She couldn't allow him to see her rising colour.

'Lexie, leave that… please.'

She felt Josh's hand on her shoulder and turned to face him.

He removed the kettle from her hand and set it down. She saw the seriousness in his face and something else. Something was seriously wrong. She glanced at his hand resting upon her shoulder then scrutinised his face, looking for clues.

He didn't remove his hand. Instead, he placed his other hand gently on her other shoulder. Her breathing quickened.

'What about Oliver?' She heard her voice wobble and cleared her throat.

'I'm sorry, Lexie. There's no easy way to say this. Oliver's dead.'

A silent pause.

Lexie's brain refused to engage.

'Dead? What do you mean dead? Is this a sick fucking joke?' Rage fuelled her hands; she beat against Josh's chest. He stilled her with a vice-like grip.

'I'm sorry.' Josh swallowed hard. 'He died yesterday. I thought you should know.'

The raw emotion in his voice confirmed it, but her brain refused to believe it.

'He can't be dead! What do you mean died yesterday? He's not away. He's at Odiham. He's finished with all that, hasn't he? I don't understand?' Her bottom lip trembled. 'Is it… is it true?'

'It's true, Lex.'

'Nooooo.'

Josh's strong arms gripped her as she swayed.

'Is he really… dead? Has he gone?'

His mournful look confirmed Lexie's worst nightmare.

'What are you saying? What's happened?' Her voice raised to a hysterical pitch. 'Was he shot down? He was coming back. He was… he was leaving fucking Afghanistan!' she yelled. 'How can this be?' She slid down the kitchen unit onto the floor.

Josh knelt beside her and pulled her to him, holding her as she sobbed.

'It'll be OK.' His voice sounded thick with emotion. 'I'm sorry, Lex. Oliver was sick.'

'But… but I would have known if he was sick.' Lexie lifted her face and ran frantic trembling fingers through her hair. 'I can't get my head around this. He's my friend. I would have known!'

'It's a terrible shock, I know.'

Lexie's brain struggled to process the news. She wanted to cover her ears with her hands, like a child who didn't want to listen.

'What's wrong with him? He's fit. Fitter than anyone I've ever met.' She refused to speak in the past tense.

'I'm sorry. He's gone.'

She hated Josh at that precise moment. His assertive, military delivery forced her to accept this disastrous news. She cried harder and his strong arms tightened in comfort. After what seemed an age, she lifted her tear-streaked face to his.

'You said he was sick?'

'Cancer, his biggest fear. Hard to believe, I know. He dreaded that more than the Chinook getting shot down.'

'I didn't even know he was ill. I can't believe this, for Christ's sake! Why didn't I know? Why wasn't I told he was sick?' Heightened emotion raised her voice to an angry accusation as she tried to contain her bitterness. It wasn't Josh's fault, and he shouldn't bear the brunt of her hurt.

'Cancer? That's not possible? I would have known.' Fleetingly, she thought about Oliver's cough and his exhausted look. She remembered his almost feral passion and the way he'd looked at her. It was all beginning to fit, triggering a fresh surge of emotion. 'I didn't say goodbye. I could have said goodbye.' As she looked at her hands, she saw her fingernails had carved crescents into her palms.

'It happened quickly and—'

'And, what? Why the fuck didn't I know? Why wasn't I told? He was my best friend!' Lexie jumped to her feet, venting at Josh as she paced like a caged lion. 'Pippa should have called me. She's a bitch! Why didn't she fucking tell me!' Lexie's voice was full of venom. She watched him, as if in a slow-motion film; his eyes scanned the room before striding across to the drink's cabinet. He poured brandy into two glasses and handed her one.

'Drink.'

Her hand shook as she reached out. She knocked the brandy back and shuddered as the amber liquid burned her throat. He refilled her glass, led her to the couch and sat her down.

'It happened suddenly. Pippa did ring you. You were out of the country; she guessed that by the ring tone. She tried twice. You didn't take the call or respond to her message.'

Lexie let out a guttural groan of frustration as she cast her mind back. She'd rejected her call, and the voicemail too.

'We'd fallen out,' she sniffed. 'I was too stubborn to take her call. I just figured it was something and nothing. I was busy in Bangalore, setting up our distribution branch. I should have called.' Lexie held her hand to her mouth. 'She needed me and I… I wasn't there. Oh my God!'

Lexie was consumed with sorrow. She gulped a second brandy.

'How is she?'

'Not good.'

'And Alex? God, Alex!' Her chest heaved in alarm. 'What are we going to do? I have to see them.'

'The funeral will be next week sometime. I'll let you know. Maybe it's best you wait till then?'

'She hates me, doesn't she? I cut them out of my life, even Alex.' Fresh tears fell, shame consuming her. 'But I…

I missed them e… every day.' Lexie searched Josh's face, as though searching for reprieve. 'What have I done? It's too late now. Oliver's gone.' Her body convulsed in waves as she bent and hugged her knees.

'You'll get through this. You have to. Pippa needs you, so does Alexander.'

TWENTY-SEVEN

Pippa

Pippa sat, with her elbows on her knees and her head in her hands, as the telephone rang. The phone had not ceased ringing, and she was too numb to communicate. She ignored it and went for a glass of water.

Flowers filled the kitchen, so many she'd run out of vases and used various other containers. White lilies and roses were the dominant choices, and her home resembled a florist's shop, emanating fragrance throughout the rooms. Their scent served only to remind her of loss.

The past two days had seemed more like a week, and she was finding it difficult to insist on being left alone in her grief. Sandy's support had been amazing, taking charge of the well-wishers and leaving Pippa in peace. The phone rang again; its tone grated on her nerves. She snatched it up.

'Hello.'

'Hello, Pippa, Dr Kerr here. I wonder if I may come over and speak with you. There's something I wish to discuss.'

'Pardon... what about? If you're offering me sleeping pills, I don't need any. Thank you all the same.' Pippa didn't mean to sound rude, but he knew her preferences. He'd been their GP for years.

'No, I... it's nothing like that.' He cleared his throat, and she could hear him rustling paper in the background. 'I have to discuss something with you... about Oliver, before I can issue the death certificate.'

'Oh. Why? It's straightforward, isn't it?'

'I'd prefer not to discuss it over the phone. May I pop over? Say in half an hour?'

'All right. I'll see you then.'

Pippa put down the receiver and frowned. What did he mean? Why couldn't he issue the death certificate? She needed it to arrange Oliver's funeral. There was no need for a coroner. Dr Kerr had seen him and certified his death, so what was he on about?

She walked the floor, rubbing her brow as time ticked slowly by. Eventually, she sat down to await his arrival and when the doorbell chimed, she leapt from the chair.

'Come through, Doctor. Would you care for a drink?'

'No, thank you all the same. Are we alone?'

Pippa was glad he didn't want refreshment. She needed to hear what he had to say, the sooner the better. 'Yes... why?'

'What I have to discuss is private – patient confidentiality.'

'Oliver's dead! There is no confidentiality now, is there?'

'I'm sorry for your loss, Pippa.' He stroked her arm. 'But there's something I must inform you. May we sit down?'

'Sorry... yes, of course.'

'There's no easy way to say this—'

'For heaven's sake! My mind's on overload as it is, Doctor.' With trembling fingers, she formed a steeple with her two index fingers, resting them on her brow, too exasperated to remain polite. 'I didn't mean to be rude.'

'Pippa, please try to relax. I need you to listen.' His face showed his concern.

'I'm sorry, Dr Kerr. I apologise for snapping.'

'Don't be.' He gave her a comforting smile. 'Now, you know Oliver refused intervention, for his... condition?' he asked, speaking in a soft voice. 'And, going by his presenting physical symptoms, his diagnosis seemed straightforward, and because he wouldn't have any clinical tests, we have to go on what we're presented with—'

'Oliver had pneumonia. You said he—'

'That's correct, he did. But we—'

'So, what are you saying? Where's this going?' Pippa's voice rose an octave and a frown knitted her brow.

Dr Kerr shifted. He gripped his chin, pondering. 'In recent days, as you're aware, I sent off a specimen of sputum and a blood test. I wanted to prescribe the most effective antibiotics to help with Oliver's breathing.' He cleared his throat. 'You were very much against it because of your, erm—'

'He was at the end stage of his life. Nothing mattered then. I wanted him to be as comfortable as possible.' Pippa was feeling indignant. Was he blaming her?

'The thing is... the results came back, Pippa.'

'Are you saying it wasn't pneumonia?' Pippa was becoming more confused by the minute.

'No, I mean yes, it was, but he had other concerning symptoms too, so I ran more tests and—'

'I know about the lung cancer.'

'Oliver's blood results revealed a low CD4 T-cell count.' Dr Kerr was attempting to explain. 'And together with—'

'His immune system was low because of the cancer, I know.'

'Oliver had pneumocystis pneumonia.'

'I'm aware of all of this!'

'The thing is, Pippa,' he interjected quickly, 'Oliver had AIDS.'

Pippa felt as though she'd been hit by a tram. Somehow, she thanked him for his visit and got him out of the door before running to the bathroom to vomit. Still reeling with shock, she leaned against the wall, opened the taps on full and ran a deep bath. She practically leapt in, not bothering to check the temperature.

Almost immediately her legs turned bright pink. She didn't care, the hotter the better, to burn the filthy germs from her body. She poured Dettol into the water for good measure then picked up a loofah brush and scrubbed her thighs until she winced in pain. Next, she used the sponge and thrust it between her legs, scrubbing frantically back and forth, adding more and more soap.

Tears streamed down her cheeks as the furious assault made her bleed. She examined the bloody sponge then discarded it and drew her knees to her breast, rocking, causing the water to splash over the side of the bath.

Why was this happening and how was it even possible? Her husband had cancer not AIDS. AIDS… she couldn't envisage what this meant. Her brain swarmed with questions and incredulity.

Dr Kerr had assured her it was true. He had urged her

to be tested as soon as possible, expressed his sorrow and left.

If it were true, she could have the disease too. Or if not AIDS, at the very least the evil HIV virus. It might be mutating inside her and all because Oliver had given in to temptation elsewhere.

How long had he had it? How could he sleep with her, knowing someone infected him? Didn't he care for her? He couldn't have loved her if he'd risked infecting her. The shock reverberated inside her with a force of emotion she'd never experienced before.

Damn Oliver!

If he saw her now, if he was looking down from wherever he might be, he couldn't possibly rest in peace. Why should he when he'd left such a disgusting legacy? Even cancer with its devastating misery was better than this.

How would she move on now? She'd be permanently tainted by his betrayal and filth, constantly reminded of his marital lie.

Try to be calm, her logical brain was telling her. But she wanted to scream, not be calm. She tried to make sense of it all. This didn't happen to ordinary people. Not people like them.

But it did, and it had, hadn't it? Now she must dig deep inside and find the strength to deal with the consequences. Consequences that weren't hers. Except they were now. She must put that out of her mind, for now at least.

There was the funeral to get through. And she would do it. There was no option, no escape. She needed to find the courage, somehow.

*

By the end of the week, the routine of normality had died, along with Oliver. When Pippa got out of the bath, a daily ritual since she'd discovered the truth about the virus, she lay naked on the top of the bed. Somehow, she needed to feel clean, so she spent long periods sitting in the bath scrubbing and soaking as though washing his deceit away. She tried to disassociate her mind from her body, not accepting it could have been infected with virulent poison.

Her body was hot, although she'd sat in the water until it was cold. Eventually, she dressed. She had to pick up Alexander from school. Pippa was trying to keep his routine as normal as possible except for the odd overnight stay at his grandparents'. They had dropped him off at school today; James insisted on allowing Pippa space to grieve and, in view of the latest revelation, she'd welcomed it.

She was emotionally unfit to deal with a simple daily routine. Despite this, she needed her son close and craved some shred of normality. A brief call from her mother, as their cruise ship docked in a port in the Caribbean, had done little to bring her comfort. 'Daddy and I could fly back today, darling, if you need us. That's if we can get a flight at such short notice. It's our only opportunity because we'll be at sea then. Unless, of course… we cancel the rest of the cruise and return for the funeral?' her mother had said.

Her parents had never had much to do with Oliver, even when he was alive, so why should they now? And, especially now. Imagine what they would think! Pippa's own mind was trying to make sense of it. Disbelief taunted her daily.

His betrayal consumed her like a toxin. Did guilt prevent him from telling her? Why hadn't Oliver sought treatment? He would still have been alive, wouldn't he? Did he feel shame or even spare a thought for her?

How could he deny her the knowledge that allowed her the chance to expose the threat to their marriage? Her fury rose, only to subside again when her mind's eye pictured his suffering, emaciated body.

As she grabbed her Macintosh, she pictured her parents with their healthy sun-kissed bodies, sipping cocktails in the Caribbean sunshine, while her life was in shreds. They barely had time for her. In fact, James's paternal role in her life outweighed her own father's, and their bond was stronger too.

Pippa grabbed her door keys, putting her parents out of her mind. She would manage, just as she always had.

The brisk walk to the school lifted her and she welcomed the crisp air. At the school gates, there were looks of pity. Why did people cross the road or avoid you when death happened? Pippa recalled a conversation she'd had with Gillian:

'People treat you like a leper when you're dying. They avoid you, never discuss the subject. It's as though they will catch the cancer.'

Pippa now understood, having experienced it firsthand. People didn't know what to say. Or, maybe it hurt them to raise the subject and witness the pain of grief? But despite this, talking was the medicine needed.

Gillian was currently in remission and Pippa felt glad her treatment plan was progressing well. Why couldn't she have helped Oliver? But he didn't have cancer. His symptoms had proved almost identical though, and everything had happened so fast.

She'd taken time off from her work to cherish Oliver

and referred some of her clients to another homoeopath. Now, she didn't believe she would ever practise again. She didn't see what the future would hold. She could not think about it now.

The days since Oliver's death had been a living nightmare. It was all she could do to summon up her strength to take care of Alexander. Thankfully, Gabrielle and James had supported her with the organisation of the funeral. Pippa hadn't shown them the death certificate; she was in turmoil about whether to disclose the cause of death. Ignorance was bliss, though she didn't have that luxury, and Dr Kerr's words rang in her brain like a stuck record.

There was a halt in the conversations of parents as Pippa stepped through the gates. She heard them whispering, then resuming their conversations behind her back. She wondered how they'd react if they learned the truth. That would certainly amount to gossip! Pippa felt shame and yet she'd done no wrong. She quickened her pace, wishing it were possible to lock herself away.

'I'm sorry about your loss,' Yvie Carter said, catching her up as she walked through the playground towards the classroom. 'If you need Alexander picking up or anything, just call me.'

'Thanks.'

'You've got my number. Anytime, OK?'

'We're fine, thank you.'

Pippa knew she wasn't fine, even as the words stumbled out. Yvie walked away swiftly. Pippa sensed her unease. Yvie was a representative of the school governors but not a companion. At least she'd spoken to her and offered support, even if only out of politeness and pity.

At the sound of the bell, Alexander was the first child to run out, followed close behind by his teacher, Miss Delves.

'Good afternoon, Mrs Sanders, I wanted to mention Alexander didn't eat lunch today. Did you, Alexander?' She glanced down at him. 'I expect you're hungry now, aren't you?' Her expression showed concern. 'He wanted to go home at lunchtime,' she told Pippa quietly. 'But he settled when I had a one-on-one with him and we did some painting.'

The teacher crouched beside Alexander. The autumn breeze lifted her long floral skirt, so she tucked it between her legs. Her frizzy red hair was unruly, reminding Pippa of one of her own teachers, an eccentric artist who had taught her when she was a teenager. The smell of weed would waft around the classroom as she floated between the easels, stoned. It wasn't long before she was dismissed from the private school. Art had never been one of Pippa's talents.

'Would you like to give your painting to Mummy, Alexander?'

Miss Delves was the opposite of Pippa's old schoolteacher. Vitality oozed from her, and she was passionate about the infants she taught. She stood up, allowing him space.

'Here, Mummy.' He thrust the picture into her hand. 'Can we go now?' His bottom lip quivered. Pippa picked him up and kissed his cheek.

'Yes, darling. What a lovely picture.' Pippa struggled to keep her emotions in check as she looked at the painting. There were two large faces on stick bodies, one smaller than the other. Instinctively she understood.

'It's Daddy and me at McDonald's.'

Pippa couldn't find her voice for a second and she felt the gentle touch of the teacher's hand at her elbow.

'We could go there for dinner, eh?'

'I want to go with Daddy.'

'Mummy will take you. I'll get you your favourite.'

'Only Daddy lets me have McDonald's.'

'Well, perhaps you and I can have one today?'

'You don't like it. Only me and Daddy do.'

Pippa hugged him closely and turned to the teacher. 'I'd better get him home.'

'OK, see you on Monday, Alexander. Enjoy your dinner.' She smiled at Alexander and turned to Pippa, giving her a look of compassion, before moving to join the other children.

*

Later that evening, Alexander refused dinner. He cried himself to sleep. Pippa couldn't pacify him, and her heart ached.

She lay beside him for a long time, only leaving his side to use the bathroom and slip into a nightie. She felt delicate, and worried about her sanity and if the latest, horrific news would make her crack.

Pippa looked at her sleeping son and her heart bled for his innocence. Her mind revisited the past, when times were happy and uncomplicated, times happiness threatened to burst from her, like the news of her positive pregnancy test. The baby inside her had been an ecstatic elation that changed her, completing her as a woman. She frequently rubbed her stomach, as did Oliver, both in awe. Watching the shapes beneath her ribs, they couldn't believe the little miracle that was moving around inside, poking out an elbow or foot.

Her body gave him protection inside her womb, giving him the gift of life. And afterwards the gift of feeding on her own reserves as she nurtured him on her breast. She fixed her eyes on him for hours, never wanting him free of her even for a moment.

She'd lived in dread of sudden infant death syndrome and stayed awake around the clock, only dozing on and off out of sheer exhaustion, much to Oliver's disbelief. She became obsessive about him, not wanting people to handle him, for fear of germs. Oliver would try gentle persuasion to ease him from her arms, to allow others to have a cuddle of their beautiful, bonny boy.

Gabrielle had voiced strong opinions about their baby. 'Oliver, you must insist Alexander be put down in the nursery. He must learn to sleep alone.'

Pippa wouldn't hear of it and kept his cot in their bedroom. Her mothering skills gave rise to friction with Oliver's mother, but Pippa would not be told how to raise her own child. Gabrielle was like a thorn in Pippa's side at times. But as time went on, Gabrielle realised Pippa did, and would do, things her own way where Alexander was concerned.

To Pippa, it was a human instinct, and though she wasn't opposed to taking advice, her own maternal instinct dictated what was right and wrong for her baby.

Pippa's parents had other ideas about parenting altogether. Pippa grew up with a nanny. Her mother wasn't tactile, and Pippa couldn't remember her ever holding her, though she must have done, surely? Pippa, on the other hand, couldn't stop cuddling Alexander or inhaling Johnson's baby powder on his tender skin, after bathing him. She would watch him as he dozed, his tiny Cupid mouth twitching as though still feeding.

Pippa drew him closer now, holding him tightly to protect him until he stirred in his sleep. She stroked his hair gently and relaxed her hold a little, not wanting to let him go, just as in the past.

She remembered securing him inside a sling, carrying him everywhere with her. She loved his tiny heartbeat against her own. She would stroke his silky, fine baby hair with gentle fingers and kiss the top of his head as he slept nestled against her body. And, when he stirred, with his rooting reflex, she would give him her breast on demand and allow him to feed – another difference of opinion with Gabrielle, who insisted a four-hourly regime was best. Sometimes Alexander would suckle simply for comfort and then go back to sleep when settled.

Pippa didn't have the comfort of her mother's breast; she'd been bottle-fed by the nanny, Miss Tiggywinkle, as she called her because she was round and motherly. Her real name was Bess, and it was her scent Pippa recollected as a child, the smell of Pears soap on Bess's hands as she bathed her.

Her mother's scent was a waft of Estée Lauder perfume as she left the house for yet another social event. Pippa hated Estée Lauder fragrances and got rid of a bottle of *Knowing* that Gabrielle gifted her one Christmas.

She thought now of her loneliness as a child. She could never have left Alexander, never, and she would not now.

There she lay still staring in the darkness, until the early hours when eventually she too cried herself to sleep.

TWENTY-EIGHT

Lexie

Three-inch heels weren't suitable footwear for a funeral, thought Lexie, as she tried to stay composed, navigating a safe path between graves at the woodland burial. As her feet sank lower into sodden turf, the patent shine on her court shoes dulled with thick mud; autumnal leaves glued on the soles, making them heavy like her heart.

She stopped at a gravelled spot beside other mourners and lowered her head, fixing her eyes on the awaiting grave. It had been the right choice to wear a veiled hat to conceal her face, but as the wind whipped up, it tilted. She reached up a hand to steady it. Pippa turned, glancing in her direction, her eyes adrift in tears. Lexie's heart thudded in response. Her mouth dried and her stomach churned. She acknowledged her with a supportive nod. Soon she would face her, offering condolences.

In a few moments, Oliver's body would be committed to the earth, his life complete. Thirty-four was too young to die. The finality hit her hard and she fought to hold back the tears that were threatening to spill. A lump choked her throat; she took a deep breath of cold air.

The priest began the psalm, but Lexie wasn't taking in the words, her mind drifting, instead, to her own private memories.

'Forasmuch as it hath pleased Almighty God of his mercy to take unto himself the soul of our dear brother here departed, we therefore commit his body to the ground...' the priest intoned.

A mournful wail from Gabrielle prompted him to raise his voice, the keening sounding louder with escalating anguish as the wicker coffin was lowered into the grave. The sky darkened, adding to the sombre atmosphere, and the soft rumble of thunder threatened rain.

'Earth to earth, ashes to ashes, dust to dust; in sure and certain hope of the Resurrection to eternal life...'

Pippa stood staring, drawing Alexander close as he watched motionless, his father's coffin disappearing into a void of clay. He shivered and turned his face up, needing reassurance. Pippa squeezed his hand.

The penetrating smell of damp earth was a stark reminder of the reality of life's cycle. Lexie prayed silently that the soul did live on.

The priest handed out handfuls of earth to drop onto the casket as it was lowered. Pippa threw a single red rose; the motion was followed by Alexander, Gabrielle and James.

Lexie watched and waited in the background. Her body was numb with the shock of it all. In the silent interlude for private thought, the sound of the wind gusting through the branches mingled with muffled sobs from Gabrielle and Pippa.

Lexie discreetly wiped her cheeks. She felt like an outsider – or was it her conscience? She wanted to comfort Pippa, but how could she? Lexie decided Pippa would now never know of her husband's infidelity, but that didn't prevent Lexie's guilt growing inside her.

Pippa was her best friend, whatever had happened between them, and somehow, Lexie had to put things right. It was time for a reality check. Pippa would need her now, more than ever.

The family was preparing to leave as bitter cold rain penetrated their shivering bodies. The priest stayed behind to offer comfort to Pippa as Gabrielle and James led Alexander away.

In the distance, the gravediggers kept to a discreet distance, waiting to complete their job. It was a harsh reality of the burial process, the weather another obstacle to their mission. Lexie was incensed by their presence, nevertheless.

She was flummoxed as to what to do next. The situation between herself and Pippa was far from normal, and Lexie was unsure how Pippa would respond to her being at the graveside for such a private moment. But at the same time, not only did she want her own closure, she wanted to be there if Pippa needed her. And if the situation had been different, Lexie knew in her heart Pippa would want her to stay.

As Pippa and the priest talked with their backs to Lexie, she moved slowly forward as respectfully as possible, to throw her own flower into the grave. Closing her eyes, she said a silent prayer for Oliver, trying to hold back her own profound grief.

Sharp needles of rain chapped her face as she raised her head up to the sky. Her hair stuck to her as it rained harder, drenching her. But at least it was a sensation. Since Josh had broken the news, she'd been numb. She couldn't imagine how Pippa must feel.

She jumped as the priest touched her elbow to offer his silent support before he moved away and left them at the graveside.

Pippa's and Lexie's eyes locked, for what appeared an age in time, though in reality, only seconds passed. Human instinct took over and Lexie threw her arms around Pippa, holding her tightly while her body rocked with hysterical sobs. Pippa's keening resounded in the stillness of the surroundings. Lexie cradled Pippa and stroked her sodden hair. A rumble of thunder intruded on the moment, alerting them to the approach of a storm.

'Come on,' said Lexie softly. 'We need to get you to the hotel and then home.'

'Home? There is no home now, only a… a house.' Pippa stared at the grave, her eyes fixed firmly on the wicker coffin. 'I don't want… to leave him… here… in the cold.' She dropped to her knees at the foot of the grave and grasped at the earth, distraught with grief, throwing her head back. 'Why?' She rubbed tears away in anger, smearing wet mud across her cheeks. Lexie grasped Pippa beneath her arms and pulled her to her feet.

'It's OK,' Lexie soothed, her heart breaking at her friend's distress. She struggled to get her words out. 'It's horrendous, I know, but you can't stay here in the rain. You'll make yourself ill.'

'I don't care,' she sobbed, her knees buckling, grief etched on her face.

'Think of Alexander, Pippa. He needs you now. Be

strong, for his sake,' she reasoned. 'Come on now, the car's waiting.' She wiped dirt from Pippa's face with a pristine white cotton handkerchief. She looked at her friend and saw only a vulnerable girl with a muddy tear-stained face, alone and afraid.

Lexie's heart sank. How was Pippa going to get through this? How would she cope? She was the strong one, wasn't she? Losing her soulmate had destroyed her, and as she looked into her red, swollen eyes, Lexie's only thought was of a desperate need to stop her pain.

She loved Pippa and always had. Why else would their conflict have hurt so much? There was one thing for sure: Lexie would remain by Pippa's side for as long as she needed or wanted her to. An almost maternal instinct arose within her. Pippa needed her mother's love, but Lexie would have to suffice for now, because Annabelle wasn't here. Annabelle never was!

Pippa's parents, Richard and Annabelle, lived in Virginia, and Lexie wondered why they weren't at the service. She recalled they'd planned a world cruise for their ruby wedding anniversary because Oliver had told her a few months before, but she couldn't remember when. Nevertheless, they could have arranged a flight back, depending on the stage of the cruise. What was more important?

Lexie wasn't fond of Pippa's parents. She found them self-absorbed and lacking in support for Pippa – traits Pippa strongly denied. She always defended them and that was commendable, but to Lexie, they didn't appear to share much of Pippa's life. They never had.

Lexie suppressed burgeoning anger, thinking of their

pure selfishness. The bond of her friendship and the support of Oliver's parents would provide her with the strength she needed now.

'I... I can't face anyone, Lexie.'

'Yes you can. I'll be at your side if you want me to?'

'Yes... please.' She sniffed and blew her nose. 'I'm glad you're here,' she said, with a strained smile. 'I wasn't sure you'd come. I, well, I hoped you would.' She turned once more to the grave and nodded. 'Oliver will be happy you came.'

'I'd never leave you alone. You know that deep down, Pippa.' Lexie shivered against the cold. A further clap of thunder boomed above them as the bitter driving rain got heavier. They moved under a huge oak tree to protect themselves from the elements.

'How's Alexander been?'

'I don't think he understands. I suppose he's had a life... a life,' her silent sobs abated, 'where Oliver comes and goes, so his absence won't be felt by him yet, I don't imagine. He's asked for him and cried though.' Pippa sighed and Lexie saw her mind ticking over as she stared at the grave. 'I don't know, Gabrielle and James have had him quite a lot since it happened. James has been a brick. Having Alexander to stay has helped Gabrielle a little too.' Pippa shivered and rubbed her arms to generate warmth.

'We should go now, Pippa. We can come back when the rain stops and people have left, OK?' Lexie took her arm in silent persuasion. 'Ready?'

'Ready,' Pippa conceded. 'Goodbye, for now, my love.' Her chest heaved and before she could object, Lexie gripped her tightly and steered her away to the awaiting car.

TWENTY-NINE

Pippa

Pippa was glad Lexie had come. She needed her now more than ever and it was good to see her. Without Lexie, she wouldn't cope with the remainder of the day. Not that Gabrielle and James weren't supportive enough, but they carried their own burden of grief and Pippa didn't want their pity.

Lexie knew how to handle things. Her organisational skills were excellent, and for now, Pippa just didn't have the emotional resources to deal with other people's mourning or condolences.

She stared out across the vast grounds of the hotel. The rain pelted against the windows, dulling all other sounds. Pippa was lost in her thoughts, and she clung to them; they were all she had now.

The six months apart from Lexie seemed an age and Pippa missed being able to confide in her about Oliver's cancer. Except, it hadn't been cancer, had it?

Pippa was angry at Oliver for leaving her. But grief took many forms: shock, disbelief, bargaining, anger and acceptance. She was stuck between disbelief and anger and would never accept her loss.

She loved Alexander, of course, but it was love of nurture, a biological bond so strong it tied mother and child eternally. A tie never to sever; a genetic fusion that lived on through the generations, passed down by genes.

Oliver had made up for Pippa's lack of parental love, doting on her, until fate tore them apart. Now there was nothing. The only love she'd know now was maternal for their son, and she would only live on for his sake, because he needed her. Pippa's desperation and inability to cope alone inspired a fear so strong, she tasted it. Memories of their happy life brought a small smile, followed by fat teardrops dropping into her lap.

'Pippa, you've been sitting here for ages.' Lexie's voice broke her reverie. 'Most of the guests have gone now. Shall I take you home?'

Pippa nodded, too emotional to speak.

'Come on, put this on.' Lexie held out a different coat, explaining as Pippa looked puzzled.

'Sandy dropped by the house to pick it up. The other one was soaking wet.'

'Oh.'

'James and Gabrielle have taken Alexander back with them for tonight. They asked me to tell you goodbye. They understand you're exhausted.'

Lexie fastened the buttons on Pippa's coat as though she were a child. 'I told them you were having a few moments alone away from the crowd to collect your thoughts.'

'Thanks,' Pippa said, feeling miffed. 'I realise they're trying to help, but I haven't kissed Alexander.'

'He fell asleep. I expect they didn't want to wake him or disturb you. It's been a long day for him.'

'I wasn't sure he should come. But he'll understand now, Oliver isn't coming back.' Pippa's eyes brimmed. 'Gabrielle insisted it was no place for a child.'

'You're his mother. It's your choice.'

'I wondered if she was right. But children need to say goodbye, or they believe it's not permanent. Especially for us; Alexander is used to Oliver being away, so he might believe he'll see him again.'

'It's hard, but you made the right decision. Don't worry about other people, concentrate on you and Alexander.'

'I know, they are just being overprotective. Alexander is the only connection to Oliver now. They're desperate to have him near.'

'Are you OK with that?'

'James has been my rock these past few weeks. We've become closer. He suggested we move in with them.'

'And… what do you feel about it?' Lexie's face expressed her shock.

'I thanked him and explained we could cope. Can you imagine me living with Gabrielle?' Pippa smiled for the first time as Lexie breathed a sigh of relief. 'As wonderful as Oliver's parents are.'

'Thank God for that!'

'Oh, Lexie, your face!'

'At least it brought a smile.' Lexie hugged her. 'I'm really sorry about everything.'

'I'd better spend a few more minutes with Joshua before I leave.' Pippa nodded towards the function suite.

'OK.'

*

The room held mainly RAF mourners now, their impeccable uniforms dominating the room, each ranked by the stripes on their sleeves.

Pippa saw Joshua glance in her direction. He was in discussion with a wing commander, whose sleeve insignia of extra stripes of blue on black bands identified him as the higher-ranking officer. Pippa wondered how well he'd known Oliver. She'd spoken briefly to their squadron leader earlier, but she'd had no real lengthy conversations with anyone.

Joshua stood out from the team, being taller and broader than most. His dual heritage showed in the full lips and the brilliant-white, perfect teeth of his Bajan mother. His almond-shaped eyes and light skin tone were dominated by the genes of his father's English ancestry. His hair was straight, if allowed to grow, but now it was typically the 'high and tight' military cut, with the back and sides shaved to his skin and a slightly longer section on top. It was the same walnut hue as his eyebrows. His smooth face showed not the faintest hint of facial hair. He was handsome, not in a pretty-boy way; his features strong, chiselled and distinguished.

The eulogy was delivered by James who talked of Oliver's life with pride. But it was Joshua who spoke of Oliver's life as a flight lieutenant in the RAF. They heard of his skill on the front line in Afghanistan, his heroics in medical evacuations, as well as the humorous antics and banter with his crew on base, which brought poignant smiles to the faces of many of the mourners. Joshua spoke of Oliver's protective human instinct for the innocent casualties of war, and his love and pride serving his Queen and country.

Joshua had stood composed, as men of war did, remembering his best friend with pride, and Pippa's heart bled for him too.

'I've hardly said a word to Joshua, only to thank him for his tribute to Oliver. Honestly, Lexie, I feel I can't breathe.' Pippa turned to Lexie.

'He understands.'

'I know he does, but I feel as though I've neglected him.'

Pippa crossed the room, aware of the expressions of pity in her peripheral vision as small groups were eulogising Oliver. It was a sad fact that funerals were common in the forces. Out on real-time operations on the front line, there were disasters and medical fatalities that created strong bonds and camaraderie. They lived in each other's pockets 24/7 out on operations, and death was part of the job.

Pippa and Oliver had attended a colleague's burial – only three years before – after his limbs were blown off in Afghanistan. The soldier had lost his fight for survival in the Birmingham Queen Elizabeth Hospital, where they specialised in treating injured troops. Oliver's funeral was different, though, because his death wasn't a result of the war.

The turnout was the same. As she scanned the area, she felt overwhelmed by the sheer number of people present. She paused and turned to Lexie.

'I thought you said that most had left?'

'They have. Did you not notice how many were at the service? There was standing room only; they were spilling outside.'

'All I saw was Oliver's coffin.'

'Of course, I'm sorry,' said Lexie, looking sombre. 'I'll mingle until you're ready.' As Pippa approached Josh, he immediately excused himself from the officer he was speaking to. He put his arm around her shoulder and Pippa's eyes rested upon the flight stripes.

'Pippa, I—'

'Don't… don't say anything,' she pleaded. 'You'll start me off again.'

His lips creased in sympathy. Pippa searched his hazel eyes, silently seeking, and he met hers knowingly. She wanted to talk privately, without others witnessing the exchange between them.

'When can we talk?'

He shifted uncomfortably at the directness of her question and Pippa knew then that he carried a secret.

'I need to talk about this,' she urged. 'I need to—'

'Whenever you're ready,' he interjected. Pippa noticed the pulse beating in his neck as the silence stretched between them.

'How about if we arrange it over the next couple of days when things have settled down?'

She stared at him, noticing a slight twitch in his square jaw. 'As soon as possible… please.'

'OK.' His face hid answers. Answers she needed, and despite the humiliation she suffered, she had to know before she went crazy. 'You think I'm—'

'You don't have to explain.' Joshua reached out and stroked her cheek. 'Just call me. I'll be there.' He lowered his arm but continued to scan her face with genuine concern.

'Thanks. I'll call you.'

'Any time.'

'And, Joshua, thanks for your help… with Lexie.'

'No problem.'

*

Pippa was glad to be home alone with Lexie after the funeral. 'Why don't I run a nice bath for you?' she said.

'No thanks.'

'It might help you relax.'

Pippa thought of her many baths, reminding her of her sense of uncleanliness since the discovery of the virus. The equation of bathing and relaxation was a distant memory now.

'I know you mean well, Lexie, but really,' Pippa sighed. 'I haven't got the energy. I want to sit, that's all.'

'All right. I can stay with you if you want me to?'

'I'd like that. I fancy a drink though, how about you?' She needed the numbness to blur the scenes in her head.

'I'll get it.' Lexie made her way to the kitchen. 'What would you like?'

'An extremely large Beaujolais.'

'Coming up,' Lexie called, over her shoulder.

Pippa flopped down on the sofa and rested her head back. She heard Lexie's voice in the kitchen, talking quietly on the phone as she busied herself uncorking the wine. She came back with two glasses, filled to the rim. She gave one to Pippa, then sat down on the armchair.

'Who was that?'

'Julian… I was telling him I wouldn't be back tonight, that's all.'

'Julian… *Julian* Julian?'

'Yes. *Julian* Julian.' Lexie smiled at Pippa tentatively.

'I thought—'

'We got back together. But my parents don't know yet.'

'I thought Serena had driven a permanent wedge between you.'

'She stopped whining once Julian signed the house over and the divorce was through.'

Pippa was unaware of what happened in Lexie's life now. She looked at her and smiled.

'You don't have to worry, Lexie. It's OK to talk. Just because Oliver has gone, doesn't mean you have to edit what you say.'

Pippa took a large sip of wine and, for the first time, relaxed a little. The day had exhausted her, and she was relieved to have it over with. She was utterly drained, her nerves shot.

'It's better now, and for the moment we're getting on fine.'

'When did all this happen?'

As Pippa sipped the wine, a warm sensation soothed her and she sipped again, unusually quickly, needing the alcohol to blank her thoughts. She had eaten little for days and the alcohol buzzed through her veins, making her light-headed. Pippa didn't care; Oliver had gone, so what did it matter? For tonight anyway, Alexander was at his grandparents', sleeping soundly by now. Lexie was keeping her company, like old times, except it had taken the tragedy of Oliver's death to reunite them.

'A few months ago, he called me and asked me to go for a drink. We were still good friends.'

'So, how did things develop?'

'I realised I'd missed him. It stemmed from there really,' Lexie said, twirling the stem of her glass. 'I've missed you too.'

'Me too.'

Lexie kicked off her shoes and curled her legs beneath her on the armchair. 'Are you ready to talk?'

'Where do I start?' Pippa stared into her glass, remembering her first observation. 'I noticed Oliver wasn't himself. It was around the time you came over last and…'

Pippa peeped at Lexie, remembering their final argument. She chose her words with care. 'When Oliver was on leave. Anyway, he had this niggling cough, but nothing to get worried about… only now, I realise it was.'

A strange look passed over Lexie's face. Did she think she should have marched him to the doctor? Pippa felt a flicker of touchiness but moved on. 'He said it was just a cough. There was a bug going around the camp, he said, so I wasn't too concerned. Only something at the back of my mind nagged. I'd seen a client with a similar cough at the clinic, and he had lung cancer.'

Pippa welled up. Lexie leaned across and patted her thigh for reassurance.

'Go on.'

'Later, he developed night sweats and had no energy. He was much leaner too.'

Pippa's mind drifted off again. She thought about Oliver's body, stripped of muscle and his transparent skin covering a skeletal frame. She remembered the sunken cheeks and deep eye sockets that made him resemble a prisoner-of-war.

'He didn't go to the doctor then? Didn't they notice anything at the time? I don't understand. How could he have been so ill and not done anything about it?' Lexie said, raising her palms towards the ceiling.

'You know Oliver, he was a private person. A little too private, it seems.'

'What do you mean? You're not making sense.'

'I'm trying to make sense of it, but my mind goes in circles. I lie awake night after night.' Pippa shook her head. 'Before he died, we talked, and it was as though he knew all along.' She held her breath as her anger rose. 'He'd given up before he started, and I was so angry at him for wanting to leave us. Oliver had no fight in him, and it made no sense. He was a soldier, for fuck's sake! Why didn't he fight?'

Pippa broke down into hysterical sobs. She clutched her knees to her chest and rocked. Lexie moved to her and put her arms around her, tucking Pippa's hair away from her face.

'It will be all right, I promise.' She stroked her hair. 'I'll stay as long as you need me to.'

'I don't want to be alone,' Pippa said sobbing. 'I can't deal with this. It's too much to bear! What am I to do? I can't cope, Lexie. I can't do this. I can't breathe.'

'You'll get through this,' said Lexie, crying now too. 'I'm going to help you. You won't be alone.'

'How could he do this to me?' Pippa shrieked, getting

angrier, wiping snot from her face. 'I did nothing to deserve this. I… I did nothing wrong. I tried to be a good wife. I was a good wife, wasn't I?' she appealed to Lexie.

'Of course you did nothing wrong. He got cancer, Pippa, that's all. You did nothing wrong!' Lexie rocked her like a child, kissing her head. 'It's a horrendous disease, everyone knows that, but nobody is safe. As much as we all try, it gets some of us. Nobody knows who will get it. It's just how it is, that's all.'

'I lived in fear of him getting shot down by the Taliban. I prayed he wouldn't be taken from me… That he wouldn't be blown apart and then… and then, he dies from a hideous fucking disease!' Pippa bounced up and paced the floor, stopping to gulp her wine. 'I was half crazy with worry every time he left us for another stint with his precious RAF! And this time it was to be his last time away. He was coming home for good. To be with us… with Alexander, and me!' She fell to her knees, her body quaking.

Lexie sighed and sat on the floor beside her, pulling her head onto her lap and stroking her back until her sobs steadied.

'Shh,' she said. 'It's going to be hard, but you have to try, Pippa. You're not a quitter and Alexander needs his mother, now more than ever. Oliver wouldn't want this. Where's your remedy kit? Have you taken anything?'

'Not since this morning,' she said in muffled sobs.

'Sit up for a moment and I'll get you something.'

'They're in the cabinet over there.' Pippa pointed. Lexie scanned the box, selected a vial and handed her a remedy.

'Here, ignatia, isn't it?'

Pippa smiled through her grief. 'You have learned

something then.' At that moment, she felt proud of Lexie for understanding what she needed. So she hadn't rejected her belief. She felt herself calming down. 'I'm sorry. I'm a wreck.'

'It's understandable. You've been through a lot. It's hard dealing with cancer, let alone to watch your husband die suffering. Oliver didn't deserve it.'

'Didn't he?'

Lexie looked at Pippa as though she'd lost the plot.

'That's a terrible thing to say, Pippa. Nobody deserves to die! What do you mean?' Pippa wondered if she should confide in her. What would she think? She wanted no one to think badly of him, especially Lexie. How was she going to break the news to people? Did she have to? Did anyone need to know? The burden lay heavy.

'Your mind's drifting again,' Lexie said. 'What are you thinking about? What on earth made you say that?'

'You don't want to know.'

'If you don't tell me, I can't help you, can I?'

Pippa stood, brushed herself down and put a hand to her brow, massaging her forehead. Her head was pounding. She paced back and forth, wine in her hand.

'Pippa, I've never seen you like this. I've never heard you utter a single swear word, unlike me. You're looking right through me. Tell me, for fuck's sake!'

Pippa stared at Lexie, observing a myriad of emotions crossing her face. 'Oliver didn't die of cancer.'

'What are you talking about?'

'Oliver had AIDS,' said Pippa as she watched Lexie's glass drop to the floor.

THIRTY

Lexie

'Oh my God, I'm so sorry!' Lexie ran to the kitchen, shock reverberating through her body. She welcomed the excuse to escape, albeit briefly. Panicking, she grabbed kitchen roll, glad to be away even for a few seconds. She mustn't allow Pippa to see her, not while every nerve ending in her body was on alert. Her brain felt as though it was shaking in her skull as her mind absorbed what she'd heard.

Running back into the lounge, she joined Pippa who was on her knees picking up broken glass.

'What? What… did you say?' Lexie used the roll to absorb the liquid. She avoided Pippa's scrutiny.

'I said,' Pippa answered, looking up, 'Oliver had AIDS. I know it's a shock, but now do you see?'

'How? I don't understand. Are you sure?'

Lexie mopped frantically at the stain, trying to process Pippa's secret. She feared for them both as the impact of the discovery registered. The consequences would be profound.

Not only would she have to deal with the shame of sleeping with her best friend's husband, but now this information would have a catastrophic effect on them all.

'That can't be right, surely? There must be some mistake.'

'That's what I said. And I still don't understand.'

Pippa's voice faded into the distance as Lexie struggled with what this meant. She desperately needed composure, not allowing Pippa to see evidence of her inner turmoil. *Focus, focus, focus*, she chanted to her mind.

'And now Oliver's gone, how will I ever know?' Pippa got to her feet, holding shards of glass carefully in her hand.

'What do you mean?' Lexie's voice rose. 'You mean you didn't know?'

'No, that's why I'm so angry, Lexie, and—'

'So, when did you find out?' Lexie interjected, desperate for the facts. There were a million things she wanted to ask. 'I need another drink, Pippa. Do you mind?'

'No, you didn't drink the last one.' Pippa nodded at the carpet. 'I need another myself.'

'I'm sorry... about the carpet.' The carpet was the least of her worries!

Lexie was relieved when Pippa left the room. Now, she paced the floor as Pippa had earlier. She shook her head in disbelief, running an unsteady hand through her hair. Lexie wanted to run. She needed to be alone, anywhere but here. Her heart bounced against her ribs. She'd never found herself in such a situation, torn between her friend's grief and her own anguish.

'Here.'

Pippa handed her another glass of wine. Her eyes were raw and puffy, her cheeks pink against her lily-white skin.

The tip of her nose shone red from the constant dabbing of tissues. 'I'm still numb, Lexie. I can't get my head around it.'

Lexie accepted the drink. The emotional torture was excruciating, and she willed herself to stop shaking as she accepted the glass.

'Right, tell me from the beginning.' Lexie tried to steady her hand as she took a gulp of the wine. When and how did Oliver contract it? Lexie wondered, but she could hardly ask, at the moment anyway. Pippa was distraught enough, and now, so was she.

'After Oliver died, his GP phoned, asking to see me,' she explained. 'I thought he wanted to prescribe me something to help me sleep. I told him I was fine… silly me. Fine, I said, and I couldn't have been further from the truth.'

'How did Oliver hide it? Why did he keep it from you?' Lexie's eyes squinted in confusion. 'I can't believe this is happening!'

'You can't? I'm living a nightmare!' Lexie saw her force the bitter emotion down. 'I don't know the answers. Only that Dr Kerr ran more blood tests, right at the end, a few days before he died.' She grabbed a tissue from the box on the coffee table. 'Oliver wanted no intervention. But towards the end, he was struggling to breathe because of the pneumonia, so I called him in. The doctor wanted to prescribe antibiotics—'

'Don't tell me you wouldn't allow it, Pippa?'

'Obviously I did. Do you think I'd let him suffer? He was dying, for God's sake!' Lexie saw colour rise in Pippa's cheeks. She must not upset her now; she was too desperate for more information.

'Of course not.'

'He prescribed the obvious drug for pneumonia, but Oliver was becoming more and more short of breath. He had chest pain too. Dr Kerr sent a sputum specimen and a blood test to the lab. His count was low, understandably, but some other readings and tests revealed that it was AIDS. Oliver had pneumocystis pneumonia and possibly Kaposi's sarcoma. I thought that was skin lesions, but it's a type of lung cancer too... I can't believe it!'

Pippa broke down again, the intensity of her sobs escalating. 'I didn't want to tell anyone, but why should I be so ashamed! I love him and hate him at the same time.'

Lexie passed her another tissue, her own eyes stinging. Lexie was scared, but as she watched Pippa's distress and anguish, she had an overwhelming urge to protect her, though she found it so hard to console her.

'I had to force it to the back of my mind, so I could arrange the funeral. Part of me was in denial; I still am, I suppose, but I needed to get past the funeral.'

Had Oliver infected Pippa? What about Alexander? What about her?

Lexie froze.

'He's gone out with a bang, eh? What a fucking legacy he's left!' Pippa said, sniffing and dabbing her swollen eyelids. 'I'm scared to get tested. And what about Alexander? Lexie, what if my baby has it?' she shrieked, as if the realisation had only just hit home. 'He couldn't, could he? What am I going to do?' Pippa's voice cracked and morphed into a distressed moan.

'Shh... it's OK. It's highly unlikely. It's passed through the blood barrier mainly, isn't it?' As Lexie reassured her, she was living the same fears as she searched her mind store for information.

'Yes, but what if I have it? I might have passed it on. I mean, how long has he had it? Maybe it was before I got pregnant?' Pippa shot to her feet again. 'We'll never know now. I can't ask him, he's dead!' Her body shook with fear and anger. 'I need to get a test! He's a fucking, fucking bastard! He might have given us a death warrant!'

'Sit and calm down, Pippa! This isn't doing you any good. You're hurting badly but we'll sort this.' Pippa's face contorted with pain and anguish. Lexie was on the verge of throwing up.

'Will you help me?' she pleaded. 'I can't do this alone.'

'I'll be with you all the way. We're in this together,' Lexie said, the irony in her answer and the situation hammering home. She wanted urgently to get tested herself, already thinking about researching the latest drugs.

Julian would help her.

Julian! Fuck! Did she have unprotected sex with him? She tried to remember. They hadn't used a condom. She was on the pill when she remembered to take it! But it wasn't an issue not being in a relationship, so she didn't beat herself up if she forgot the odd one or two.

How could she ask Julian? She'd had unprotected sex with Oliver too! Things were looking more disastrous by the minute. And how could she keep it from Pippa now? Would she have to tell her? Oh God!

'What would I do without you?' said Pippa, her breathing becoming more controlled. Lexie was screaming inside and silently begged her mind to separate her emotion from facts as she focused on Pippa. The loyalty of the friendship that bound them might now destroy them.

'You've always been there for me, despite our differences,'

Pippa was saying now, each word crucifying Lexie's heart. 'I'm so glad you're here. It makes all the difference, and if I didn't have your friendship and sincerity, I wouldn't get through this.'

'It's OK,' said Lexie, pulling her close and stroking her hair. As Pippa lay cradled, with her head on Lexie's lap, she looked like a small child, tiny and vulnerable. Lexie's gut knotted with the shame of her betrayal. She wanted to run and hide. It took every ounce of willpower she'd ever possessed to remain here, with Pippa, comforting her whilst her own mind was in turmoil.

*

Back home at her apartment, Lexie sat with her iPad, researching everything possible about HIV and AIDS. She looked a mess and couldn't eat or sleep from worry and constant nausea.

She swiped the screen, tapping and searching each link. Her vision felt gritty from studying research papers, and the situation seemed more positive than she'd first imagined.

HIV treatment had advanced, but that did little to ease her fear. She'd already phoned several private clinics, not wanting to visit her GP or any other; she knew many through her job, so how the hell would she present herself as a patient? Thankfully, discretion was a major factor when it came to seeking help and there was so much information on the internet. She'd discovered a simple finger prick of blood could detect HIV antibodies and she could post a sample to the laboratory for a small fee. There was also the option of a saliva test. They offered these two simple tests online with the results only taking around three days, and sometimes a few hours. But Lexie wanted the traditional medical option of visiting a clinic because she wanted the results to be foolproof. Not everything online could be trusted. Or was she being paranoid? But did she want to visit a clinic and be surrounded by infected people? She could drive into London and find out almost immediately while maintaining her anonymity.

Her tired brain continued to scan the same links, allowing the information to sink in. She learned the early onset symptoms; she'd had a recent cold and lacked energy, but that was her gruelling schedule, surely? But she'd also had an unexplained fever…

Her stomach cramped and water brash filled her mouth. She flew into the bathroom, dropped to her knees, cradling the toilet pan, and vomited. Her ribs heaved and she retched as bitter bile filled her mouth. Her stomach was empty, which made the sensation worse. But her physical distress was nothing compared to her psychological state.

Lexie sat with her back against the wall, knees bent to her chest, too drained to move for a second. She clutched at her stomach and wiped her mouth with a piece of tissue. She'd vomited a few times lately, she mused, throwing the tissue down the toilet; no wonder her ribs ached.

Lexie felt torn about the test. If she did have it, and it revealed HIV, what then? Would she get full-blown AIDS? According to research, not necessarily. She would, however, live on drugs for the rest of her life. How ironic would that be for a pharmaceutical rep? It didn't bear thinking about. But if she didn't have the test, she'd never know until it was too late to do anything.

Lexie stood up and cleaned her teeth, then glanced in the bathroom mirror as she rubbed her face with the towel. She looked wretched. Thank God it was the weekend, and she didn't have to face anyone. She was lounging around in a baggy T-shirt.

Wrapping a soft comfort blanket she'd grabbed from her bedroom around her shoulders, she padded to the kitchen for a glass of water from the fridge. She popped an energy tablet into the glass and watched it fizz. The effervescent bubbles tickled her nose as she sipped the fruity amber liquid. The drink refreshed her palate, diffusing the foul taste of bile that even toothpaste didn't dispel.

Lexie sat at the window seat, staring out. The world, as she knew it, had changed in an instant with that single sentence, 'Oliver had AIDS.'

Was this her punishment? Did she deserve this torment? Was it divine retribution? She'd betrayed her best friend in the most unforgiveable way possible.

She'd betrayed herself too, for allowing Oliver to possess her body, and the realisation she might have contracted the virus filled her with horror.

Her anxiety was fuelled further as she replayed every moment, like a video recording in her brain. She'd played a dangerous game that had now come back to haunt her.

Her phone rang; she felt the urge to throw it through the window. If she hadn't answered Oliver's call that day, none of this would have happened and she wouldn't be in this situation. Damn Oliver, damn him to hell! The ringtone stopped as Lexie ignored it and continued to sit curled up in a ball with her arms wrapped around her knees. The uncertainty of her future consumed her. She felt isolated and alone.

Who could she tell? Was there anyone to confide in, anyone at all? All her life, she'd dealt with her emotions and problems privately, but this burden overwhelmed her, to the point of mania. She would not tell her mother, for sure; she didn't need another burden to carry. Miriam had lived life to the full since the shock of possible breast cancer. And, after everything Lexie's mother had been through, she'd probably be hysterical if she found out. Lexie didn't have the energy to deal with other people's emotions right now, Pippa was challenge enough. The bitter reality was, she must keep it to herself.

The phone rang again. Whoever it was wasn't going away, so this time, Lexie picked it up.

'Hi, baby, are you home?' The sound of Julian's voice triggered a release of emotion. She longed to be secure in his arms. Why had she made the stupid decision to separate in the first place? If they had stayed together, none of this would have happened. A picture of Julian's expression of disbelief flashed in her mind when she told him it was over. He couldn't believe that she was prepared to relinquish their relationship by giving Serena her imaginary power over him, despite the decree nisi being issued from the court. In truth, their bond was special even before they became partners. Looking back, she knew Serena was doing everything in her power to drive a wedge between them, and in the end she'd succeeded. But now Lexie had a second chance. Would she lose him for a second time?

'Yes, I left Pippa this morning. She had to fetch Alexander from Gabrielle's.'

'How is she?'

'Not good. I'm worried about her.'

'How did... funeral go? Did you... make m... apologies?'

The line wasn't good, though Lexie could decipher his words.

'Yes, I told her about Bangalore. She was fine about it.'

'I felt bad abou... but I couldn't—'

'She knows you would have been there otherwise, don't worry. Anyway, it was packed out. I think the whole of the RAF attended!'

'I do hope your eyes didn't roam with all those uniforms.' She heard his mischievous chuckle.

'I only have eyes for you, sweetheart. You know that.' Lexie placated him, thinking that was the furthest thing from her mind. 'Besides, it was a funeral, so don't be so disrespectful,' she admonished.

'I love it when you scold me. Are you missing me?'

'Yes. Are you missing me?'

'Goes without saying. Look, I've got to rush... meeting in a min...'

'Good luck with that.'

'I'll call you tomorrow. We can talk then.'

'OK, bye for now.'

'And, Lex?'

'Yeah?'

'I love you.'

The call ended before she could reply. Lexie missed him, and needed him, though she was relieved he was away. She couldn't face Julian or more guilt. She'd come to the realisation she loved him, truly loved him. So she had a duty to get checked out for his sake. It was unfair to be selfish. He was the innocent party, and he deserved none of this.

Lexie picked up a pad with various clinic numbers on it and chose one. She made the call and booked an appointment.

Then she bowed her head and cried.

THIRTY-ONE

Pippa

Pippa pulled up the collar on her chunky jumper as she climbed out of her car at the woodland cemetery. The brittle autumnal leaves whipped past her legs in a wind akin to a mini-hurricane. She was glad she'd put on sensible boots.

Her hair slapped her face and flew across her eyelids. She grasped the tendrils, twisted them around her fingers and secured them with a clip from the glove box. She shuddered and reached across the passenger seat for the flowers. Today she'd chosen petunias, their meaning resentment and anger because she considered it appropriate. She wanted to bring flowers from the mock orange shrub, to symbolise Oliver's deceit, but it wasn't the season.

At the grave, Pippa dropped to her knees. She split up the bunch of petunias in a frenzied display of emotion and scattered them between the other bouquets, on top of the new burial mound.

'Why, Oliver? Why did you do this to me?' She grabbed

handfuls of soil and let it fall again. 'Are you at peace, you bastard?' She wiped the grief-induced snot from her nose. 'Well, I'm not!' She sat at the foot of his plot, leaning back on her heels, head slumped.

'It's tough, isn't it?' a man's tender voice asked beside her. 'My wife died three months ago.'

Pippa glanced at the supportive palm on her shoulder. She couldn't find words but felt compelled to listen to the stranger. Pippa looked up at a face of maturity.

'Don't worry, my dear, we all deal with it differently.' His kind, rheumy eyes almost reached into her soul. 'I come daily to sit with Eleanor. I sit on that donated bench, just above the Japanese maple tree, next to her plot.' He pointed his walking stick to an adjacent grave, separated by a small pathway sectioning the plots. 'I talk to her as though we're having our normal morning chat,' he told Pippa with a gentle smile. 'Our grandchildren planted the tree in her memory.'

She could see the signs of grief etched in his face.

'It's all very raw for you at the moment,' he said, turning and nodding at Oliver's grave.

'Sorry, you must consider me very peculiar.' Pippa bowed her head in shame at the use of her bad language and dug for a tissue from the pocket of her jeans. She rose and brushed herself down, drying her eyes with the balled-up tissue.

'We are all different. Anger is part of the process. I'm Raymond, by the way.' He changed his walking stick into his left hand and reached out with his right.

'Pippa,' she answered, shaking it rather awkwardly. This empathic soul would probably be her graveside companion now, she mused. If he came daily, they would be bound to meet sometime.

She wondered how long he and his wife had been married. Judging by his advancing years, more than half a lifetime, she guessed. Pippa was humbled by him.

*

By the time the evening came around, Pippa's anxiety had risen to a pitch. At least Alexander was sleeping, after much deliberation and persuasion. He had asked why his daddy had gone to live in the sky. Pippa told him Oliver was an angel and needed to look after children who'd died and lived in heaven, alone without their parents.

'But now I haven't got a daddy. Are you going too?' he'd asked her. Pippa's heart was breaking as she tried in vain to assure him that she would never leave him. 'Daddy said that and now he's gone. And why are your eyes leaking, Mummy?' Pippa tried to reason with him, but eventually he'd cried himself to sleep, and she was broken.

In her bedroom, Pippa sat at her dressing table and combed her hair. She looked into the mirror and stared at the stranger reflected there. Dark shadows, pale complexion, sunken cheeks. Maybe she should conceal her pallor before Josh arrived? She took up a neutral-coloured lipstick and applied it to her lips then smudged the surplus onto a tissue. The action sparked a thought. Did Oliver's other woman wear lipstick? What was unique about her that caused him to stray? Or was it several women? A stab of jealousy pierced her heart. She wiped the lipstick off with the back of her hand.

Downstairs, she squirted Rescue Remedy into her mouth and waited for Joshua to arrive. Pippa hoped he would have answers about Oliver's secret life. If he could shed light on the situation, Pippa knew she'd process things better. Now, her mind questioned everything.

Now that she had to consider how Oliver might have contracted the virus, she knew how foolish she'd been to assume he'd remained loyal. How naïve was she? She couldn't mourn him in the normal way now. Their marriage was a lie. He'd slept around! Not only did she have to picture him with other women but she pictured his type of sexual companion. Pippa felt dirty, tainted and violated.

Pippa had researched remedies specific for HIV and started homeopathic treatment, first by strengthening her immunity with the more common remedies, to build up a resistance to the virus, then working out a sustainable constitutional plan.

She'd contacted a previous university tutor who treated many HIV clients in a clinic in Manchester. When she trained, she'd been lucky enough to observe his method of prescribing at the clinic and his results were amazing.

It fascinated her then, but now with the possibility of having contracted the virus herself, the fascination was the last thing that mattered.

The tutor emailed notes and a PowerPoint presentation to her, assuming it was for one of her clients. Pippa didn't correct him. She'd perused the notes but found it hard to stay detached. Her thoughts and professional judgments clouded her prescribing technique, so she sought advice from an unknown professional.

Pippa sprang to her feet at the sound of the doorbell.

Joshua stood on the step, carrying a bottle of wine and a huge bouquet. His crooked smile immediately eased Pippa, and she smiled back as he handed her the flowers.

'Thank you.' She kissed his cheek. 'They're beautiful. Come through.'

'Where's the corkscrew and I'll open this?' He held up the wine and glanced around the kitchen.

'It's hanging up, there.' She motioned to a hook in the shape of a bunch of grapes, next to the wine rack.

'That's posh,' he said, admiring the silver corkscrew. He uncorked the wine.

'A gift from Lexie's parents. It's from St Emilion.'

'That's nice. Glasses?' he asked, looking up at the cabinets. 'I'm only used to going to the fridge for a beer.'

'Second shelf on the right in the Welsh dresser.'

Pippa arranged the flowers, not for precision of the arrangement, but to stall for a little time to calm her jumping nerves.

'Nice crystal too,' Joshua said, pouring wine. She knew he was talking small talk.

The glugging of the wine sounded familiar these days, thought Pippa, who waited eagerly for the evening – once Alexander was sleeping – to indulge in alcohol and numb her mind.

'I've never drunk so much. I've had more wine this last couple of months than in my entire life. Shall we go through?'

Pippa led the way into the lounge and sat on the sofa. Joshua sat opposite, crossing an ankle over his knee. He was taller than Oliver and his frame filled the seat.

'A few glasses won't harm you. How are you doing? Stupid question I know, but…?'

'Do you want the truth or a dressed-up version?'

'The truth.'

'Hurt, upset and angry. How do you expect me to feel? Oliver shouldn't be dead!'

Joshua's jaw tensed. 'He shouldn't, Pippa. What can I say?'

'You can start by telling me how long you were aware he was ill, and how come I didn't know?'

'He kept things close to his chest, you know that.'

'It seems he confided in his friend, more so than his wife.'

Joshua looked at a loss for words. He bowed his head and stared at the floor.

'Pippa I—'

'Please, Joshua, spare me the bullshit and answer me honestly. Don't treat me like a hysterical bimbo. My husband is dead. Dead! I'll never see him again. Can you imagine what it's like to lie awake wishing I could still hear his heartbeat when I lay my head on his chest? How it feels not to have his body lying against me? Not to hear his voice or the touch of his lips on mine? I'm falling apart. I can't breathe.'

He moved to cradle her in his arms.

'OK, I'll tell you what I know.' He moved her hair back from her brow.

She sniffed, embarrassed, wiping her face with her fingertips. She leaned forward to pull a tissue from the box.

'I must have gone through ten boxes of Kleenex.'

Josh cupped her shoulder then moved back to his seat.

'A few months ago, I noticed he wasn't himself. He was often tired. Training seemed hard for him – we'd push a few weights at the base when things were quiet – and he made excuses for his fitness. Oliver was always the one who'd put us to shame.' Joshua smiled fondly.

'Anyway, the lads assumed it was a one-off, but I spent more time with him. He was broody and spent time alone, didn't bother coming to the Mess. When he did, though, he downed the beer with a vengeance. And that was unusual too.'

Josh frowned. 'I reasoned it was PTSD. We'd had tough tasks on the last mission, one in particular where our winchman lost half his face. Honestly, this shit is hard to handle—'

'Oliver didn't discuss work much,' Pippa interrupted. 'He wanted to leave it behind when he came home. Too traumatic, he told me.'

She looked at Josh, prompting him to continue.

'Anyway, this went on for weeks. I saw him growing weaker by the day. He looked drawn and struggled with the long flights, even losing concentration sometimes. Navigation is crucial when we do a supply drop. It has to be accurate. Piloting the Chinook is a skill, as you know. We fly in the dark when approaching Camp Bastian, for obvious reasons.' Joshua looked uncomfortable as he continued. 'One day, we had words, and I flipped out.'

'Why?'

'His concentration wasn't the best. His mind wasn't on the job. It affected the team.'

'What happened?'

'Oliver broke and said he thought he was dying.' Josh looked away, shaking his head. 'I told him to stop chatting bollocks. He stared at me for the longest time, without saying a word. That look haunts me.' Josh put his elbows on his knees and his head in his hands. Then he turned to Pippa. 'I still can't believe it. He asked me to take care of you and Alex. Told me that was the hard part, not the dying.'

Pippa felt hot tears sliding down her cheeks.

'I asked him what made him so convinced. He hadn't seen the medics, because we were always together and I would have known. Oliver talked about his uncle and how his cancer had 'eaten him alive'. He wasn't prepared to go down the same path and have you nurse a 'withering, decaying man with a soul that left his body behind to rot', he told me. I argued with him, telling him he could be wrong. He was adamant and—'

'Do you mean he never wanted help?' Pippa screeched. 'How dare he make that decision? It wasn't his alone to make!'

'He was thinking of you, Pippa, not himself.'

'What a selfish bastard,' she spat out, eyes ablaze. 'He left us without a fight!'

'Oliver had seen the end result, with Ronnie. He didn't want to put you through it. Oliver wanted quality of life rather than quantity. Surely you can understand that?'

'Oliver assumed!' Pippa said with bitterness. 'He could still be here, with us.'

'I understand how much faith you have in homeopathy,' Josh said tentatively. 'But this disease eats a man alive. He didn't want that. It beats any medicine. Oliver was the ultimate macho man, who didn't want to wither away to skin and bone. To have chemotherapy and radiation only to die anyway. It's a matter of pride.'

'Fuck his pride! That's why he's dead!'

Josh reeled, his eyes wide.

'He should have come to me!' Pippa broke down and felt Josh's arms around her again.

She curled up into a ball, allowing the raw emotion to escape.

She no longer had the energy to fight against it. It was akin to holding back a tidal wave, and it exhausted her.

Josh allowed her to cry as he held her. When she finally looked up, she saw his pain.

'You miss him too, eh?'

'More than I care to admit.'

As she searched his face, she realised what he said was true. But Oliver would have confided in him, surely? Men stuck together. Her mind swarmed with questions, but her instinct, at that moment, told her he was telling the truth.

'I want to ask you something, Joshua, and I need you to be truthful, OK?'

'Sure.'

'How many women did he sleep with?'

'What?' His brows rose almost to his hairline. 'Where did that come from?'

'I need answers.' Pippa sat up and stared at him.

'What are you saying? Oliver was besotted with you. Other women never entered his mind, never!'

'I wish I could believe you.'

'I swear it. Where did that ridiculous notion come from? He didn't tell you he was ill, but that's different.' He looked bemused. 'Your mind's all over the place, understandably so, but to think—'

'Not think... know,' Pippa said coldly; her mouth

tightened. 'I never thought he would betray me, never! It goes to show you never really know anyone, do you?'

'He's never betrayed you, Pippa. Your mind is doing overtime, that's all! Oliver wasn't like some others. He was a one-woman man and not ashamed to admit it. Oliver was a gentleman, proud of his wife and family. Jesus, he had your picture in the flight deck, for Christ's sake. The lads took the piss, but he didn't give a damn. He only hoped to make you happy, that's why he decided to leave the RAF. Then he got sick.'

'Then either he kept a low profile, or you're lying.'

Josh flinched. 'You're wrong, Pippa. Oliver kept nothing from me, nothing!'

'So why didn't he tell you what was wrong?'

'He did. I just told you. What are you talking about?'

'Oliver didn't have cancer, Joshua... Oliver had AIDS.' Pippa almost felt the resonating power of his shock as it registered on his face. He hadn't known. His expression confirmed it.

'You're lying!'

'You really didn't know, did you?' Pippa's eyebrows met in a frown.

'I don't understand what's going on in your head, but you need help, Pippa. Your thoughts are governed by emotion, not reason.' Joshua took a gulp of wine. He looked consumed with rage.

Pippa stared silently, her face deadpan while Josh drained his glass. She rose to her feet and left to collect the bottle. She refilled their glasses, giving him time to process the news.

'I'm sorry, Joshua. I thought you knew.' She sat next to him on the couch, and they sipped in silence. Pippa turned to look at him. 'That's why I had to ask you.'

'I can't take this in. It's not possible.' He scratched his head. 'He didn't go near the medics, so he couldn't have been tested. I told you, I was like his shadow. And he would have told me.'

'He probably wanted no one to know... in case they thought ill of him.'

'No.' He shook his head. 'It makes no sense. Did he go to his GP then, when he was back?'

'No, never, I always treated him. Why do you ask? He was never sick, anyway. That's what I can't understand. He only ever had the flu once, a few years ago, and apart from the odd headache, he was fit.'

'Well, Oliver couldn't have known either. He talked for hours about lung cancer and was convinced he had it. If he'd known it was HIV, he would have got treatment. Don't you see? It wouldn't have developed into full-blown AIDS. He was desperate to live, desperate!'

Josh rose and walked back and forth, his hand rubbing his chin. 'How did you find out?'

'The GP ran tests the week before he died. The pneumonia wasn't responding to any drugs, so he sent specimens off.'

'They must have got them mixed up with someone else's. Is that possible, for labs? I mean, to mix up results?'

'I asked the same thing. He told me he'd run different tests on different days and repeated them. I wish that were true. I didn't believe it either.'

'I'm so sorry, Pippa. It's not that I don't believe you, but Oliver never slept with anyone else. So there must be some other explanation.' His expression changed suddenly, and his eyes widened.

'What?'

'Erm, it's nothing,' he said, trying to avoid eye contact, his jaw twitching.

'Tell me, please! I can't live not knowing. It's killing me!' Pippa leapt up and turned him to face her.

'I can't, he swore me to secrecy.'

'He's dead, and I'm living with this torment. It's bad enough being robbed of my husband, don't allow my pride to be robbed too. I'm begging you, Joshua, please! Don't you see, I can't grieve for him until I know.'

'I... it's not... it's not something he'd want you to know. Please, Pippa!'

'Fuck you!' She stormed through to the kitchen. Pippa needed the answer, however painful it might be. She couldn't bear to picture Oliver in someone else's arms.

She bent over the sink, crying in frustration. She heard Joshua approach and turned.

'Are you sure you want to know?' he asked gently, searching her face for the answer. Pippa nodded.

'You're wrong about him. Oliver was loyal until the day he died.'

'Then how? How is all this possible?'

'You need to sit down.'

Pippa obeyed his request, trying to still her chest sobs.

'This will be painful, and I won't deny, I'm worried you're already under too much stress.'

'Nothing could be worse than not knowing. Can't you see that?'

Josh sighed, his distress evident. 'Do you remember our stint in Morocco? It was about ten years ago.'

'That training exercise?'

'That's right. We had to train across desert terrain, and

it was damn hard. Obviously, in that country, things are different to back home, aren't they?'

'Are you preparing me for an excuse now?'

'Not at all. What I'm trying to say—'

'What? It limits the social life, so you had to find pleasure elsewhere?'

'No. This is not helping. Let's forget about it.'

'No! I can't, Joshua. Spit it out.'

'It's not what you think.'

'So what is it then?'

'We went out to a bar.' He paused and looked at the ceiling.

'Carry on.'

'This is difficult,' he said, moving to the tap for water. He took a drink. Turning, he leant back against the sink and put the glass down. He wrung his hands and blew out his cheeks.

'Joshua?'

'The lads got out of hand with squaddies, drinking in the same bar. It was banter at first. They called us 'toffs of the forces' so we humiliated them with intellect. One of them took a distinct dislike to Oliver and kept baiting him, so Oliver left the bar.'

'What's this to do with anything?'

'Everything,' he said, shaking his head. 'Now it's all fitting into place.' He turned and gulped more water and cleared his throat. 'Two of them followed him. I'm... I'm sorry. I—'

'Please, Joshua!'

'The thing is, they got the better of him, called him a puff.' He swallowed hard. 'The squaddie with the mouth got the other to pin him down.' Josh's breathing quickened. 'I'm sorry to tell you this, Pippa… the bastards… raped him.'

THIRTY-TWO

Lexie

'Lexie... can you come over? I need you, please, I—'

'Pippa, calm down. What's wrong?'

'I need to talk to you,' sobbed Pippa. 'I can't talk over the phone.'

'OK, I'll be there. Give me an hour, the traffic's horrendous.'

When the call ended, Vivaldi's *Four Seasons* filled the car. Lexi hit the off button, concerned for Pippa. It was one thing dealing with the loss of Oliver, but quite another having to deal with the possibility of the disease he'd left behind.

Oliver had a lot to answer for. How many women were there? He'd affected all of their lives now. Pippa had been the only one, according to him, but Lexie knew how untrue that was; he'd slept with her, hadn't he?

A moment of lust, need, or what? She didn't know, but she'd learned the hard way and now, she was paying for it.

'Bastard, bastard, bastard!' she shouted out, smacking

her hand on the steering wheel as she halted at the traffic lights.

Glancing across, she saw a driver alongside her, his dreadlocks splayed down his back like the gnarled roots of a tree. His thumb drummed the steering wheel in time to the bass beat of music vibrating his Saab. He winked, so she gave him the two-fingered salute pulling off with speed, leaving him at the lights.

'Tosser,' she mouthed at him through the rear-view mirror. Supercilious moron, she thought, gaining momentum through the lanes. Men! Most of them were cheating. She'd worked herself into road rage because she was emotionally out of control. And she hated being out of control.

Oliver, look what you've reduced us to. She peeked out at the grey sky.

Her mood was as ominous as the clouds overhead. Pippa's call instilled yet more worry and Lexie was already drained. Her work was as demanding as ever, and she didn't want to be there. She needed a break. She'd slogged away for months without a day off and Rupert kept badgering her for more. It wasn't enough that her sales were the best, he wanted her at his side, expanding revenue prospects in the Bangalore project.

'They like you, Lexie, and I can see why,' he'd told her with that lecherous look in his eye, as usual. 'Everything helps for new business, I mean, your assets equal your excellent sales and negotiating skills.'

Well, he'd have to take somebody else this time. She was sick of his suggestive remarks and constant unwanted attention. Julian was right, Rupert was creating opportunities for her to be alone with him. But Rupert was careful in his delivery and waited for moments of privacy before passing comments. Lexie wondered how he'd react to a claim of sexual harassment in the workplace. Maybe it was time for her to drop a subtle hint if he continued with his unprofessional tactics?

She'd been to India twice in the past two months and had done nothing but vomit since her last trip. The food or water obviously didn't suit her, and she felt washed out. Julian insisted on him having a quiet word with Rupert, but Lexie didn't want to create waves, she could handle him herself. Rupert was devious and ruthless, and the last thing she wanted was for Julian to be sent permanently to Shanghai or Bangalore. Rupert was already doing his best to keep them apart since Lexie's relationship with Julian was now common knowledge.

But performance had been the least of her concerns in the past couple of weeks. Oliver dominated her thoughts once again as she cast her mind back to the night of her fatal mistake…

His eyes had held a mystery that night, something unvoiced that plagued her. Their sex was frantic, and it didn't fit with Oliver's character.

Lexie and Pippa discussed sex, as best friends did, and Pippa said Oliver was a considerate, patient and gentle lover, who took his time. That was not her experience; there had been nothing slow and gentle that night.

Had Lexie awakened a deep feral instinct, an instinct unknown to his spiritual wife? Did he have an intimate secret desire he sought elsewhere?

Lexie would never know now and couldn't unleash her

fury on him. Nor force him to pay for what he'd done. She wanted to visit his grave and stamp on it; at least that would give her some release. Oliver had snatched away their planned future and Lexie could do nothing about it.

*

Lexie pulled onto Pippa's drive with the realisation that each time she came here, her body flipped into alert mode. She sighed, mentally preparing herself for the next horrendous piece of drama. Had Pippa discovered something from Josh? Pippa mentioned he'd be paying her a visit. She hoped he hadn't delivered more disastrous news about ex-lovers or else it would shatter her heart beyond repair.

Her heart jumped into her mouth as Pippa opened the door, grief and pain etched on her face. Lexie hoped Oliver hadn't revealed their secret to Josh! She'd automatically assumed it would remain between them. But knowing what she did now, perhaps Lexie had been only another notched-up conquest. Lexie leapt out of the car and sprinted up the path. As she approached, Pippa's expression sent her heartbeat into a frantic rhythm.

'What is it?'

'Oh, Lexie, Joshua came over last night and told me something hideous!'

'OK, come inside and we'll have tea,' said Lexie, trying to compose herself. 'Where's Alexander?'

'He's on a school field trip in the Forest of Dean. Sandy is picking him up for a sleepover. She's been an angel, helping me out, giving Alexander some sense of normality, and to be honest, I'm relieved. He's asking all sorts of questions about Oliver, questions I can't answer,' she said, shaking her head. 'He's lost his father and I'm useless to him. I feel so guilty.' She rubbed her temples and bowed her head.

'Don't worry. Things are raw at the moment, it's only natural. You'll find a way. Don't be hard on yourself.' Lexie stroked Pippa's shoulder, feeling an irrational stab of resentment at Sandy's recent closeness with her, but at the same time, so grateful for her support, especially for Alexander. 'Come on, let's make that tea.'

Indoors, Pippa explained how she'd verbally attacked Josh, trying to prise information from him. She told Lexie how Josh defended Oliver, denying he'd had partners.

'He even implied that I needed help!'

'What a cheeky bastard!' said Lexie incredulously, her breath quickening at Josh's insensitivity. How dare he defend his precious mate? 'What audacity, coming here, taking Oliver's side.'

'That's what I thought. We went round it, talking about when exactly Oliver got sick. He told me Oliver was ill months ago. He even covered for him at work.'

'But why?'

'He didn't want me to know. He didn't want to hurt me, he said.'

'That's fucking rich!'

Pippa looked taken aback.

'I'm sorry, Pippa,' she said, trying not to sound bitter. 'I'm pissed off with him for what he's put… you through.' She stopped herself just in time; she'd almost said, 'us'.

'Don't be too quick to condemn him, Lexie.'

'Oh, Pippa, how can you defend him?' Lexie fought to keep the venom from her voice as her frustration rose.

Pippa was so forgiving, always protecting the underdog. Lexie both pitied and envied her qualities. Didn't she understand she was the victim? 'And why is Josh protecting him, knowing he might have infected you too? They're bastards, both of them. There's no excuse!'

'He didn't know.'

'What do you mean, he didn't know?'

'That's what I've been trying to tell you. That's why he said – for want of better words – that I was going mad.'

Lexie was inclined to agree, Pippa did sound mixed up. 'I don't understand.'

'Oliver told him he had lung cancer and didn't want me to watch him suffer. He didn't want treatment, only for it to fail. Then I blurted it all out, venting my anger. When I told him about the AIDS, he said I was lying and the shock on his face confirmed he really didn't know about it.'

'So, Oliver deceived him too?'

'No, that's just it, don't you see? *He* didn't know, either.'

Now Lexie was even more confused. Oliver was a liar and a cheat and now, Pippa was making excuses for him. Loyalty bound people like nothing else ever could. Perhaps that's how she handled her grief and, in fairness, if it got her through, that's what mattered.

'Think about it. If he did, he'd have gone for treatment for the HIV. It would never have progressed into full-blown AIDS! He wouldn't have thought he—'

'Oh… now I see.'

'And he would still be here.' Pippa's eyes brimmed.

'Oh God.' Lexie's head was spinning. She was saddened by the consequences he'd suffered. One slip, and now, drastic consequences. Consequences both she and Pippa faced; ones that had to be contended with, and soon.

'So, what did Josh tell you?' asked Lexie, remembering Pippa's original statement.

'It's awful, I'm appalled and so sick inside.'

'It's OK,' said Lexie. She couldn't blame her. Lexie wondered how many secret affairs he'd had. She still didn't believe it somehow though, having known Oliver for so long. Perhaps it was only one lover, one mistake? But Pippa had said, 'something hideous'. Was she going to tell her he'd slept with a prostitute? Could Oliver be bisexual and have a male lover somewhere? No, that couldn't be possible, could it?

'Go on.' Lexie braced herself for the details. Her brain was conjuring up ridiculous scenarios.

'Joshua was adamant about Oliver's loyalty, and so convinced, he asked me if the GP had mixed up the test results. I told him I had arrived at the same conclusion. But he refused to accept it, telling me how they confided in each other about everything.'

Lexie felt a familiar burst of adrenaline and her pulse pounded in her ears. 'He would say that though, to protect him.' Oh God, she thought, was Josh his lover? The thought horrified her, and it would almost have been better if Oliver had been involved in a long-standing affair with another woman!

'Then I saw his face change, as though he'd recalled something. And, he had.' Lexie listened intently as Pippa explained. She watched Pippa as her emotions rose to a crescendo, before she finally blurted out his secret.

'A brutal squaddie raped him while another bastard pinned him down. My poor baby!'

Pippa's sobs burst from her soul, tears mixing with nasal mucus and saliva as she wept into her hands.

Lexie sat, unable to move, unable to speak. The news shocked her core, and she was mortified for Oliver! How horrific he'd endured such humiliation and how unfair!

He was the victim in all of this, and they were the victims of circumstance. Now things made more sense, the missing details fitting into place.

'I can't believe this is happening,' Lexie managed, in a choked voice. 'It gets more horrendous by the minute!'

'When I searched my mind, I remember Oliver behaving strangely after his stint in Morocco. I thought it was because the sex turned him off. You know, when we were trying to conceive and it all got clinical.' Pippa touched her stomach as if back in that moment. 'When you're first together, sex is urgent and hot, isn't it? And we couldn't get enough, especially when Oliver had to go away, sometimes for months.'

'I remember, you were convinced he'd gone off you.' Inside, Lexie's blood boiled, and she immediately wanted justice for Oliver, her brain already deciding how to go about it. But years on, she doubted whether she could successfully track them down through the MOD. Maybe Josh could help? She hadn't been fair to him either, she reasoned.

'But now I know, all these years later! He must have felt abused and violated. And all I wanted was more sex, obsessed about getting pregnant when all the time he must have been desperate inside!'

Pippa's voice rose, reliving his pain. 'And… he… never told me.'

Lexie was at a loss for words. Rape was soul-destroying,

and Oliver's humiliation at being the victim of rape and buggery would have eaten at him. She turned to Pippa and held her, searching for words of comfort to appease her broken heart.

'At least he was ignorant about his condition; that would have destroyed him!' Lexie tried to give her something positive to hang on to, but she despaired about how unpredictable life was. One comment, action or event could change a person forever and had.

Everything was about cause and effect, always. Pippa looked up.

'You're right, at least he was spared that. In my heart I know it was better for him to believe that he was dying from something incurable. For me, though, I can't stop thinking he would still be here, with us, now… if only he had been checked out. I mean, one blood test would have been all it took.' She blew her nose. 'Things could've been so different if only—'

'Oliver could never have lived with the guilt if he thought he'd passed anything on to you,' said Lexie, her thoughts turning to the impending HIV tests. She didn't want to broach the subject at that precise moment, but it needed saying, and soon.

'Talking of which,' said Pippa, 'I've made an appointment with Dr Kerr, to get the blood tests done. Putting it off any longer won't make the problem go away, will it?'

Relief flushed through Lexie. 'Do you want me to come?'

'No, I'll be fine. It's when I get the results I'll need you.' Pippa looked down, in torment.

'I'm worried though.'

'Understandably so,' said Lexie, thinking what an

understatement that was. She was worried sick herself, and Pippa had had so much more to deal with. 'But try not to worry about that just yet. You've had a lot going on and you haven't had time to grieve, and now this.'

'But at least I have answers now.'

'Yes, but painful ones.' Lexie wondered how Pippa coped with it all. She looked drawn and skinny. 'When did you last eat?'

'Yesterday sometime, I couldn't face food today. I keep going over the past and I keep thinking, what if?'

'You must eat. How about if we order Chinese? Or shall I rustle up a dish from your cupboard contents?'

'I can't face anything.'

The truth was, nor could Lexie, but she had to act normal, whatever that was.

'My cooking, you mean.' Lexie grinned to lighten the mood. 'What about getting a bite to eat at a quiet pub then?'

'No, I don't fancy going out. Not to face people, especially looking like this.' Pippa attempted a smile.

'That's settled then.' Lexie pulled her phone from her handbag and dialled the local Chinese. She covered the mouthpiece with her hand and said, 'I'll order the usual, even if— Yes, I'd like to place an order, please.' She smiled at Pippa as she cut their conversation short to speak to the person on the line.

She warmed plates in the oven and set the table. Pippa went to the bathroom to freshen up. Lexie was glad of the breathing space. She glanced at her Cartier watch and wondered what time to call Julian. She missed him so very much; she'd never imagined feeling like this. She longed to be with him and craved the solid security of his arms.

Why did it take pain to make a person change? She'd gone along, giving her all, to a multi-billion-dollar company and for what? To miss out on what actually was important: life itself!

Life is what happens to us while we make other plans, according to Allen Saunders, or was it Zsa Zsa Gabor? She couldn't remember; her brain recall had been dismal lately. She was so busy trying to plan for the future, she was missing the here and now. How many times had Pippa told her she was forgetting how to live in the moment? And Lexie had dismissed that as people's excuse for stagnating without ambition.

But Pippa's choices were already decided for her by what fate had dished out. How cruel and unforgiving.

Lexie felt helpless. What if they both had the virus? How could she deliver yet another blow when Pippa already had a huge cross to bear? For now, she needed her, and their friendship was one of the few solid things left in her life. Lexie was paralysed with shame, but she couldn't tell her.

After the food arrived, they sat down to eat. Pippa picked at the meal, taking only minuscule bites of vegetables, but Lexie was grateful that she'd eaten, at least. They talked at length and drank wine until exhaustion set in.

Lexie stayed over, then left early in the morning to go home and change before work. Pippa needed her, and when she had listened to her talking on the telephone to Alexander, her heart struggled with the sorrow for their loss.

She didn't know how to make things right for them, and to watch Pippa's pain tore at her heartstrings. Her guilt was an overwhelming burden and one she'd have to live with for the rest of her life.

It amazed her how resilient some people could be in the face of adversity. Lexie felt ashamed by her fickle behaviour and the unimportant life goals she'd set herself to prove she was good enough. But for now, she would have to deal with that, until she could change things.

The first hurdle was to get tested and deal with the results, whatever they might be. The second was to learn how to live with the fact that she had betrayed her best friend. She was determined to become a better person; change things she despised about herself and make new lifestyle choices.

*

Later, Lexie couldn't switch off, following another day of emotional turmoil. But a new fire burned in her… justice! She wanted Justice for Oliver and intended to get it. Lexie was determined to hunt down the men responsible.

It was too late for Oliver, but she would make sure they held those bullies accountable if she found them. Years had passed but she would try. The army had a responsibility and Lexie would take them on. They could not hush this up and hide it away like a dirty secret. It would take hours of research to start the process. But start she would, and her first step would begin with Josh. She needed his help for dates and background. She needed him on her side too, though Lexie understood it would be hard in view of his career.

Aware it was late, Lexie decided she'd speak to Josh the

following day. She knew she was too wired to sleep, so she switched on her Mac and made a start on her research.

*

The following morning, Lexie struggled to push open the heavy oak doors on the ground floor of the Victorian building. A brass plaque on the wall indicated which floor the rape crisis centre was on. Nervously, she climbed the stairs, the sound of her heels echoing in the silence. The place was a stark contrast to the plush, carpeted pharmaceutical offices she was familiar with.

Rape crime was usually committed in seedy toilets, derelict warehouses, subways and obscure places. But it wasn't always the case. Rape happened anywhere, and to anyone, even within the sanctuary of marriage.

Lexie thought about Oliver and the humiliation he must have suffered. It was horrific for women to report rape, but men? Lexie doubted many would reveal their abuse; male pride had to be an enormous factor. Lexie wondered about the statistics. Such a thought hadn't entered her head before learning of Oliver's assault. She needed to clear her head and focus on her appointment.

Her heartbeat had risen by the time she reached the top floor, but it was nothing compared to what a less fit person might experience, she thought.

She pressed a buzzer on the wall and waited, tucking her hair behind her ear and adjusting the belt of her jacket, fidgeting and fiddling with her appearance. Her poise expressed a confidence that belied her feelings. She was out of her comfort zone, wondering what to expect.

A tall woman opened the door and held it ajar, greeting Lexie with a beaming smile. It wasn't often she met women who almost matched her height. Lexie returned her smile.

'Hello, do come in. I'm Amanda, one of the counsellors here. Take a seat.' She pointed to a worn chair in the small reception area. 'Can I get you a coffee or tea?'

'Yes please, coffee, black, no sugar.'

There were fine wrinkles on the counsellor's cheeks. Under her kind eyes was the puffy look of sleep deprivation. Her face was warm and welcoming, and Lexie was at ease in her company.

'I won't keep you a minute. It's Miss Philips, isn't it?'

'Yes, Lexie Philips. I have a ten o'clock appointment. I'm a little early.'

'Nice to have you. I'll just get your coffee and then we'll have a chat.'

'Thank you.' Lexie sat on the edge of the chair, tucking one foot behind the other.

The wall displayed posters with advice and information about rape. Plastic holders contained leaflets with contact numbers to help victims. Lexie selected one and absorbed the information, wondering if Pippa should see a counsellor. After all, she was living with the consequences of Oliver's rape, wasn't she?

Lexie slipped the leaflet into her bag to give it to Pippa later. For the first time in her life, she understood the need for counselling, no longer believing it to be a self-indulgent therapy for people needing to vent. Instead, it was a lifeline for those in desperate emotional crises.

How Lexie's opinions had changed. It had taken death to shock her into real life, a life Pippa had always understood.

But wasn't that the reason people buried themselves in work and activities, to distance themselves from feeling? Lexie was one of those people, because to deal with emotion equated to dealing with pain, didn't it? And emotional pain differed from physical, remaining deep-seated and buried until a time when trauma made the heart bleed. Her grief was like that now, a bleeding heart. Lexie needed to give something back, and she was here to do just that.

'Black, no sugar,' Amanda said, returning and breaking Lexie's reverie. She handed Lexie a mug and sat opposite her. 'It's great you're offering your time to our team. We're short on the volunteer front. So when you've finished your coffee, I'll show you around first. Is that all right?'

'Absolutely and thanks for the coffee.'

As Amanda twisted towards her, the low sunlight caught her tiny crystal nose stud. Pippa would know exactly what crystal it was, but Lexie didn't have a clue. Lexie knew about the amethyst; Pippa had several. 'My healing crystals', she called them. The only other one she knew was rose quartz, for Pippa had given Lexie a heart-shaped one as a gift to symbolise love, apparently. Lexie felt a little guilty thinking about it sitting in a drawer at home.

The morning passed quickly and gave Lexie a renewed sense of purpose. The people she'd met were not, as she'd imagined, saccharine and gushy. The dedicated team was made up of strong characters on a mission to question policies and fight for changes in the law. They helped vulnerable women to come forward and press charges against their aggressors.

Lexie was surprised to learn how many rape victims knew their assailants. But fear and shame prevented huge numbers from revealing the crime. Not only had the victims suffered horror and degradation, but for some, the added humiliation of sexually transmitted diseases. Others were emotionally scarred for life and needed extensive therapy.

Lexie was introduced to a tiny woman in her late forties. She'd suffered years of abuse from her husband, who'd frequently dragged her out of bed on his return from the pub. It was only when she'd needed surgical repair of her rectum that the surgeon had gently encouraged her to talk. The outcome meant she'd been referred to a safe house, away from her abuser, until she was strong enough to press charges and force him to trial.

Lexie almost broke down as the woman told her how proud she was for coming so far on her journey. Her freedom was liberating, she told Lexie, and for the first time in years, she could finally speak of her trauma. Lexie had to suppress her pure outrage towards a man she didn't even know. She wanted to cry, 'Put the bastard in prison, let him have his come-uppance!' But how totally inappropriate that would be!

THIRTY-THREE

Lexie

Lexie sat in the plush waiting room of a private clinic, thumbing through a glossy magazine. She gave the impression she was relaxed in the presence of the only other client, a rotund businessman reading a broadsheet newspaper. Instead, she was churning inside.

She scanned an article, taking in none of it. She peered at her wristwatch for the third time, feeling restless. As the second hand ticked, it emphasised her life could change in a single moment.

What was the point of private medicine if one was kept waiting?

A few minutes later, a mature nurse dressed in a crisp white uniform approached her.

'Miss Philips? Please, come through.'

'Thank you.' Lexie stood with a false confident smile. Now the moment had arrived, her nerves were jumping. The nurse led her into a small consultation room and offered her an armchair. What Lexie wanted was to leave, and her logical brain conflicted with her emotional state. She knew she had to have the test, but her fear was paramount. Following a detailed medical history, Lexie rolled up her sleeve, as instructed, for the blood test.

'A sharp prick.' The nurse used gloved hands to test the vein and plunged a needle in to draw blood. 'Good, all done. If you press there for a moment, that will avoid a bruise. I'll get you a plaster.'

'Thanks.' Lexie pressed her finger on the cotton wool bud covering the puncture site. She glanced sideways at the vial of blood and shuddered, wondering if her blood held the virus. Staring at the sample, fear overwhelmed her. Never had she been more afraid. The burgundy tube held her future, and soon she would know.

Lexie was alone in the waiting room. Her mouth was dry, and she felt light-headed. Moving across the room, she helped herself to some cool water from a dispenser in the corner. The dizzy spells were a daily occurrence, and she deduced her erratic lifestyle must be the cause. Her stress levels rose to breaking point. Her stomach knotted with the constant dread she'd become used to.

A wave of nausea prompted her to take a complimentary mint from a glass leaf-shaped dish that lay in the centre of the mahogany table. She unwrapped it and popped it into her mouth, hoping to dispel the bitter taste. Another wave of nausea had her rushing to the restroom. Her eyes watered from the retching, and Lexie dabbed them with a tissue.

She rinsed her face and wiped away a streak of mascara from her cheek. She reapplied lipstick and a light dusting of blusher to her pale cheeks. Taking a deep breath, she returned to the waiting room.

It wasn't long before the nurse appeared. She gave Lexie a reassuring smile and sat beside her.

'There's no need to return to the consultation room,' she said to Lexie, leaning closer.

'You're the last client and I'm glad to tell you, your tests are negative. You've nothing to worry about.'

Lexie let go of the breath she'd been holding. 'Thank God!'

*

In the gym later that week, Lexie worked the power trainer as though her life depended on it. The beat of the music through her earbuds prompted her to move faster. One of the personal trainers wandered over. Lexie pulled out an earpiece.

'Hey, Lex, you've been hitting it hard today, haven't you?'

'Yeah.' She panted for air. 'I need to put in extra work.'

'You're gonna suffer later if you don't ease up.' Carl was short yet ripped, his build reminding her of a rugby player. He'd been at the gym as long as she remembered. He had a nice way about him. Now, though, Lexie felt irritated by his intrusion. Why didn't he mind his own business and let her get on with training?

'I'm fine, Carl. I know my limits.' She stepped off the machine and wiped the sweat from her forehead on her wristband. Bending, she inhaled to grab her breath and picked up her water bottle for a drink.

'Something hassling you?'

'Should there be?'

'Only asking. I've been watching your session. You've put yourself through the paces. You do that when things are happening.'

'Thanks for the psych talk, but I'm fine.'

'OK, OK. I was just lending a friendly ear.'

'Look, Carl, no offence, but if I needed to do emotional stuff, I'd visit a therapist, not a gym. So if you don't mind…' Lexie was annoyed it was so obvious to him. She bounced off to get changed into her costume.

Lexie pushed through the pool like an Olympic swimmer. She'd already swum twenty lengths and the pace had tired her. The alternating sounds of muffled activity around her suited her fine as she glided along the allocated swimming lane. She slowed her crawl, turning at the top. This time, she thrust off into a breaststroke, to reduce her aerobic activity. Pushing her head below the water, she blocked the sounds, listening to her heartbeat and the wisps of her breaths as she came up for air.

She preferred the serenity below the water. The echoing tones of voices above enabled her to switch off for a while. Normally, she wore good earplugs to deaden the sounds further, but in her haste to get away from Carl's further questions, she'd forgotten them. Her only desire had been to get into the pool and work her body harder.

Lexie completed a few more lengths and pulled herself up onto the edge where she sat for a moment to catch her breath. Her eyes itched from the chlorine; the smell was almost toxic, so she stood to leave.

In the changing rooms, Lexie showered and dressed. The day's punishing exercise had distracted her thoughts, albeit briefly. But all too soon, the guilt was returning, gnawing away at her. She tried to block the torment while she blasted her hair dry wishing she could turn back the clock, but it wasn't an option. Now, she was suffering the consequences of her actions.

Gathering her Burberry leather gym bag and slipping into her Loewe jacket, she left the building.

'Thought I'd find you here,' said Julian, approaching Lexie as she crossed the car park. 'I've been trying to reach you for hours.' His fringe flopped over his eye, and he shook it aside.

'Oh, sorry. I left my phone in the car. What's up?'

'Nothing. I just wanted to see you. And, as your phone is normally an extension of your arm, I worried. But then I remembered how obsessive you are and figured you'd be here.' He pecked her lips. 'Fancy a bite to eat?'

'Shouldn't you be somewhere?'

'Yes, here with you.' Julian pulled Lexie into his arms and kissed her.

'Jules… stop it,' said Lexie pulling away. 'We're in public.'

'So? I've missed you.' He gave her one of his cheeky grins. 'And if we don't get lunch, I might take you round the back of the car park to have my wicked way with you.' Lexie chuckled, despite her mood. Julian was always full of surprises and always lifted her mood.

'We'd better go to lunch then. I'll follow in my car.'

En route, Lexie's emotions were mixed. She felt torn about telling him about the test. Was now the right time? When would it be? It was his right to know, wasn't it? She wondered if he'd slept with anyone else. It was possible, she mused. A stab of jealousy pierced her heart. What was wrong with her? It wasn't like her to be possessive and jealous.

Julian parked outside Giovanni's, a small friendly Italian restaurant. Lexie smiled as he approached her car and held open the door for her.

'We haven't been here for at least a week.'

Lexie laughed at him as he led her into one of her favourite places to eat. For the briefest moment, things appeared normal. It didn't last, however, as her brain refused to co-operate and her inner tension built as she battled with her conscience. She could no longer pretend life was simple. Julian didn't deserve it. Lexie made the conscious decision to tell him.

So, when they returned to her apartment, Lexie found she couldn't bear to wait a moment longer.

'There's something I must tell you.'

'You've gone serious.'

'This isn't easy, Jules.' Lexie chewed her bottom lip.

'Let me guess, you're getting cold feet again and want to end it?' Julian folded his arms across his chest as he perched on the arm of the sofa.

Lexie's heart jolted. 'No.'

'That's a relief,' he said blowing out a breath. 'I was getting used to the notion of us having a future together.'

Would he still think so once she'd told him? A future with him was far more important now. Perhaps she'd lost that choice. She recalled another of her mother's many quotes: 'You never know what you've got until it's gone.'

Taking risks was easier when alone. Now, there was Julian to think about. She wanted to freeze the moment and not blurt out her mistake.

'You're not pregnant, are you?' Julian's eyes widened.

'No, I'm not pregnant.' That might have been easier news, and he looked a tad regretful.

'I know you won't guess, so it will be better if you just listen.'

'What is it, Lex? You're worrying me. Are you ill?'

'No, please listen.'

'All right,' he answered with a worried frown.

'I've made a tremendous mistake. I've done something I'm not proud of.' Her hands shook, so she curled them into her lap.

'What is it, honey?' Julian moved beside her and wrapped her hand in his. 'You're shaking. Nothing can be that bad.'

'Oh, Jules... I'm so sorry.' Tears of shame filled her eyes.

'Have you been seeing someone else? Is that it?' Julian stood and peered down at her.

'Yes, no. I mean, not since we've been back together.'

'Who? When then? What do you mean?'

'I can't say who.' Lexie could not meet the accusation in his face.

'Why not? It's not my brother, is it? He's been meeting someone on the sly.' Julian's nostrils flared with male pride.

'No! What do you take me for?' Lexie felt her own frustration build.

'Sorry.'

'Julian, I'm not ready to tell you who yet, because it's complicated, and that's not the—'

'Complicated? Why?' He gave her a hard, suspicious stare.

'It just is! Anyway, it doesn't matter who he is, that's not the issue.' Lexie felt ashamed of the hurt she was causing him. But it was against her instincts to admit more.

'So, what is the issue here, Lex?'

Her eyes closed briefly in misery. 'He had AIDS.'

The colour drained from Julian's face. Panic rose within her. She gulped.

'What?' He looked astonished.

'I...'

'You can't be fucking serious?' His scared eyes challenged her.

'It's the truth. I'm sorry.'

'You're sorry?' he said incredulously. 'I can't believe this! What does this mean? Have you got it? Have I? Fucking hell!'

Lexie's breathing quickened. Fear surged through her as he glared at her.

'Calm down.'

'Calm down? Calm down!' His face twisted with contempt and rage. 'You deliver that bombshell, then tell me to calm down?' Lexie winced and pulled her head back as he thrust his face into hers.

'Have you been tested?'

'Yes.'

'And?'

'It was negative.' Tears splashed down her cheeks as she witnessed his sigh of relief. 'I'm so sorry,' she said, lifting her hand up to his arm. He shrugged her off and moved away. Lexie had never seen him so angry. She didn't know how to reach him and dipped her head, regretful of the pain she'd created.

Julian stood with his back to her, staring out of the window, his body tense, his anguish palpable.

'What do I have to do?' His tone sounded defeated.

'Nothing, because I'm clear. But if you prefer to put your mind at rest, it's a simple blood test. I'll come with you. I could take you?'

'Thanks, but no thanks. You've done enough already!' He turned, picked up his jacket and left without a backward glance.

When the door closed, emotion burst from Lexie with such force she could barely breathe. Her body was wracked with sobs until she was depleted of energy. Her limbs felt too heavy to lift, so she slumped back on the sofa and stared into space.

The conversation played on a loop in her brain and the gravity of her behaviour sank in. She was alone once again. It was her own fault for letting her guard down. She was angry at herself because it had taken years to build her defences and now, she'd allowed them to crumble.

She'd let love in and exposed herself to pain – pain like nothing she'd known before. Now Lexie was left empty and bereft, and she deserved it.

She had hurt the people who loved her and was beyond redemption. If Julian despised her, he couldn't despise her more than she despised herself.

She had watched him reel in horror and disbelief, his face distorted in shock. Lexie wondered how she would have acted, had the situation been reversed. It didn't bear thinking about. It only gave rise to more shame.

Her world was falling apart, but all of this was nothing to what Pippa had to endure. Lexie was hiding secrets from both Pippa and Julian, but she could never expose the truth. The worst was, Lexie worked alongside Julian, and she would be constantly reminded of the pain she'd inflicted upon him.

Work had always been her saviour, but no more. She wondered about her future. Perhaps she would move to Bangalore instead? But in her heart, she was sickened by the cut-throat industry. Maybe she should go to France, to the sanctuary of her family. But what of Pippa and Alexander then? She could not leave them now.

Lexie felt bloated and uncomfortable. She forced herself up and moved to the bathroom where she ran a bath and submerged herself beneath the bubbles.

When the water was turning cold, she got out and wrapped herself in a towelling gown and flopped onto her bed, too tired to dry herself.

*

At home two days later, Lexie started at the sound of the intercom and peered through the blinds. Julian stood outside with his head bowed. Was he here to end their relationship officially?

She released the door and gave her hair a quick groom. 'Hi.' Lexie remained still, unsure of what to do or say.

'Aren't you going to ask me in?'

She stepped aside, and Julian walked past her. She wanted to rush into his arms and bury her head in his chest.

'Would you like a drink?'

'No thanks.' His head was bowed, his hands in his pockets. 'I'm not staying.'

'Oh.' Her heart sank, and she sat on the edge of the sofa, not sure what else to do. 'Why did you come in then?'

'Because the subject matter is better talked about in private.' His face was deadpan. 'And you weren't in your office, nor at the meeting today, and I've never known you miss a meeting.'

Lexie had called in sick at work, something she'd never done in her entire life, but she couldn't face him. Even when they had parted before, when it all became too much with Serena's baggage, Lexie had gone to the office, avoiding Julian, until the pain of their break-up was not so raw. She fidgeted, the familiar guilt surfacing.

'At least sit down for a minute.' She'd missed him, more than she thought possible. Julian sat in the chair opposite her. He was crestfallen.

'I had my speech all worked out on the way over,' he said, wringing his hands together. 'Now, I…'

Lexie waited for him to continue, at the same time fearing his words. An overwhelming sense of doom made her stare at the floor.

'Look, I'll make this easy for you.' She crossed her arms protectively. 'It's over. That's what you want to say, don't you?'

Julian stood. 'I don't know what I want, Lex. I feel angry and betrayed.' There was agony in his voice. 'But now… now I'm here,' he said, striding over to her. 'Now I want to do this.' He tugged her to her feet and kissed her with a fierce passion.

When he pulled away, Lexie's fingers reached her bruised lips. He'd never been so rough. He'd kissed her in punishment.

They stood locked in a silent moment as though in another world, a world without complication and pain. Lexie didn't know how to respond.

She needed him more than she'd ever needed anyone but couldn't bear to be rejected and humiliated.

She knew his mind was full of questions. Questions she did not choose to answer. His face softened, making her cravings more desperate.

'Just looking at you sends me crazy.' Julian's eyes roamed her face. 'You're like a drug and I'm the addict. I should give you up, but I need you to make me function. You possess me entirely.'

He moved his face nearer. She was aware of his breath. She closed her eyes as his lips touched hers, gently brushing her mouth. He drew her closer, and she wrapped her arms around his neck as his kiss deepened, daring to hope.

'I'm sorry,' she said when they came up for air. 'I am so, so sorry. Can we get through this?' She hoped he couldn't sense her fear of rejection.

He took her hand and led her to the bedroom.

THIRTY-FOUR

Pippa

'Are you going to eat any of that?'

'Sorry, my appetite's not brilliant these days.' Pippa put down her cutlery and rested her chin on her hand despondently.

'Understandable, I suppose. Have you booked in for the test yet?' Josh's wary expression revealed his reluctance to ask.

Pippa took a generous sip of wine, her stomach tensing at the reminder. 'I'll call the surgery. I ought not to put it off, but part of me wants to remain ignorant. Can you understand that?' Pippa swallowed hard, trying to avoid thoughts about that part of her future.

'Absolutely. They say ignorance is bliss, don't they? These sayings come from somewhere.' He stretched out and patted her hand. 'Want me to come with you?'

'No, thanks for the offer but it's something I need to do alone. I must admit, though, I'm scared. And... and

I'm constantly churned up inside.' She lowered her lashes, trying to avoid his scrutiny, not wanting his pity. 'Anyway, I can't have you observing an emotional wreck,' she said, in a braver tone.

'Keep positive. It might not come to that.'

'It will be highly probable,' Pippa said, spinning her wedding ring round with her thumb. 'I can't erase it from my mind. Shall I tell you something sick? I would accept the hideous virus in exchange for Oliver's life.' A sob sounded from deep within, causing her lower lip to tremble. 'But I can't bargain with Him up there, can I?' She raised her face up. 'He's taken Oliver and I still might be positive, anyway. And they say there's a God. What did Oliver do other than good?' A fat tear escaped, and Pippa dabbed at her eye with a napkin. 'Perhaps I'm being punished for something, but why take him away from his innocent son? I mean Oliver was coming home, no more separation. But now, we are… and for good.'

'The truth is, I don't know what to say. Except you don't deserve this, any of it.'

'Sorry. I'm not great company, am I?'

'You're always good company so don't apologise. It's good having it out in the open. Part of the healing process. You of all people know that.' His face twisted into a half-smile.

'You're right, but at this moment, I don't feel I'll ever heal. It's funny how we think we've got all the time in the world, isn't it? We all plan for our future and then there is no future. It's all bullshit. I've spent my life helping others deal with grief on a daily basis as though I can't be touched. What's that all about? Suddenly I'm catapulted into a world that's alien to me, and yet it's not.'

'Why don't you call your mother?'

'For what? Comfort, compassion?' She gave a wry smile and dipped her head, staring at the patterns on the crystal glass as she twisted the stem slowly in her fingers. 'It's Oliver I want to talk to, if only I could. This will sound stupid to you, but I've been searching for a medium. You know, to contact him. Sometimes a good one can bridge the gap.' Pippa felt her cheeks flush. 'I can tell by the look on your face you think I'm crazy.'

'Not crazy, no, I guess we all have our own views. I can understand why you want to. But there are charlatans who prey on the bereaved. Just be careful.'

Joshua wasn't the person for this conversation. She would talk to Gillian instead. Gillian would understand her desperation. And she was a believer.

'When do you go back?'

'Next month.'

It relieved her to learn he would be around for a while longer. He'd been her saviour, filling in all the gaps. She couldn't believe she might never have had answers. And to think she almost didn't reveal Oliver's diagnosis to him!

She pushed the thought away, trying hard not to turn into a blubbering wreck again. Once had been enough. And, as kind as Joshua was, Pippa was aware he was uncomfortable around emotional women; put him amongst conflict and crisis, he came into his own.

Oliver had spoken highly of him and told her he'd choose him every time to cover his back in the war zone. Joshua was the solid, dependable type, and Pippa's only wish for him was to find a loving partner. But he was married to the RAF.

'Do you still love your job?' She didn't understand why she asked as soon as the question left her lips. 'I mean, how do you do it? Face those atrocities day by day?'

'Programming. You take emotion out.'

'Or be devoid of it completely. Sorry, I didn't mean—'

'I understand.'

'People don't understand though. I mean really, do they?' She moved her plate to one side. 'Oliver told me once about a farmer complaining—'

'The Salisbury Plain exercise? Said we were flying too low. Spooked his chickens.'

'Yes, he's the one. He said they fled into the coop and suffocated other birds.'

'And because of it, his other hens produced too much calcium and could no longer be classed as organic. I mean, he had a point but, eggs compared to war training…'

'That's just what I mean. People can't comprehend. Or don't want to.'

'It won't be the same now,' he answered, sighing. He rubbed his jaw.

'It will be strange co-piloting somebody else, won't it?' Pippa thought of their long working relationship.

'There's the talk of us pulling out of Afghanistan, as you're probably aware, but I'm thinking of throwing in the towel myself.'

'What? Never! You've got to be kidding me.' Pippa couldn't be more surprised. She noticed indecision in him and realised it would be hard for him too. 'The RAF is your life. How many times have we had this discussion in the past?'

'That was then. Things are different now.' He picked up his beer and tipped his head back to drink.

'What would you do?'

'Keep my eye on you and Alexander.'

'We're not your responsibility.' Pippa felt humbled.

'I need to be around for you both. Oliver's my best mate... was, I mean.' He picked at the side of his nail, then took another slug. 'Besides, I promised him.'

'Don't even think of putting your life on hold for us. We'll be fine. We have to be.'

Pippa clasped her hands in front of her and leaned forward to meet his eyes – eyes that lacked sparkle with dark shadows beneath them. He'd probably lost sleep too.

The new stubble on his chin suited him, she mused bizarrely, though she wasn't used to seeing him looking anything but clean-shaven.

'You're not responsible for us. I must learn to live a life without Oliver, so don't make choices based on us. I can't, and I won't let that happen.' She hadn't stopped to consider the impact of Oliver's death on him. How could he give up his life, for them?

'Pippa, I—'

'No, look, I'm not saying we don't need you in our lives because we do. So check on us from time to time. Come and spend time with us. Be normal, as though Oliver were alive, but don't,' she said firmly, 'don't change your life for us.'

'Mummy, Mummy!' Alexander wailed from the stairs.

'I'm coming, darling,' she called, springing up from her chair. 'He wakes a lot, asking for Oliver. I'll try to settle him, though I don't know how successful I'll be. He keeps getting into our bed.'

'I'd better go then,' Josh said, standing.

'No, put some coffee on. I'll be down soon,' Pippa said

over her shoulder, sprinting up the stairs. The nights were long enough.

*

Pippa stood at the foot of Oliver's grave a week later and marvelled at the volume of hand-tied bouquets. A few white lilies were dead. The roses, carnations and other varieties weren't too bad, although wilting. There were no cellophane wrappers or pretty bows at this woodland burial, only biodegradable substances reverting to nature, decomposing as Oliver would be.

She knelt for what seemed an age. She could not contemplate the thought of her beautiful husband as a corpse, a decayed skeleton, a disembodied state. No beautiful facial features, or skin and muscle. No mind and no life force. She only found solace in the knowledge that his spirit would now be free to live on and she hoped he would find sanctuary.

Pippa craved her own peace but knew it would never come. Her only respite was the unconsciousness of sleep, and even then, dreams haunted her. Learning of Oliver's rape gnawed away at her by the fact of not knowing, or to offer him support in his desperate hour of need.

Pippa picked up the dead flowers and walked up a small hill. She placed them on the mound with others waiting for the tractor to collect them. She stood a while taking in the charm of the surroundings. The autumnal colours were spectacular, offering such beauty.

Oliver would love it here. Fresh teardrops slid down her cheeks. He wouldn't want her sad. She dried her eyes on her sleeve and walked back, thinking about life and its meaning. How did evil survive? How could Oliver's rapists walk the streets, leaving devastation behind in their wake? She raised her face up to the heavens, questioning her faith, then she knelt and stroked the earth, wishing she could reach inside the coffin and touch his skin. Oliver deserved better.

As she rearranged the rest of the flowers, a family of rooks gathered nearby, squawking their dominant chorus above smaller birds. She watched them tapping the soil, imitating raindrops to attract worms to the surface. The wintery showers would soon come and moisten the earth.

Pippa picked up the memorial cards from the grave. She would keep the cards forever as tokens of dedication and appreciation from friends, colleagues and family.

As she lifted them, she read some of the goodbye messages and her heart constricted.

The remaining floral array of colour overflowed the plot, a testament to Oliver's popularity.

'Will you come and let me know you're safe?' she asked wistfully. 'Will you find a way to get through? I need you to find a way to be with me to comfort me and love me like you always have.'

She hugged her arms around herself, feeling alone, abandoned and desolate, devoid of any positive emotion. 'Oh, Oliver, what am I to do?' The salty residue forming around her lips reminded her she would only ever feel grief, loss and pain. Somehow, she must go on for the sake of their son. It remained true Alexander would bring happiness into her life. He was a precious gift and Oliver would live on through him.

A sudden breeze brought goosebumps to her skin. A

robin, with the most amazing red breast, glided down and balanced upon Pippa's wreath: purple hyacinths she'd chosen to express the floral meaning *I am sorry, please forgive me*, blue hyacinths, *constancy of love* and pink carnations, *I miss you*. A smile brightened her face. Pippa looked to the sky, stopped crying and laughed aloud. Oliver had given her a sign.

As a spiritual believer, she knew robins were signs that loved ones were still near after death. Generally, the bird represented strength, industriousness and resilience, symbolising the ability to bounce back, as well as the rebirth of new beginnings. Most of all, the robin stood for patience.

She would cope.

A tiny seed of doubt made her wonder if the bird would have landed there anyway? But it was in synchronicity with her words to Oliver, and he was sitting on her wreath.

'Did Oliver send you?' If anyone saw her talking to a bird, they'd think her most strange! He sat still, chirruping, as though to answer, before flying off.

'Thank you,' she said to Oliver and walked to her car.

On her wing mirror sat a red admiral. Its black velvety wings were intersected by red, orangey stripes. Its colours told her it was a male, as the female's wings would be a browner shade. Pippa grinned, her doubts answered. The butterfly symbolised metamorphosis, transformation and change. It was time to discover her own fate. She would book the appointment, she decided.

That evening, Pippa was reading a book to Alexander.

'I want a different story, Mummy.'

'Don't you like this one?' Pippa's emotional state was fragile, and she was tired. 'No, I want that one,' he said, pointing to another book. His sweet cherubic face looked up at her. *From Caterpillar to Butterfly…*

Pippa's eyes brimmed as she reached for the storybook.

*

Two days later, in great trepidation, Pippa walked back into the surgery for her test results. Lexie was collecting Alexander from school and taking him for a McDonald's treat.

Pippa needed to deal with her demons alone. She sat, looking quietly dignified, but was shaking inside. She knew her movements were fidgety, and it seemed an age before she was called into Dr Kerr's office, to hear what fate had dished out next.

'Have a seat, Pippa.' Dr Kerr's mood was sombre. His dismal expression confirmed her fears without him having to utter a word.

Her gut churned and her palms went clammy. She settled her hands in her lap, wringing them. She sighed deeply to prepare for the shock and the impact of a possible positive result.

'Now, the good news is, Alexander's test is negative.'

Pippa exhaled the agonising breath she held, elated at least her child was free.

'Yours, however,' he said glancing at the computer screen, as though to read it for the first time, 'I'm afraid—'

'No!' Pippa closed her eyes in disbelief as his voice became a murmur in the distance.

'It's not all doom and gloom, Pippa. We have excellent drugs to manage the virus,' he said, but she wasn't listening.

Her heart banged against her ribs, beating its loud tattoo, and sounds hissed in her ears. All her composure vanished.

Dr Kerr stood and strode around the desk, hand stretched out, offering her a tissue.

So much adrenaline coursed through her body she felt dizzy. Her lungs heaved as she hyperventilated, and her vision blurred into blackness.

Pippa woke on the couch sensing a tightness on her arm. Her eyes flickered open.

'Lie still for a minute. I'm checking your blood pressure. You passed out.'

She prised them open again, this time with lucidity, seeing the doctor's kindness. He unfastened the cuff and handed her a glass of water.

'I'm going to sit you up slowly, but don't stand yet.' He raised the backrest of the examining couch. 'Is there anybody who could pick you up and take you home?'

'I'll be fine,' said Pippa, heat scorching her cheeks.

'I'd prefer you didn't drive.'

'I'll get a taxi then,' she reasoned.

'If you wait a little while, I can take you. Afternoon clinic is over now.' He moved back to his desk. 'I have to go out to do some home visits. It's no trouble, I'm passing through anyway. Besides, we can talk about treatment options on the way if you'd like?'

'If you're sure I can't go myself?' Despite knowing Dr Kerr for years – he had always been their family GP – what she truly wanted was to be alone to let the information sink in.

This was her life now and it was time to face her anguish. Pippa had cried a lake, let alone a river, and she would cry no more. She needed a change of perspective. Loss was one thing, regret entirely another. Pippa would not live the rest of her life with regret.

She had given Oliver the gift of a humane death, sparing him the hospital setting of floodlit rooms and beeping machines. He had found dignity in his journey to transcendence and spiritual peace.

Pippa would continue to live well. Not in spite of Oliver's death, but because of it.

EPILOGUE

Six Weeks Later

Alexander sat next to Lexie, his small hand rubbing her stomach. 'Is the baby big now?' he asked.

'He's much bigger,' Lexie confirmed with a smile. 'He'll soon be as big as you,' she said, turning to Pippa as she walked into the lounge, armed with popcorn and a DVD.

'Come on, Alexander. Leave Auntie Lexie and her bump alone now.' She bent to slide the DVD into the player. 'Right, sit by Mummy and we'll all watch the film.'

'Can I have the popcorn?' He jumped up and down with excitement, wriggling his backside in anticipation. 'I love popcorn.' He licked his lips.

'Be quick before the film starts,' Pippa said, patting the couch. 'Pass some to Lexie first.'

'*Auntie* Lexie,' he corrected.

Pippa and Lexie burst into laughter.

'Does the baby like popcorn?'

'I'm sure he does.' Lexie stroked her stomach, silently thanking God she hadn't contracted the virus.

She was still in disagreement with Pippa about her treatment, but she appeared to be doing brilliantly with her homeopathic medicine. It impressed Lexie as she studied more about it. She discovered Hugo's progress had been because of homeopathy. The results were amazing. Lexie was surprised to learn even Gabrielle was taking Pippa's remedies to support her through the grief of losing her son.

Their conflict had disappeared once they agreed there was a place for both types of medicine. Lexie had witnessed first-hand the efficiency of remedies in an emotional crisis and had even agreed to try a natural birth, though she knew if she needed drugs, she would definitely take them!

'Grandma and Grandpa like popcorn too, don't they, Mummy?' Alexander grabbed a handful of corn. 'And Jasper and Bailey,' he added, chomping.

'They certainly do, though Grandma doesn't like you feeding the dogs, does she? Or speaking with your mouth full?' Pippa grinned at Lexie.

'Can I have a dog, please, Mummy?'

'We'll see.' Pippa rolled her eyes.

'I can buy a puppy with my savings money,' Alexander said, his eyes wide with excitement.

'We'd better top up your money box then.' Lexie looked at Pippa from the corner of her eye.

'But remember, dogs need lots of walking too.'

'We can take him to the daffodil fields by Grandma's house, can't we, Mummy? And Auntie Lexie can come, now she's left work.'

Lexie watched Pippa's lips twitch and knew Alexander had won that particular battle. For Lexie, there was still an internal battle: the battle with her conscience. It would be a battle she would live with, for Pippa and Julian would never learn the truth.

Some secrets have to remain, to protect those we love. Lexie and Pippa's bond of friendship had survived and was stronger than ever.

Things could have been so different. Lexie silently thanked God her baby was Julian's.

Acknowledgements

There are many people to express my thanks. If I've omitted anyone, it's unintentional.

Thanks to Jackie for our creative days together all those years ago, clacking keys on old typewriters, and Pat, for our book exchanges and discussions. Devoted friends since our school days!

A warm thank you to all members of Cornwall Writers, Wednesday Writers Online - gratitude to our talented tutor, Kerry Hadley-Pryce. Nine Online, and RedPen sessions where our nag buddy, Anne Rainbow, keeps us accountable.

Special love and thanks to my children, Dean, Adam, and Grace for listening to my writerly stresses and supporting me.

To my grandchildren, without whom, this book would have been finished years earlier! I adore you all.

To friends and family who have waited patiently to hold this book.

Immense gratitude to my husband, Kevan, for your unwavering faith, encouraging me to succeed despite life's stress and heartache along the way. Thanks for your positive words and for giving me the courage to put my story out there.

Deepest gratitude to my mother, Evelyn, an avid reader, who truly believed I would be published. I wish you could have read this book - my mother earth. I miss you every day. And my father, Ronald, who insisted I read the dictionary when asking the meaning of a word! Your love, sacrifices, guidance, and wisdom have been my greatest blessing, and I'm proud to have had you as my parents.

A heartfelt thank you to everyone whom I've loved and lost and been privileged to have in my life. Some of you appear in these pages. In loving memory of my beautiful friends, Gillian, for your strong faith in homeopathy and our chats over a glass of wine, and Sue for our homeopathic conferences and a shared love of writing. Not forgetting a beautiful lady, Maureen Dillon, the first reader of the original draft; you loved it - RIP

For research, my nephew, Ian Linney for RAF, and Terrence Higgins Trust for HIV. Any inaccuracies are mine alone.

To Claire Linney, for reading draft 1 and requesting a sequel!

Thanks to beta-readers Nicky Benton-Simcock and Anita Hunt, who gave time to critique later drafts, and for positive feedback. I owe you both a signed copy!

To Ali Luke, for an early critique and for introducing me to Lorna.

A special mention to my amazing editor, Lorna Fergusson, who pushed me that little bit further to add more scenes, when all I wanted to do was type The End! You gave me faith and encouragement when I was close to giving up. I owe you the biggest thanks of all, for without you, Bitter Pill would still be a file on my Mac!

Huge thanks and praise to all the team at Troubador, especially Chloe for the perfect cover design - you executed my ideas to perfection, and Jessica for guidance and support throughout the publishing journey.

Finally, a sincere thank you reader for choosing my novel.